CURVING FOUL

A Story About Baseball
A Story About Life

Harris Frommer

Gray Productions
Guttenberg, New Jersey

Copyright © 2018 by Harris Frommer

Published by Gray Productions
JudyCorc@aol.com
www.judycorcoran.com

ISBN-10: 1719169705
ISBN-13: 9781719169707
Cover design by Jim Bennett
Book design by Judy Corcoran
Printed in July 2018

To my father, Thomas Frommer.
My fondest childhood memories were
talking baseball with you.
Every son should be so lucky.

Acknowledgements

I'm not one for similes, but writing a book is like embarking on a long journey with many people involved each step of the way. And on this incredible trip, I'm grateful to every person who helped me in one way or another.

I began writing this book in 2013, but put it down after the first chapter and returned to a life of Netflix, couches, and naps in my spare time. John and Bonnie Schleimer didn't know it then, but the encouragement they offered a faithful night in 2016 went a long way in reviving Curving Foul. I hope they know it now.

I'd like to thank my copy editor, Diane Sinitsky, and my book designer and publisher, Judy Corcoran, for their guidance, professionalism, and words of encouragement, which have meant everything to a first-time author. I'm also appreciative of my cover artist, Jim Bennett, who took a vague idea and turned it into a beautiful painting, and Iris Blasi, for her numerous plot edits and marketing advice.

Baseball is a wonderful game that has provided me with thousands of hours of joy but, more importantly, it has also sparked some amazing friendships. In April 2001, I randomly called Lynn Henning, a columnist at the Detroit News, to discuss the upcoming MLB draft. Seventeen years later, Lynn remains a close confidant. Not long after meeting Lynn, I crossed paths with Dave Chilton, a gifted speaker, entrepreneur, and lifelong Detroit Tigers fan. I thank you both not only for your support on this book, but also for your friendship. Also with me every step of the way for the past 40 years have been Dan Crolius and Jeff Brazer. What a ride it's been!

I owe a big thank you to my mom, Molly, who taught me the importance of not just sports, but embracing a healthy lifestyle. I hope this book will ease some of the sting from me not becoming an orthopedic surgeon. And I'm grateful to my siblings, Ariella, Heather, and Eric, for tolerating my baseball fetish all these years. Also, my in-laws, Joe and Marlene Gabriele, were tremendous with their support for this project, as was my brother-in-law Vin.

My beautiful wife Jessica has more to do with this book than anyone. I couldn't have asked for a more loving and devoted wife. And to my kids, Tommy and Stella, not only do I wish you both a lifetime filled with good health, lots of love, and success, but I hope each of you finds something that gives you as much happiness in your life as baseball has given me.

Finally, there's my dad, Thomas, to whom this book is dedicated. Although his German upbringing kept him from knowing how to teach me to hit a fastball or spin a curve, he was always supportive of me playing baseball and following the sport that meant so much to me. In fact, it was my father who took me to my very first game, on October 4, 1980. Reggie Jackson hit a home run as the Yankees beat the Tigers 5-2 to clinch the American League East. Thank you for taking me to that game and for everything else you did. I miss you and always think about the good times we had and can only hope to be half the father to my kids that you were to yours.

Pregame

Since word of this book leaked out, I'm sure you've seen all the features about me on *Outside the Lines, Undisputed,* and *First Take.* You've probably read the likes of Ken Rosenthal, Buster Olney, Peter Gammons, and Will Carroll meticulously examine my career, game by game, at bat by at bat, pitch by pitch, like a fourth-year medical student dissecting a fresh cadaver. And you've heard my name shredded to pieces by Colin Cowherd, Howard Stern, and even President Trump, who called me a loser. And, yet, you still don't know my story. Not even close.

I'll make you a deal. If you read this book, I'll take you on one hell of a journey—a real roller-coaster ride. You'll read not only about all the highs I've experienced both on and off the field—the pure exhilaration of turning on a 100-mile-an-hour fastball, the thrill of becoming a world champion, and the unbridled ecstasy of making love to three stunning supermodels (after seeing them satisfy one another, of course)—but you'll also learn about the heartbreak I've experienced and demons that haunt me every day.

Oh, and I'll tell you why I used performance-enhancing drugs for over a decade.

Kansas City

Monday, April 6, 2015

So, here we are, 4-1 in the bottom of the seventh inning with Royals pinch hitter, veteran Jack Carter, stepping up to the plate to greet Chicago White Sox right-hander Dan Jennings. You've gotta think nearly all of the 40,000 fans in the stands know Carter's sitting at 499 home runs for his career. And with the cold drizzle and bitter wind blowing in, 500 will certainly be a tall order for Carter. Carter's gotta be anxious—he's been one away from 500 all winter and has had months to think about it. Let's see what he can do here.

Jennings sets and deals. First pitch of the at bat . . . a fastball outside at 93 miles per hour. Ball one. Not a bad pitch, but it missed the plate by about two inches. Good take by Carter. Seems like he got a good look at that pitch. Leave it to Carter, a real pro, to come up to the plate in this situation and take a close pitch for a ball.

Jennings toes the rubber, looks in to the catcher Flowers for the sign, and deals . . . a breaking pitch just above the letters for ball two. Jennings better be careful; a little lower and that's in Carter's wheelhouse. Carter doesn't have the bat speed he had earlier in his career with Detroit and the Yankees, but if Jennings leaves a breaking pitch out over the plate, it could be 5-1 in a hurry. And wouldn't that be something!

Jennings gets back on the rubber and peers at his catcher for the sign. Both the infield and outfield are playing Carter straight away. Here's the pitch . . . Carter swings . . . belted to deep right-center, Eaton turns and

11

Curving Foul

races back . . . no chance! That baby is gone! Wow, he hit that a ton! Home run number 500 for Jack Carter! Eaton turned around and ran back about five steps before he realized that the ball was going to carry over the fence. Carter is trying to hide a smile as he rounds the bases, and this crowd of 40,000 is on its feet. Ha-ha, easy does it, Jack! The entire Royals team has left the dugout to greet Carter at home plate.

Cooperstown, here we come!

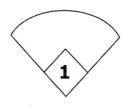

Tough Start

April 11, 1985, was the worst day of my life. It was the day I lost my best friend, my biggest fan, my first batting-practice pitcher, and, most important, my father. It's a day, over 30 years later, I still haven't recovered from.

Let's back up for a minute.

I was born on February 15, 1975, in Fullerton, California, to Michael and Janet Carter, who were both 25 at the time. Looking back, my parents seemed like the closest thing to the all-American couple. They were native Southern Californians (with the good looks to match), bright, and seemingly happily married and deeply devoted to one another. Though they had both come of age in the late '60s and early '70s, they'd never bought into the hippie craze and instead had concentrated on getting their college degrees and starting a family.

I inherited my athletic genes from my father, who, with the exception of football, played every sport you could think of growing up—basketball, volleyball, tennis, and even soccer, which was still in its infancy in the U.S. in the 1960s. But his best sport was by far baseball. An All-Orange County shortstop in both 1967 and 1968, Mike Carter was selected by the Cleveland Indians in the 29th round of the 1968 amateur draft—the same draft that produced Thurman Munson and Bill Buckner, as well as the immortal Roger McSwain and Carlton Exum. However, the Vietnam War was already in full swing, and my father knew that by going to college he'd be able to put off the military draft by four years.

My dad graduated in May 1972 from UC Santa Barbara with a bachelor's degree in urban planning. Shortly after leaving UCSB, he accepted a job with the city of Anaheim as an urban planner. It was the only job he ever had.

Janet Downing was just three months younger than my dad and also graduated high school in 1968 and college four years later. Despite looking fit for the early part of her life, she wasn't into sports, save for an occasional game of tennis or swim in a neighbor's pool. My mom majored in early childhood education at UC Irvine and began working as a special education teacher in the fall of 1972.

Some guy I never met, Todd Glass, had the honor of introducing my parents in the spring of 1973. The story goes that it was during a happy hour on a Thursday night at a random bar in Orange County. Glass was actually in the process of flirting with my mom, though she wasn't interested. It was raining that night—a rarity in Southern California—and my father walked into the bar soaking wet and literally bumped into my mom. Glass, who'd roomed with my dad in college, figured it wasn't happening between my mom and him and therefore decided to do my dad a solid and introduce him as his buddy who "cares too much and volunteers too often." My mom completely fell for it, and she and my dad spent the next three hours immersed in deep conversation (or so I was later told). Anyway, they hung out every night for three months after that and were engaged by Halloween and got married on Valentine's Day.

From what I remember, I had a typical early childhood. We lived in Fullerton, on 1520 Maurine Place. It was a pretty, ranch-style house in a cul-de-sac, ideal for Wiffle ball, basketball, roller hockey, or any other game where at least one kid would trip, slice open his knee, and probably have a gruesome-looking scar for the rest of his life. But that never deterred me—if I wasn't in school or eating, I'd be out there under the warm California sun pretending I was Freddie Lynn, Magic Johnson, or Marcel Dionne. What a life.

To my parents' credit, they never tried to deter me from my sports obsession. I don't remember us being super rich, but my dad made enough money so that my mom didn't have to work and could spend her weekday afternoons and evenings chauffeuring my younger sister, Dana, and me around to various games and friends' houses. And my father—no matter how tired he was after work—was always there to pick us up. With a smile on his face.

Like my dad, baseball was my favorite sport. I started playing T-ball when I was six, and from the first moment I ever held a bat, I knew I was meant to play the game. I don't think a day went by in which I didn't do something baseball related. I'd either play with my buddies in the cul-de-sac or throw a tennis ball against the wall in the garage (I would make my mother pull her car, a 1982 Buick

Curving Foul

LeSabre, out of the garage and park it in the driveway so I could make the garage into my own personal bullpen). And my father was always a willing accomplice. He was younger and in better shape than my buddies' dads and was often "that dad," meaning a 350-pitch outing on a random Saturday afternoon throwing to my friends and me was par for the course.

Our neighborhood was teeming with kids, and luckily many of them happened to be my age and loved sports as much as I did. You had Bobby Rossi, a tough Italian kid whose father, Vito, owned three Italian restaurants and everyone thought was connected; Johnny Kelly, the youngest of four red-headed boys; Justin Finkelman, a kid with Coke-bottle glasses who could make a Wiffle ball do whatever he wanted; Kenny Lapitka, who was quick-witted, even in grammar school; and Nicky Ruggiero, supersmart and with a sister so smokin' that she had half the guys in Orange County in hot pursuit. I met these guys before I even stepped foot into kindergarten and stayed buddies with all of them until we graduated from Fullerton Union High School.

It shouldn't surprise anyone that my first season playing baseball ended with me making the all-star team. As did my second, third, and every one after that until I got into pro ball. I was always tall for my age, and, unlike most big kids, I was coordinated. So, even when I played against older competition, I never had a problem. Like all the best athletes in Little League, I played shortstop and pitched, and on the rare occasion there was a kid on my team better than me, I would slide over to first.

I've been asked a bunch of times why I throw right but bat left-handed. The answer's an easy one: Freddie Lynn.

16

Despite my father's Southern California roots, he was a die-hard Red Sox fan who patterned my swing after Lynn's from the moment I picked up my first bat. And that, of course, included teaching me how to hit left-handed even though I was a natural righty. You can't imagine his excitement when Lynn broke in with Boston in 1975 and not only won the American League Rookie of the Year but also was voted the league's Most Valuable Player.

There was another reason why my father was such a Lynn guy: Lynn was just two years younger than my dad and the two were on the same team one year in summer ball. Anyway, Lynn signed with the local California Angels (who were my team, by the way) as a free agent in 1981, about the same time I was starting my T-ball career. Though his first year with the Halos was injury plagued, he was an All-Star in 1982 as the Angels made the playoffs and I was hooked. To this day, he's still my favorite player.

So, April 11, 1985. It's crazy, because when I talk to people from New York about 9/11, they say that they remember that horrible day like it was yesterday. But I remember 4/11 like it happened about 20 minutes ago. The sights, sounds, smells, and especially the hurt is still ensconced in my brain like time has stood still all these years.

It was a Thursday. The day after what had been a banner game for me. Against Carmine's Fine Tailoring, the first-place team, I pitched a complete game and hit two home runs as we won 7-1. The game ball, signed by all my teammates, still sits prominently in my trophy case with my MVPs and Silver Sluggers. After the game, the whole team went to Jimmy's Pizza to celebrate, and I'd be hard-pressed to tell you of a happier moment in my life. At that instant, my life seemed perfect. We didn't get home until nine or ten that night—late for a school night—but neither of my parents seemed to care. When my mom and dad came to tuck me in and kiss me good night, I remember my father telling me how proud of me he was. Those were the last words I ever heard him speak.

The following morning was beautiful. It had to be in the mid-70s without a cloud in the sky. As they did every morning, Kenny, Justin, and Bobby swung by on their bikes to meet me at the corner of Maurine and Lindendale and we rode to school together, picking up Johnny and Nicky on the way. It was another boring day in the hallowed halls of Acacia Elementary School until music class, which was right after lunch. Suddenly, the classroom phone rang. Obviously, no one thought anything of it, but when the music teacher put the receiver down with a serious look on her face and said, "Jack, would you please go to the office," a bunch of kids—including my buddies—chirped in unison, "Oooooooo," implying trouble was ahead. Little did they know.

When I got to the office, I immediately knew something was wrong. I saw my neighbor, an elderly lady who used to babysit us when my parents went out, standing next to the school principal. The principal was a stern man with a crew cut and a take-no-prisoners attitude, which even 30 years ago was a bit much for a guy who ran a school populated with nothing but preteens. But on this day, he had a look of compassion on his face as he said, "Jack, your father has been involved in a car accident and your neighbor, here, is going to take you to be with the rest of your family." As a gigantic lump filled my throat and my eyes began to swell with tears, I started to walk with my neighbor to her car for what would be a quiet ride home.

When we arrived at my house, my mom was a complete wreck, shaking and sobbing. Both of my mom's parents, Carl and Barbara Downing, were there. My grandfather, who I later learned was already terminally ill with cancer, looked completely lost, while my grandmother was holding my mother, trying in vain to calm her down. It was my mom's best friend who gave me the dreadful news. I was so numb, I don't even think I shed a tear. There could have been a nuclear war going on all around me, but I was so oblivious I don't think I would have noticed. I was just thinking how my father had put me to sleep the night before and couldn't be dead.

It's crazy to think how much the world has changed over the past 30 years. If this all happened today, no doubt there would have been a therapist at the door to offer counseling and probably some type of sedative. But not in 1985. Instead, we were on our own. By nighttime, all the friends and neighbors who had come over to offer support went home to be with their own families and my grandparents weren't far behind. My mom also had a younger sister, Nancy, who hadn't yet made it to Fullerton from her home in Seattle. Also, it being nearly 15 years before the advent of the internet and 25 before the widespread use of social media, some people, even those who were local, didn't find out for days that my father had died.

The funeral was the following Monday, and it was exactly as you could imagine—a wide-open cemetery on a cloudy, unseasonably cool morning with lots of crying people. Because we were in laid-back Southern California and my parents weren't big church people, I didn't even have a sport coat or a pair of dress slacks that fit. So, I ended up borrowing a tan corduroy suit from Nicky Ruggiero that was at least two sizes too small. I can't recall if it had suede elbow patches.

The graveside service lasted barely a half hour, but it felt like an eternity. I don't remember much of what the minister said, but there was one sentence that I'll never forget. It was a quote from Dr. Seuss, whose books my father read to me when I was a little boy. *Don't cry because it's over, smile because it happened.*

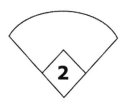

When the Going Gets Rough...

I have no concrete memories from the first half year after my father's death. To this day, I have no idea how I functioned in school, on the ball field, and in life in general. My brain turned back on sometime before that first Thanksgiving. My mother and her sister never got along that well, so it came as no surprise when my aunt called two days before the holiday to give some flimsy excuse why she and her family couldn't make it down from Seattle. By this point, cancer had ravaged my grandfather's body, forcing him into the ICU, where the nurses and my grandmother tended to him night and day. This left my mom, sister, and me home alone for Thanksgiving dinner.

When I was younger, we always had a minor skirmish just before the holiday because my dad and I hated turkey and would beg my mom to make something else. But my mom, the house chef, always won that argument and we'd all be forced to consume that big, ugly bird. Yet in a cruel twist of irony, my mom on this particular Thanksgiving was simply too exhausted and depressed to slave over the turkey and instead boiled hot dogs and corn on the cob that the three of us ate in absolute silence.

Christmas wasn't much different, except that we had microwave pizza and an ice cream cake from Carvel. My aunt thought of another bullshit excuse to avoid coming down to spend time with her grieving sister, and my grandmother was still consumed by my grandfather, who by this time was under hospice care. The other thing about that Christmas that I've never forgotten was my mom tearfully telling us that she could only afford one gift for each of us, a Barbie Corvette for Dana and a *Baseball Encyclopedia* for me.

That Christmas was the first indication of how tight things would be for me financially until I received my first Major League contract over a decade later. My mom, who hadn't worked since before I was born, found it nearly impossible to land a steady, decent-paying job and had to settle for a number of part-time gigs such as babysitting and tutoring, which, combined with the pittance my grandmother could give, barely enabled us to stay current on the mortgage. It wasn't long before the penny-pinching was evident in all facets of our lives. Summer camp was out of the question, as were new toys, school field trips, nonessential clothing, and cable TV. Dana and I were even discouraged from inviting our friends over to play because my mom was afraid that if these kids stayed for dinner, she'd be forced to feed them.

It was during these lean times, however, that I saw the good side of so many people. My friends' parents all went out of their way to let just a little bit of sunlight back into my life. The Lapitkas must have taken me on at least five vacations with them, including trips to San Francisco, the Grand Canyon, and Yellowstone. The Rossis allowed us to eat at their restaurants dozens of times free of charge. And Mr. Finkelman on more than one occasion bought me baseball spikes and a glove. Complete strangers also went out of their way to help.

There was one specific instance that's stayed with me all these years. Less than a year after my father died, we were clothing shopping and my mom had picked out a pair of jeans for me she thought were on sale for $16. It turned out they were mislabeled and instead cost $22 (remember, this was the mid-'80s). Because my mom only had a $20 bill in her pocket, she couldn't afford them. Despondent at the thought of not being able to even afford a pair of jeans for her son, my mom began to cry and begged the cashier and the store manager to give her a break as her husband had just passed away. Suddenly, a young lady with a toddler of her own who had been watching the episode unfold handed my mom $20 and said how sorry she was for our loss and that she'd like nothing more than to buy the jeans for me. This stranger then bent down and whispered in my ear, "I'm sure your daddy was a wonderful father who loved you and your sister very much. Be brave and take care of your mother, Sweetie."

Obviously, the impact of my father's death on the three of us extended far beyond money, and my mom was affected the most. Once a vivacious, funny, confident, and caring person, she gradually withdrew into a shell and her personality changed dramatically. My father had clearly been the love of her life, the only man with whom she'd had a serious romantic relationship, and after he was gone she had no way to cope with this huge loss.

Curving Foul

She spent more and more time alone in her room crying and increasingly less time with her kids, who were also grieving, albeit in a different way. As time progressed, my mom became more detached, and not just from her own kids but also from most of her friends, the community, and the realities of everyday life.

Lorraine Crowley was one of my mom's friends she did keep in touch with, but unfortunately it was for all the wrong reasons. A divorcee in her early 40s with a daughter who was a high school dropout, Lorraine was a walking caricature. At about five feet seven, at least 30 pounds overweight, and often clad in leopard-skin leggings and high heels, Lorraine's main goal was to find a man, or two, or three. And at some point in the months following my father's accident, she convinced my mom this should be her calling in life as well.

Eventually, Lorraine's influence over my mom grew, and before long my mom was leaving two preteens home at all hours of the night to hit every seedy pick-up joint west of Long Beach. Never a big drinker while my dad was still alive, my mom began hitting the bottle hard as she hit the OC singles scene with Loose Lorraine. She also began to smoke, something I'd never seen her do when I was younger. If losing my dad wasn't traumatic enough, seeing my mom evolve into a cougar who invited stranger after stranger into her bed left me devastated and asking whether this was the person who'd loved my father, sister, and me so much just a short time ago.

With a mother who had checked out, my performance in school began to suffer. Now, don't get the wrong idea because no one would have ever confused me with Einstein, but with nobody around to make sure I was doing my homework or to ask how I'd done on a recent test or project, my grades began to drop. More important than falling test scores, however, was the fact that I failed to develop good study habits and a solid work ethic when it came to school, something that would plague me later on.

As cliché as it sounds, the one constant in my life remained baseball. Regardless of how poorly I was doing in school, what guy my mom was having a one-night stand with, or how many holes were in my sneakers or jeans, I continued to excel on the diamond. As an 11- and 12-year-old, I was the starting shortstop on the Fullerton Little League team that advanced to the California State Championship two years in a row. As a 13-year-old playing on the professional-sized field for the first time, I made Fullerton's Mickey Mantle team, which was comprised solely of 15- and 16-year-olds. Looking back, this was probably the first time it struck me how much better I was than kids my own age. While guys like Ruggiero, Finkelman, Rossi, and Lapitka were all good ballplayers in their own right, by my early teens, I was already bigger and more coordinated than they were and able to hold my own against kids with big-time velocity and breaking stuff.

The other thing I started to notice around this time was how much better baseball is in California and elsewhere in the Sunbelt. If you look at the rosters of big-league clubs, it's no accident that an overwhelming majority of the guys are from the Caribbean, California, Arizona, Texas, and Florida. Baseball is such a nuanced game with simply no substitute for repetition, and in a warm climate like California you have so many more chances to get these reps. At 13, 14, and 15, we occasionally played in tournaments against teams from cold-weather places

25

like New England, New York, and the Midwest, and I was shocked when I realized how much better we were than them. While many of these northern kids were just as big, strong, and fast as we were, they were not nearly as polished at the various parts of the game. Their pitchers threw hard but lacked command or had no legitimate off-speed pitches, and their hitters could punish balls in batting practice but wilted at the sight of premium velocity or anything that spun. As a result, we won more trophies than we knew what to do with.

Evidently, my mom's hard work paid off in August 1988 when Conrad Dickinson asked her to marry him. For starters, Conrad the Dick as I would soon nonaffectionately call him, was far from a catch and couldn't even have stood in the same room as my father, let alone slept in the same bed. But my mom, overcome by grief, loneliness, and near insolvency, felt that a thrice-married man 12 years her senior with a horrific temper was better than nothing and decided to take the plunge. By the time my mom "settled down" with Conrad, she'd already been with dozens of men, most of whom she'd known for only one night and were long gone by sunrise. Though Conrad enjoyed the idea of being in the permanent company of a much younger woman, he wanted nothing to do with Dana or me. My mom, relieved at having a live-in partner again, as well as someone whose income allowed us to stay above the poverty line, was fine with this.

I was supportive of my mom and Conrad's relationship in the beginning. If nothing else, I figured this new guy in our lives meant I'd soon have my old, happy mother back, we'd be able to afford to stay in our house, and maybe, just maybe, Dana and I would once again have something that remotely resembled a normal childhood.

To put it mildly, things didn't exactly turn out the way I had hoped. While Conrad did move in shortly after his and my mother's wedding that September and his monthly mortgage payments allowed us to stay in the house on Maurine Place, he quickly showed us just how big of a douche bag he really was. His arrival in our home ushered in years of verbal and even physical abuse that tore apart what was left of our family. Conrad the Dick would frequently come home at night from his job as manager at a roofing company in a sour mood and do nothing but berate us, and if anyone dare talk back or raise their voice, things quickly got physical. There was one particular exchange between Conrad and my mom that eats at me even today. One night before I had arrived home from a game, my mom asked Conrad several times if he could change the light above the garage. After the fourth request, my mom, sensing she had a snowball's chance in hell in getting Conrad to perform that easy chore, muttered something under her breath. Conrad heard this, charged at my mom, and smacked her across the face. I walked in the door just as my mom began applying ice to her wound. Seeing my mom with a gash under her left eye, I cursed at Conrad, earning a welt to match my mother's.

As I grew older, I wondered more and more why my mother, a woman who'd already been in a decade-long healthy relationship where mutual respect was evident from the beginning, would allow herself and her children to put up with Conrad's abuse. I initially thought back to the years immediately following my father's accident and realized the predicament my mother had been in. By the

27

time my mom and Conrad tied the knot, we were almost broke. Conrad's money kept us in the house and food on the table. As a result, when he started using my mother's face as a punching bag, she had a big decision to make: take the abuse but keep the house and be able to feed her children or take legal action and possibly lose everything.

But finances weren't the only reason why we had to endure Conrad's reign of terror for so long. While there should be absolutely no place in society for domestic violence, I think that prior to the O.J. Simpson case in 1994 and the revelations of the abuse he inflicted on his ex-wife before her murder, America—and the American justice system as a whole—paid far less attention to the horrors of domestic violence than it does today. And because of that, in the late '80s and early '90s, battered women, like my mother, were still unsure what the response of the authorities and legal system would be in the event they did step forward.

In September 1989, I began my freshman year at Fullerton Union High School. If you think you've heard of it, it's because you probably have. Over the years, numerous notable athletes and dignified members of other fields have walked the halls of the school and donned the Indians jersey, including former president Richard Nixon, Hall of Fame baseball players Walter Johnson and Arky Vaughan, NFL All-Pro Keith Van Horne, and, most recently, Michael Lorenzen of the Cincinnati Reds.

Because of my success on the travel-ball circuit, the coaching staff at Fullerton Union, or FU, knew who I was the minute I walked into the school for the first time. For some reason, Ed Orbison, the varsity coach, took a liking to me and went out of his way to ensure I stayed out of trouble and made a smooth transition to high school. I later found out that he'd been buddies with my paternal grandfather, who'd died before I was even born.

Coach Orbison was a tough, no-nonsense type, which was exactly what I needed with all the chaos going on around me. He had three simple rules—be on time, be ready to play, and go all out on every play—and if you didn't follow them, you'd have big problems. But if you did, I swear, the guy would have your back 100 times out of 100. Coach Orbison quickly noticed not just my talent but also my passion for the game; however, he also figured out that my home situation was far from ideal and that he'd have to double as the authoritative male figure in my life. Coach Orbison's first cameo in that role came at the end of the first quarter of my freshman year when I received a D in algebra.

"Son," Coach began, "D's don't play baseball for Fullerton Union. I don't expect straight A's or even A's and B's from you or anyone else on the team, but I expect a full effort out of all my players. Now, I don't think you gave a full effort this quarter. Don't ever come by here with a D again."

I never received another D in high school.

By the time I got to FU, Coach Orbison had built a tremendous program. In his 21 seasons at the helm, the Indians had won 12 conference titles and five state sectional championships. The program was so strong that Coach Orbison had never had a freshman starter on the varsity. I had every reason to believe that streak would continue until a week before the start of the season Coach called me into his office to tell me I'd be playing left field and batting eighth in the opener against Buena Park High.

Curving Foul

From a talent perspective, there were other guys on the team probably more deserving of a spot in the lineup, Coach said, but he appreciated the way I'd hustled my tail off in fall ball and spring practice. He also thought that consistently facing older players as a freshman would help me develop into a core player by the time I was an upperclassman.

I'd love to be able to say that I was an instant success as the first freshman to start for the vaunted Fullerton Union Indians, but the fact of the matter was that I sucked the first several weeks of the season. For the first time in my life, I was facing fastballs in the 90-mph range and seeing off-speed stuff in counts other than 0-2 and 1-2. But, unlike some of the Major League clubs I would eventually play for, there was no backstabbing or bickering by the upperclassmen I had forced to the bench, and in time, I made adjustments and was soon back to hitting ropes.

By the end of the season, one that ended with yet another conference title, I'd hiked my average to the .250 mark and delivered a bunch of extra-base knocks, including a key double in the playoffs. While .250 may not sound like much, again I'll point to the unbelievably high level of baseball played in California. As a matter of fact, I faced three guys who would be drafted that June and two others who ended up pitching for Division I schools the following year. Coach Orbison was dead on—that year of facing such good pitching worked wonders for my long-term development and put me on the fast track.

By my sophomore season, I had grown several inches and was over six feet. With most of the starting infield from the prior season having graduated, I moved back over to shortstop, where I would stay for the remainder of high school. My arm was only slightly above average and I didn't have the best range, but my soft hands and quick release enabled me to make all the routine plays and occasionally a spectacular one. My calling card, however, remained my bat. I started the season in the two hole, but midway through I was moved to third in the lineup and never looked back. I hit about .350 with four home runs to earn all-conference honors as well as second-team all-section. And once again we were the conference champions while also making it to the state sectional finals. All the winning notwithstanding, the most gratifying part of the season occurred when all my childhood buddies joined me on the varsity. Though Kelly, Finkelman, and Lapitka didn't play much, Rossi hit a home run in the conference playoffs and Ruggiero contributed a diving catch in the sectional finals. Just sophomores, we all thought the best was yet to come.

By the end of my sophomore year, my home life had evolved into a mess. My mom, after years of physical and mental abuse by Conrad, had put on 50 pounds and become an alcoholic and diabetic who rarely left the couch. Dana, now in middle school, had a wide array of emotional issues that were reflected in her own obesity, in addition to multiple facial and body piercings and shaved head. Conrad's outbursts were nearly a daily occurrence. He'd often hurl vicious insults at my mom and sister, and because they were so used to the horrific treatment, they rarely even reacted. I wasn't immune to the prick's attacks either. His favorite verbal jabs usually were focused on my lack of a steady part-time job and subpar grades, and he took great pride in calling me a loser who wouldn't make anything out of my life. Unlike my mom and sister, however, I did my best to get as far away as possible from that asshole. Luckily, I had a bunch of cool friends with understanding parents who had no problems with me inviting myself to their homes for impromptu sleepovers, even on school nights. One night I'd be at the Lapitkas' house, the next night at the Finkelmans', and the following night at the Rossis' or Ruggieros'. These people provided a roof over my head, fed me, did my laundry, and even gave me some spending money despite having their own kids to worry about. There's no way I would have made it through high school without them.

Things finally came to a head between Conrad and me during the final week of my sophomore year. And of all things, it was over $3. I had come home one night after a game just to pick up some things before heading over to the Rossis' to spend the night. Just as I was about to leave, Conrad pulled up in his Pontiac. As usual, I didn't have a dime in my pocket and felt bad about again imposing on Vito and Maria Rossi, who'd been so generous. So, I politely asked Conrad if I could borrow three bucks from him and promised to pay him back as soon as possible.

"What did you just ask me for?" came the dick's reply.

"Just $3 so I can buy lunch tomorrow."

"Just $3?! Just $3?! Do you know how hard I bust my ass for you guys and none of you do shit! Your fat mother pissing her life away on that couch, that freak sister of yours, and you with your stupid baseball! I'm so sick of all you guys! You want money? Here's some fucking money!"

Just then my stepfather, completely unprovoked, took a swing at me. I should have been ready for it because it surely wasn't the first time he'd hit me, but I wasn't. He got me right in the mouth, and I instantly tasted blood. He then followed up with another right, but this time I was ready and sidestepped the blow. Rage, like none other I'd ever experienced, suddenly came over me, and I unleashed a barrage of blows against the man who'd caused my mother, my sister, and me so much pain.

With each punch, I was releasing all the pent-up anger that had been building inside of me for years. Before I knew it, Conrad was a bloody pulp writhing in pain on the driveway, and my neighbor, who'd heard the commotion from his backyard, was peeling me off him. Good thing, because I likely wouldn't have let up until the prick bled out.

Like most bullies, Conrad backed off after that. In fact, the words we exchanged that night were the last we ever said to one another. Sadly, this episode also marked the end of my relationship with both my mom and Dana. During my final two years of high school, I spent an increasing amount of time with my friends and their families and found any excuse I could to avoid going back to that house of horrors, where my mom and Dana's downward spiral continued. By the time I graduated high school, I hadn't spoken to either in two years.

You would think that between my exploits on the diamond and dashing good looks, the girls of FU would have been foaming at the mouth at the mere thought of dating me. Not quite. I was a quiet kid, and that was before my father died and was "replaced" by a jackass who took great pride in constantly berating me. Thus, when the hookup train left the station, I didn't exactly have a prime seat.

You have to understand something. While all the girls

at school might have seen a decent-looking, athletic guy, when I looked in the mirror, the kid staring back was everything that the primary male figure in his life told him he was—an imbecile who'd never amount to anything. Try getting laid with that opinion of yourself! While I had a couple minor hookups in the back of Bobby Rossi's Chevy Blazer on the way to the beach and at some house parties, I didn't begin to feel confident enough with the ladies to lose my virginity until my freshman year of college. By then, I was far enough away from my stepfather's insults and mother's self-destruction to realize how much I had going for myself.

Early in the fall of my junior year, Coach Orbison met me outside my last class of the day as the final bell was sounding and asked me to take a walk with him. As we strolled around the campus of FU, Coach and I had what would become one of the most important conversations of my life.

"Jack," Coach Orbison began, "given that you were only a sophomore last year, you had a great season."

Because my miserable home life didn't expose me to such lavish praise, I didn't know how to react and just kept my eyes glued to the floor as we walked.

Coach continued, "I'd wager I've coached over 300 of my own guys and coached against thousands of kids in the nearly 25 years I've been here and am certain I've never seen an underclassman as talented as you."

By now, my face was turning a bright shade of red.

"And I'll tell you another thing. I'm not the only one who feels this way. Talk to any other coach from our conference and they'll say the same thing. What I'm trying to say, Jack, is that you have a gift. A real God-given gift.

Now the question is what do you want to make of this gift. Do you want to be satisfied with a couple years at Cypress County Community College or do you have bigger plans for yourself, like a big-time D1 school and perhaps the pros?"

If Coach Orbison didn't have my attention earlier, he surely had it now. Though he'd drop hints in the past that I may be good enough to play at the college level, this was the first time he'd ever indicated I could be a prime-time guy.

"Hear me out, Jack," Coach warned. "You've got some big decisions to make. It's going to take a lot of work. No, an unbelievable amount of work. It's a big world out there, and there are thousands of guys who are great ballplayers and want the same things you want. You're not just going to have to outplay them; you're going to have to outwork them. Do you want it, Jack?"

You better believe I wanted it! After that pep talk, I started to work my ass off. I convinced the whole gang—Lapitka, Ruggiero, Kelly, Rossi, and Finkelman—to meet several times a week before school to do soft toss, work on the batting tee, and do a bunch of other drills. Then after school, we hit off the pitching machine in one of the school's auxiliary gyms.

Once junior year started, Coach looked prophetic. I was red hot right out of the gate, smashing a home run and two triples in the season opener. The entire team soon followed suit, and before we knew it, we had won our first 20 games in a row and were smelling blood. As good as FU baseball had been under Coach Orbison, no team had ever posted an undefeated season. In our 23rd game, we were down 8-2 after the first six innings. But with one out in the seventh, we strung together eight straight knocks—including a blistering triple by yours truly—and we won 10-9 in extras. We finally lost in our 26th game, but not before I notched another three hits, including my eighth home run. When all was said and done, we cruised to a 34-1 final record and were conference and state sectional champs. With a .450 average and nine home runs, I received more publicity than I could ever have imagined. I was first-team all-county, all-conference, and all-state. Even *Baseball America* said I was a third-team All-American. All this and I was only a junior. What would I be able to do for an encore?

Youth baseball has changed dramatically in the last 25 years. These days, the top amateurs throughout the country assemble for wood-bat showcases that match the best against the best in front of college coaches and pro scouts on beautifully manicured major and minor league fields. I feel old saying this, but back in my day we had none of this. After the high school season ended, we'd merely switch uniforms and play American Legion, usually on the same fields against the same kids we had faced during the spring. Occasionally, our Legion team would play in out-of-state tournaments, but these opportunities were few and far between and we never played with wood. That's why it was such a big deal when I was invited to Dodger Stadium—along with 100 other high school players from the greater LA area—for an informal tryout during the summer after my junior year. The tryout itself meant little because I still had another year of school left, but dressing in a Major League clubhouse, stepping onto that big ball orchard in Chavez Ravine, and hitting with a wood bat made me realize that despite all the shit I'd gone through, I still had so much to live for.

In addition to the proliferation of showcases, the other way in which amateur baseball (and amateur sports as a whole) has changed has been the entire college recruiting process. I can't help but chuckle when I hear of a high school sophomore or even freshman signing with a school he's not going to be attending for another three years.

When I was a kid (there I go again), the college recruiters and coaches would keep tabs on you during your junior season, followed by some dialogue during the subsequent summer. Then finally you'd decide which college you'd commit to by signing day, which was in the autumn of senior year. During my junior season, there were five schools that scouted me harder than all the others: USC, UCLA, Cal State Fullerton, Fresno State, and Cal Irvine. USC, which still had all the cache from being hands-down the best college team two decades earlier, was my first choice, but two potential roadblocks stood in the way of me becoming a Trojan. First, as the only private school on the list, USC was by far the most expensive, and because college baseball offers far fewer scholarships than football and basketball, it was out of my price range. Additionally, my mediocre grades and SAT scores were likely not going to be enough to meet its tough admission standards.

Coach Orbison, who by now had become a surrogate father to me, was aware of my precarious financial situation and academic limitations and did all he could to steer me in the direction of Cal State Fullerton. Not only was tuition a fraction of what USC charged, but because it was literally down the street, Coach Orbison even offered to let me live with him and his wife. But I would hear none of it and longed to follow in the footsteps of my boyhood hero, Freddie Lynn, as well as those of Tom Seaver, Roy

Curving Foul

Smalley, Steve Kemp, and Mark McGwire.

At the end of the day, Coach called in every favor he could to get me a full ride to the school of my dreams. Finally, on a picture-perfect September afternoon, Coach Orbison interrupted my senior English class to give me the amazing news. And though it was from just the other 17 students in the class, I received the first standing ovation of my life.

Even with the full scholarship to USC in my back pocket, I hadn't ruled out the idea of going straight to the pros if a team was willing to take me somewhere in the top five rounds of the 1993 amateur draft and give me a signing bonus large enough to enable me to forego college. I'll admit, prior to the start of my senior season, I spent a lot of time agonizing whether I should take a team's money right out of high school or head to the college of my dreams. After the monster season my teammates and I had enjoyed the previous year, I was certain my senior year would bring more championships for FU and another all-world season for me. Man, was I wrong.

No one was more disappointed at the outcome of my final season than I was. Although I had been a three-year starter, my senior season was vastly different from any other. For the first time in my baseball life, I was the guy with the target on his back, the guy opposing coaches and pitchers wouldn't let beat them. I found that out during the first three games of the season when I was walked a total of NINE times and barely got anything good to hit.

What made things even worse was that we lost all three of those games. So, with my team behind the eight ball this early in the season, I tried to carry everyone on my back and hit a five-run home run each time I stepped to the plate. I began to press and expand the strike zone, and it was only a matter of time before my timing and hitting mechanics were all screwed up and I found myself in a doozy of a slump. What was supposed to be the best season of my life, one last hurrah with all my boyhood pals, turned into a nightmare.

What complicated things even more that year was all the preseason talk of me being a likely high draft pick and the throngs of Major League scouts swarming around our field like bees circling around honey trying to determine whether one Jack Carter was worth a six-figure signing bonus. Having played in an ultracompetitive Southern California conference the past three years, scouts in the stands and behind the backstop were nothing new. But when it's you they're there to see and it's not just three or four scouts but instead 20 or 30, the thing put to the test is your ability to focus and perform under pressure, not your 60-yard time, power, or throwing arm. I guess you could say I failed that test miserably.

It probably wasn't a coincidence that as soon as all the scouts lost interest in me and disappeared, I started to hit again. I hit .500 over a 12-game span with seven home runs, but it was too late. I'd blown my chance at a large, six-figure payday, and FU didn't make the postseason for the first time in 11 years. Ultimately, the Cubs drafted me in the 33rd round and offered me a measly $6,000 signing bonus, making my decision to attend USC an easy one. To an extent, I was relieved that I'd gotten drafted so late because it meant I'd be heading off to college with a clear head and would never be forced to play "what if." As much as I loved my teammates and coach, when my senior year ended, I felt this overwhelming desire to move on and see what awaited me in the next chapter of my life.

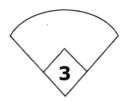

Big Man on Campus

Featuring a lineup that more resembled a Double A team than a college squad, USC captured five consecutive College World Series titles from 1970 to 1974. To put this into perspective, no school has ever won more than two championships in a row. Though the program had won just one CWS since that great run, it had claimed four Pac-10 championships and made it to the NCAA Tournament six times, including five of the past six years.

This was the powerhouse I joined in the fall of 1993. To give you an idea of just how stacked we were, seven (SEVEN!) of the guys from that team made it to the Major Leagues, including future All-Stars Geoff Jenkins and Aaron Boone.

Piloting the Trojans' ship in those years was Mike Gillespie, a tall, thin, nondescript-looking guy who looked more like a CPA than a renowned baseball coach. Gillespie had taken over for legendary skipper Rod Dedeaux following the 1986 season. Dedeaux was to college baseball what Bear Bryant was to college football and John

Wooden was to college hoops. In 45 years at the helm of the Trojans, Dedeaux had amassed over 1,300 wins and a .699 winning percentage. Gillespie, though not nearly Dedeaux's equal, still oversaw a program that was good enough to rank among the best in the dog-eat-dog world of Pac-10 baseball. I've always asked myself, however, how much of USC baseball's success under Gillespie was because of Gillespie himself and how much was the result of him simply being able to leverage what was still college baseball's premier name brand in attracting the nation's best talent.

I quickly learned that baseball at USC would be a far cry from what I had been used to. My somewhat disappointing senior year at FU notwithstanding, I had won every award and accolade you could win in high school and had trouble imagining that many guys my age could be as skilled at hitting a baseball as I was. I was in for a rude awakening.

I'll never forget my first round of batting practice during fall ball my freshman year. I was in the same hitting group as Jenkins, Boone, and a young freshman from San Diego who you might have heard of, Jacque Jones. Boone was the first to step into the box, and all he did was launch rockets all over the park. It seemed like every ball broke the sound barrier and landed at least 400 feet away. Next up was the sophomore Jenkins, who at not even 20 was already 200 pounds and built like a brick shithouse. And with each swing, Jenkins tore the cover off the ball. On his last swing, the future Milwaukee Brewer put the ball onto the top deck of the parking garage beyond the right-field wall. And the crazy thing was that not one person said anything. Did this beast put 'em onto the roof on a regular basis, I asked myself.

When Jones, who in those days was five feet 10 and 170 pounds soaking wet, stepped up to the plate, I breathed a sigh of relief from the on-deck circle. Finally, the laser light show would be coming to an end and the bar would be lower when it would be my turn to take a couple swings. Wrong. I'd never seen a guy generate such torque with his swing as Jones did that day. The little guy blasted missiles with each cut. Before long, I was at the plate, already psyched out by all the cannon fire I'd witnessed. While I hit some line drives and deep fly balls, several of which barely cleared the fence, it was clear to anyone watching that I wasn't in the same class as the guys who had hit before me.

As dispirited as I may have been following that first practice, I wasn't discouraged. To the contrary, what I had just seen made me work even harder. For the first time in my life, I started lifting weights and also began a habit of something I would do for the remainder of my baseball career, squeeze rubber balls whenever I was watching TV or reading. This is a common exercise in baseball that builds wrist and forearm strength, which, in turn, increases bat speed. And like the last two years of high school, I resumed taking extra BP and doing more hitting drills whenever I had the chance.

In this regard, USC was ideal for me. The facilities, even over 20 years ago, were outstanding. Because of generous donors and a massive athletics budget, we had all the equipment you could ask for. The most up-to-date pitching machines, tees, balls, gloves, bats, weight-training equipment, you name it, we had it. And to my credit, I made use of all the resources that were offered to me.

It was a good thing that I made use of all the baseball resources available to me, because I certainly didn't take advantage of the academic perks USC offered. Though not a top-tier school like Stanford, Princeton, or Harvard, USC was competitive and presented students with the opportunity for a solid, if not spectacular, education. But, truth be told, I was there to get my BA in hitting a baseball and couldn't have cared less about hitting the books. As a freshman, I took as many easy courses as I could—phys ed, Introduction to Acting, The Role of Sports in American Society—so I could put as much effort into baseball as possible. It was a good thing, because aside from mandatory study sessions, I rarely cracked open a book.

Other than getting used to the fact that everyone on the team was as good or better than me, the toughest thing about my transition to college was making friends. Outside of the half dozen guys I'd played baseball with since grammar school, I didn't have any close friends. And with all of us now scattered across various colleges in California, it was high time for me to branch out and meet new people. Easier said than done. I was still an intensely private, shy kid not over the trauma of losing my father when I was just 10 and then having to deal with years of Conrad's abuse. I also had an inferiority complex when it came to money, or more precisely, my lack of it. USC was, and still is, a wealthy school, and I realized early on that I was one of the select few "have-nots" on campus.

While many kids, including a bunch of guys on the baseball team, were cruising around in their parents' leftover BMWs, Saabs, or Jeep Cherokees and partying in some of LA's toniest bars and nightclubs courtesy of the fake IDs they bought at $50 a pop, yours truly couldn't even afford a car and delivered mail to the dorms to earn some extra cash.

The baseball team was the obvious place for me to find new buddies. With the exception of a couple guys who were spoiled douche bags, most of my teammates happily welcomed me into the clan. Boone, who would one day be part of a three-generation baseball family as well as hit one of the biggest home runs in Yankee playoff history before becoming manager of the Bronx Bombers, was the leader of the pack. Because of his big-league bloodlines and an entire childhood spent in the Phillies', Angels', and Royals' clubhouses alongside the likes of Pete Rose, Mike Schmidt, Reggie Jackson, and George Brett, Booney, as we called him, was a cool customer who carried himself like USC was a mere pit stop on the way to bigger and better things. From the first day of practice when he came up to me and warmly introduced himself, Booney was a class act who did his best to make me feel at home.

Though not as outgoing, Jenkins was another guy who became a good friend. Heavily pursued by several pro clubs out of Rancho Cordova, Jenkins opted to refine his skills at USC, where he quickly established himself as one of the most prolific power hitters in school history. Other guys I quickly built a solid rapport with were Chad Moeller, who carved out a lengthy Major League career as a backup catcher, Griffin Dengler, a glove-first infielder who could play anywhere on the dirt, and Eric McMurry, a lanky right-handed reliever.

Being a baseball player at USC definitely had its benefits, especially socially. Let's just say there was not a party we couldn't get into. And, rest assured, in the

1990s USC had some party scene going on. In the fall, the fun revolved around the football team. Though not a powerhouse like the Pete Carroll-led teams of the 2000s, USC under John Robinson was a perennial top-25 team that didn't have any problems capturing the attention of the student body and filling the 93,000-seat Coliseum on fall Saturdays. On game days, we'd finish our fall ball workout, shower, then head to 901 Bar, or the "Nine O" as we called it, for some pregame. Though most of us weren't yet 21, things were far different back then and many bars in and around USC didn't card. Usually we'd just stand in the corner and shoot the breeze while drinking a lot and killing time before heading to what would often be a Trojan victory at the Coliseum.

Following the game, we'd make our way to the USC landmark Traditions, or "Traddies," where we'd survey the scene and plot the strategy for the rest of the night. If there was a good amount of "DS," or Designated Snapper in English, we'd stay and play the field, but if things were quiet, we'd try our luck at either another bar or club or hit an off-campus party. Either way, things were always bound to get out of control.

It was during one of these Saturday rituals when I popped my cherry. McMurry's girlfriend from high school was visiting and brought some friends to the Nine O with her. One of them, Samantha I think her name was, thought I was cute and instead of being discouraged by the customary Carter silent treatment became even more interested and practically threw herself on top of me right in the middle of the bar. I wasn't even that attracted to her, but with my new teammates, who still hadn't gotten a good read on me, watching like hawks, I figured now was

45

as good a time as ever to prove to all those interested that the batter's box wasn't the only venue where I excelled. So, we went back to my dorm room, and I emerged 20 minutes later, a new man.

It's hard to put into words what I felt after that first sexual experience. Joy? Fulfillment? Sense of belonging? Probably all of the above, but relief more than anything else. Prior to sealing the deal with Samantha, I felt that my virginity served as a note of caution to my teammates in the brave new world of USC that I was a loser who couldn't get laid and wasn't worth a millisecond of their time. But that all changed the minute I rejoined my buddies in the stands of the Coliseum. I was greeted like a folk hero, with multiple high fives, pats on the back, and inquiries on Samantha's technique. An hour earlier, I would have done anything to get these guys' acceptance and suddenly I was a stud.

My good fortune continued for the rest of the fall semester. More at ease in my new surroundings, I got closer with some of the guys, notably Jenkins, McMurry, and Moeller, and even made some friends who weren't baseball players. I also noticed an improvement on the field. Though not in Jenkins' or Booney's class, I started to drive the ball in the Red and Gold World Series, which was held at the conclusion of fall ball, drawing praise from the usually stoic Gillespie and his coaching staff.

I alluded to this briefly earlier, but what struck me that first semester was the preferential treatment athletes received at USC. Not only did we live in nicer dorms, get to work out in a better-equipped gym, and enjoy access to special study sessions, but socially we were also at the top of the food chain. I couldn't tell you how many times we'd show up at a party or on-campus bar only to be asked, "You guys are on the baseball team, right?" Free drinks and adulation would usually follow.

The benefits of being an athlete extended to my love life. Though I wasn't ready to butt heads with George Clooney, my newfound confidence after my experience with Samantha and acceptance by my teammates opened doors for some good times with several other chicks. There was Michelle, the baseball groupie, Cara from my freshman writing seminar, and Giovanna, who lived down the hall. For the first time in a long time, life was good.

Back in the 1990s, the college baseball season began during the second half of January, which meant that right after returning from winter break we got down to business. Unfortunately, despite coming on toward the end of fall ball, I couldn't crack the starting lineup and found myself riding the pine for the first time of my life when the season started. With Booney and future big leaguer Gabe Alvarez anchoring the left side of the infield, there was no room for me on the dirt, so I was moved to the outfield, where, politely stated, I was a work in progress. The problem was, however, that Jacque Jones was ensconced in center field. With Jenkins manning one of the corners and a slew of upperclassmen splitting time between the other corner and DH, there wasn't a spot for me. Rather than sulk, I kept taking extra BP and doing my extra hitting drills because when my opportunity came—and I was sure it would—I was going to be ready.

It took longer than I expected to get that opportunity. In a rare Wednesday game against Cal Irvine in the season's sixth week, I finally got a chance to play. After a makeup game that Monday and regularly scheduled contest on Tuesday, Gillespie started some reserves after games on five straight days to give the regulars a breather prior to the upcoming weekend's marquee series against crosstown rival UCLA. Because I was taking up a full scholarship in a sport where each team only gets 11.7 of them, Gillespie was chomping at the bit to use me. Also, I think he appreciated the fact that I continued to work hard and not bitch when I was on the bench to start the season.

Batting seventh and playing left field that night against the Anteaters, I singled three times and made a sliding catch to save two runs in a 5-4 win. Gillespie, whose communication skills would never evoke comparisons with Joe Torre, greeted me in the dugout after the victory with some music for my ears.

"Nice game, son. I think I may have just found a spot for you."

Gillespie was true to his word. That Friday night I was in the lineup, hitting seventh again and DHing against hated UCLA. I hung tough against the Bruins' ace, lining out and working two walks as we won 6-1. I sat against the lefty on Saturday but was back in there again for Sunday's rubber game. I slammed a triple and single to help us win the series.

Over the next month and a half, I played mostly against righties, holding my own but still not doing enough to warrant a full-time role. Then, in a mid-April series versus Stanford, I went off. I hit my first collegiate home run against future San Diego Padre Jason Middlebrook, a no-doubter to right, and followed it up with a ringing double. In all, I had six hits and drove in seven runs in the

48

series. I caught fire down the stretch and began to play regularly, usually hitting fifth behind Jenkins and Booney and playing left field. By the time the regionals started, I had gotten my batting average up over .360 and had already slugged five home runs.

As a top 16-ranked team, USC got to host a regional. In our pool was Kent State, San Diego State, and Texas San Antonio. We breezed through the first two games but found ourselves down in the final against Kent State. With future first-round pick Dustin Hermanson in to preserve the Golden Flashes' 7-5 lead in the bottom of the eighth, Booney and I hit back-to-back home runs to tie it up, and an inning later Jones crossed home plate on a passed ball to send us to the super regionals.

My hot hitting continued as we were just two wins from advancing to Omaha as one of eight teams to make the College World Series, college baseball's version of Mecca. I hit another big fly in the first game and socked two doubles in the second, but unfortunately we lost the deciding third game when a skinny shortstop for Georgia Tech named Nomar Garciaparra hit a walk-off two-run triple.

The pain of not making it to Omaha notwithstanding, I'd had a tremendous freshman year, which was capped by me being named a Freshman All-American and receiving an invitation to play for the Bourne Braves in the prestigious Cape Cod Baseball League. To this day, that summer I spent on the Cape remains one of the best experiences of my life. I not only developed as a ballplayer but also for the first time had the chance to spend a large chunk of time outside California.

Until 1999, when rules were introduced to dampen

the power of aluminum bats used in college baseball, the sport was commonly known as "Gorilla Ball" because of the plethora of high-scoring games. You would commonly hear scouts say that a certain hitter had an "aluminum bat swing." Such a hitter was a guy who'd be able to put a charge into a ball when he was swinging a lighter aluminum bat, but when he had to switch to wood he was quickly exposed as a non-prospect. Enter the Cape Cod Baseball League, which was like truth serum for college hitters. Guys would arrive on the Cape full of confidence after putting up gaudy numbers hitting with aluminum during the spring only to wither away when forced to use wood against the best pitchers from all over the country.

I'll admit, I had my doubts as to whether I'd be able to prove my mettle when they took the metal out of my hands (yes, pun intended). Seriously, you have to realize that 20 years ago, before wood bat showcases became the norm, guys' first long-term exposure to wood bats usually occurred on the Cape. And regardless of how much success we may have enjoyed during the spring, none of us had any idea of how well we'd take to the wood bats until we stepped into the box in the CCBL.

My first experience hitting with a wood bat was rough. Against Clemson's Kris Benson, who would eventually be picked first overall in the draft, I went 0-4 with three pop-ups and a strikeout. Fortunately, before any doubts could seep into my head, Miles Jansen, an outgoing septuagenarian New Englander who was Bourne's hitting coach, approached me after the game with some reassuring words and useful tips. He said he liked my swing because it was simple and fluid and didn't contain a lot of moving parts. However, like a lot of college hitters, he believed that the aluminum had "spoiled" me into thinking I could pull everything with power. This caused me to become pull happy and fly open with my front shoulder too soon. Instead of spraying line drives to the opposite field, I was trying to pull pitches on the outer third of the plate. This was why I had just popped the ball up three separate times. Miles also encouraged me to look for certain pitches in the zone to drive, preferably those on the inner half of the plate that were thigh to waist high. Finally, Miles' last suggestion was for me to take BP right before the game with the biggest, heaviest bat I could find, then move to a lighter bat once the game started. This would enhance my in-game bat speed.

Miles ended up offering similar tips to a lot of guys who were struggling that summer, but only a select few listened and implemented the changes he recommended. Rest assured, I treated his words as gospel. In fact, the next day Miles and I were on the field several hours before game time, working on what he had told me a day earlier. With a 36-ounce bat that felt like lead after a few swings, I tried shooting outside pitches the other way while pulling and driving pitches that were in my "wheelhouse." Miles was amazing. Not only did he offer commentary and encouragement after each pitch, but he also just kept throwing despite the intense 90-degree heat and high humidity that I was learning was so commonplace on the East Coast. And when we finally did stop after over a hundred pitches, it was because I had to conserve some energy for the game.

The old man proved to be a wise sage. Though I didn't get a hit that day, I lined out sharply to third base and left field on two outside strikes and pulled an inside changeup deep to the warning track in right.

"Progress," said Miles.

As the summer wore on, my progress became more evident. Although I didn't hit with the power I had during the spring at USC, I still drilled three home runs to go along with a boatload of doubles. With the season winding down, my .320 batting average ranked among the league leaders and earned me a trip to the Cape Cod All-Star game at majestic Fenway Park. As I stretched and ran some sprints in that beautiful outfield before the game, I was gripped by the same longing to be a Major League baseball player as when I attended the tryout two summers earlier at Dodger Stadium. The only difference was that I was now a little closer to realizing that dream.

That summer on the Cape was about so much more than just baseball. Together with Seton Hall ace Matt Morris, who would later be a 20-game winner for the Cardinals, I lived with Anne Honeycutt, a 50-something widow with no kids who worked as a writer for a local paper. Anne wasn't much of a baseball fan, but because her late husband was, they had started serving as host parents to visiting players about 20 years earlier.

Anne was fascinating, the most interesting person I'd met up until that point in my life. Because she and her husband, a freelance journalist, had never had kids, they took the opportunity to travel the world. Woodstock for the big concert in '69, Sarajevo for the '84 Olympics, Rio de Janeiro for Carnival, Munich for Oktoberfest, Jerusalem for Easter, you name it, Anne and Ron Honeycutt were there. As a kid who had never been east of the Mississippi until that summer and whose seminal moments in life had occurred on a baseball field, I was mesmerized by Anne's stories. Looking back, the time I spent with Anne was more valuable than any course I ever took in school because it opened me up to a world I had no idea existed.

Morris wasn't around much because he had several pairs of aunts and uncles in the area, so Anne and I had the opportunity to talk for hours. Maybe it's because she was a writer, but at times she seemed just as fascinated by my meager past as I was about all the adventures she had embarked on during her exciting life. I remember one night, late in the summer, after we had finished eating a late dinner and loaded the dishwasher, Anne invited me outside. Unexpectedly, she removed a small plastic bag from her pocket that contained two joints already rolled up.

"Care to join me?" she asked.

A couple times when I was in high school, Kenny Lapitka, Johnny Kelly, and I would drive to a nearby beach to smoke up, but weed never really did it for me. Still, if it meant another enthralling conversation with this worldly woman, why not? True to form, I coughed up a lung when I first inhaled, evoking a laugh from Anne.

"You don't do this much, do you, Jack?"

"No, definitely not. A lot of guys I play with drink and some chew tobacco, but not too many get high."

"Interesting," she mused. "You know, Jack, I've hosted at least 40 guys your age over the years. White, black, Latin, mixed race. Some Ivy Leaguers who went on to bigger and better things on Wall Street and in Washington and others who I'd bet were illiterate. And I've hosted some guys who brought a new girl to their room each night and others I was sure were in the closet. And, yet,

53

you are by far the most intriguing. No family photos in your room. No letters for me to mail. You are unfailingly polite and have a friendly disposition. Yet, when we've spoken, you haven't told me anything about yourself. Who are you, Jack?"

I inhaled, then gave her the CliffsNotes version of my life story. When I was finished, Anne took a drag of her own, then stared into space for a moment. During that moment of silence, I thought about how she would respond to my life story. I didn't expect anything to the effect of "you poor thing," and I was proven right.

"You've been through a lot for such a young person, Jack," Anne began. "As a matter of fact, you've already lived a fuller life than most people my age. My husband, Ron, if he were still alive, would have turned 64 later this year. His first-ever assignment was as a reporter embedded with an Army unit in the waning days of the Korean War. He was in Dallas the day President Kennedy was assassinated, then covered the race riots in Watts, Detroit, and Newark before doing the war in Vietnam. Ron, through his work, came into contact with all sorts of people. Heroes, cowards, tyrants, realists, idealists, rapists, murderers, the list goes on and on. But once he told me of another type of person, one which was his favorite to cover. Do you know what type of person that was? It was a survivor. Someone who, despite all the horrible things that happen to him, succeeds in life and makes something of himself. You know what, Jack? You're just that, a survivor. You've been through so many hurdles in your life and you're still not even old enough to drink. And, despite all the long odds, here you are, standing out among the best in the country. It was a privilege to host you this summer, to get to know you, because you're going to accomplish some amazing things before all is said and done."

And with that, my summer ended. On the flight from Boston to LAX, I looked back over the past year and couldn't believe how much my life had changed. Just a year earlier, I was just a shy, insecure kid unsure of whether he'd ever be able to shed his demons and realize his dreams. But now, with Anne's words playing over and over in my head, I was heading back to school more confident than I'd ever been. That was a good thing, because during the next year that confidence was going to be tested in ways I never would have imagined.

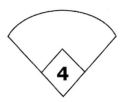

Rock Bottom

A strange thing happened to me almost immediately after I returned to USC to start my sophomore year. The day after I got back, I was grabbing some food in the cafeteria and a nondescript-looking kid who couldn't have been more than five-foot seven with thinning hair and glasses made his way over to me with his hand extended. Not knowing exactly what to do or say, I just smiled and shook his hand.

"Jack Carter," he began. "Brian Goldstein. Great to meet you. Tremendous summer! .324 on the Cape with almost 15 extra-base hits and more walks than strikeouts! Fantastic, man!"

"You a reporter?" I asked, still somewhat bewildered. Remember, this was still years before the internet enabled fans to access reams of obscure data, such as stats from the CCBL, with just the click of a mouse and I was shocked how this guy knew my numbers better than I did.

"Nah," he answered. "Just a fan. A big fan. I was devastated when you guys lost in the Super Regionals but am super pumped for next spring. Even without Boone, you guys should definitely make it to Omaha. And YOU will be one of the premier bats in the Pac-10."

I had no idea who this guy was nor how he knew all this stuff, but, man, I liked what he had to say! So much so that I invited him to sit down to talk some more baseball. During the conversation, it became evident that my new buddy was quite the savant. He didn't follow just the Major Leagues but was also an expert on the minors and even college. Like this guy, I ate, slept, and drank baseball and could talk about it morning, day, and night. First Anne and now Brian. I'd met the two best conversation partners I'd ever had in just the last two months.

After about an hour of discussing whether Jenkins, Nebraska's Darin Erstad, or Rice's Jose Cruz Jr. was the best college outfielder in the nation, I had to excuse myself to get to the gym. But before I did, I took down Brian's number and promised to call soon so we could continue the conversation.

Later, when I met up with a bunch of my teammates and excitedly told them about my new friend, their reactions were far from what I expected.

"That little shit's a real pain in my ass with all of his stupid comments and questions!" someone who should remain nameless declared.

"Yeah," added another. "He was all in my business like it was SportsCenter or something. I told that fucker to get lost."

"C'mon guys," I almost pleaded. "He's a good dude and a huge fan. What's the big deal?"

"I'll tell you what the big deal is," chimed in a third teammate, an upperclassman. "If that creep wanted to be someone's mascot, I'm sure he can call the football team and set something up. Unless he's got some grade A pussy he's been hiding from us, we don't need him around. Carter, it's on you to make sure that jackass knows his place."

Wow, that was a side of my teammates I hadn't seen before. What a bunch of dicks. You have to realize something here. When you spend a large part of your childhood the way I did, always low on cash and constantly on the receiving end of insults, you become nonjudgmental and accepting of others. I may have been better looking and a better baseball player than Brian Goldstein, but I can assure you there were about 54 things he did much better than me. Heck, after the miserable childhood I'd had, if some dude who loved talking baseball as much as me wanted to be my friend, I was all in. So, despite my teammates' boorish behavior, Brian and I became quick friends, often meeting to grab a quick bite and talk baseball. In addition to my heroics on the ballfield, the friendship I struck with Brian was one of the best parts of my time at USC.

Another odd thing happened early sophomore year. I was stalked by someone who eventually became my first-ever girlfriend. It started the week I returned to school. Wherever I went, I'd see the same tall, blonde chick. In the cafeteria, walking on campus, at Traddies, whenever I turned around, there she was. At first, I thought it was merely coincidental, but after about the 19th time, I realized it was more than just happenstance. Finally, when I saw her lurking five feet behind me at the school bookstore early one morning, I finally called her out.

"C'mon, legs. That's the best you've got?"

"Ha, it took you long enough, Carter," she responded.

"I was beginning to think you'd never notice."

"I didn't realize USC offered a stalking major. I'll bet you make Dean's List this semester."

"We'll see. Maybe you'll help me study."

"Why don't you give me your name first and then we'll discuss my tutoring business. Oh, and speaking of names, how in the world did you know mine?"

"My name's Amanda, but friends and foes call me Mandy. And get your head out of your ass, Jack. After that show you put on the end of last season, everyone knows who number 18 with the cute ass is."

Apparently, Brian Goldstein wasn't the only one who appreciated my heroics on the diamond.

Within several weeks, Mandy and I had gotten real close. Real close as in she was already telling anyone who'd listen that I was her boyfriend. Real close as in she would tag along to any bar or party I went to with my teammates. And real close as in she told me that she loved me after not even two months of dating and demanded the same line from me.

"*Tell me you love me, Jack. Tell me!*" still occasionally echoes in my brain.

Despite Mandy's control issues and "overzealousness," I didn't issue her walking papers. In fact, I doubled down—by mid-semester I was spending more time with her than anyone else. Save for fall baseball and weekly lunches with my new buddy Brian, I spent nearly every waking hour with Mandy. I guess I figured I could do a lot worse than a five-foot nine Amazon with a killer body who lavished me with attention, even if she was a tad overbearing. Anyway, before I knew it, we were on our way to meet her parents. It was just like any other drive we'd taken—

in her custom-built, mint condition 1978 Mercedes 450 SL convertible—until we turned off Route 10 and entered plush Bel Air. One minute we were passing Tom Hanks' house and the next we were pulling into a driveway just three doors down from former President Reagan. Things got even more crazytown when Mandy's father burst out of his front door, clad from head to toe in starched white tennis garb, shouting "How's my princess?" And Mandy's mom was not far behind, wearing sunglasses way too big for her face, cradling a white, fluffy poodle in her arms like a newborn baby.

Mandy's parents couldn't be more gracious (and neither could the two housekeepers, dog walker, and three landscapers all working on the grounds of the estate that day). It turned out that Mandy's father, Roger McDougal, was a big-time entertainment lawyer who'd represented Clint Eastwood, Paul Newman, Steve McQueen, and a wide variety of other household names. And here was lil ol' me from the other side of the tracks hobnobbing with Southern California's rich and famous. If only these people knew.

I woke up one morning that December with the realization that I had a serious problem on my hands. Lost in all the excitement surrounding my first girlfriend and monster fall ball numbers was the not-so-trivial 2.0 minimum grade-point-average requirement, which if I did not maintain would result in me losing my scholarship. After learning that I'd probably not earn any higher than a C in Pre-Calculus, it struck me that a 2.0 might require nothing short of a minor miracle. The problem was that because I had taken so many worthless classes freshman year, my sophomore year schedule was filled with legitimate courses that required time and effort. But with me burning the midnight oil juggling baseball and Mandy, I had barely opened a book all semester.

With several weeks remaining, I assessed my chances of achieving that magical 2.0. With a B in Spanish all but assured, the aforementioned C in Pre-Calc, and a D in Introduction to Physical Science, where I hadn't had a clue since the first week of class, it all hinged on my grade in US Government. I'd earned a C on the term paper but received only a D on the midterm, and the final exam was worth 50 percent of the semester grade. This meant I would need at least a B on the final to achieve a C for the semester and avoid falling below the coveted 2.0.

The situation looked bleak, to the say the least. But with five minutes left in the last lecture of the semester, Professor Saunders, a Birkenstock-wearing former hippie with a gray ponytail and earring, suddenly stopped the lesson and started discussing our final exam. Instead of a standard in-class final, Saunders explained that the exam would be take-home with three essay questions. He then passed out the sheet with the questions and added that we could use any class materials we wished to answer the questions; however, we couldn't consult one another as that would be considered cheating. A take-home final! I felt like I'd just been awarded another lease on life.

All the good vibes I'd been feeling were tempered that evening when I opened my textbook to see if I could get a handle on what some possible answers to the three-question exam would be. Nada. Zip. Zilch. I didn't have a clue, which was not a surprise since I hadn't even looked at the book in weeks. But then I remembered that this guy McMurry had gone to high school with had Saunders two years earlier and had aced the class. Maybe he'd be able to give me a couple pointers.

Krishna Patel, who'd graduated from Laguna Hills High School a year before McMurry, seemed happy to help when I called him. He even invited me to his dorm room right away to talk about the exam.

Notebook in hand, I made it to Patel's place, which was on the other side of campus, in less than 10 minutes. I was all business. Patel noticed this and didn't bog me down with any small talk.

"Old man Saunders has you stressed out, eh?" my new friend asked.

"Yeah," I answered. "I got behind the eight ball this semester with the reading and never really caught up. And now all these questions look like Greek." I pulled the question sheet out of my notebook and said, "I was hoping you could give me a couple ideas on how I could best approach these questions."

Just then Patel burst out laughing, this strange, high-pitched snort, and strangely, I felt I was the butt of this joke. "Dude," he began. "I can do a lot better than that. Everyone knows that moron gives the same questions on the final year after year. Why don't I just give you my exam from two years ago, which I nailed." As he was saying this, Patel went into his desk drawer and fished out some papers that were stapled together. He then handed them to me. "I'll tell you what," he offered. "I was gonna give this to you for $100, but since you're a buddy of Big Mac, how does $50 sound?"

My head was spinning. This was almost too good to be true! I'd been prepared to spend the next week holed up in the library busting my ass, but if $50 was all it would take to guarantee that I'd be able to keep living the dream, then so be it. As far as I was concerned, Christmas had come early. Just then, I thought of something that sobered me up a little.

"Say, Krishna, there's no chance I could get busted for doing this, is there?"

"Hehehe." There was that fucking laugh again. "Dude, how do you think I got this A? I'm pre-med and had an Organic Chemistry and Advanced Calculus final the same week this exam was due. Do you think I had time to answer stupid questions about the Founding Fathers and the Bill of Rights? I bought this fucking exam, Dude! Just like you! Except it cost me $100, which is what I should be charging you. Plus, what's Saunders, about 70? He's a fossil. There's no way he'll figure this out; the guy can barely make it through class."

And with that, I decided to meet Patel the next morning to give him his hard-earned $50.

With two days to go before Christmas, I was in a mad rush. Mandy's parents had surprised us by giving us an all-expenses-paid week-long trip to their luxury time-share condo in Acapulco. Though I badly wanted to take five minutes to lie on my bed and pleasure myself while imagining Mandy's unbelievable body in a hot string bikini, I couldn't because I had a long list of errands to run before we flew to Mexico later that night.

Realizing I would soon be in paradise, I was in excellent spirits. Although I had not yet received my grades for the semester, I was confident that I'd made it through unscathed, thanks of course to my $50 donation to the

Krishna Patel Medical School Fund. However, I was well aware of how lucky I'd been and made a promise to myself that I would spare myself the 11th-hour drama next term and open a book before it was almost too late.

As I wheeled the suitcase I had borrowed from Jenkins onto my hall, I was intercepted by Tim, my floor's resident assistant, who had a solemn look on his face and appeared eager to speak with me. Because of my busy schedule, Tim and I had exchanged maybe seven words since late August, so I found it somewhat odd that he was so interested in talking to me.

"Jack, you haven't spoken to anyone at the Dean of Students office today, have you?" he inquired somewhat anxiously.

"No, I haven't," I responded. "What's up?"

"The dean's office has called me twice looking for you. They said they haven't been able to reach you and it's important they talk to you before all students go home for the holiday. I'm supposed to send you down there as soon as possible. I'll give them a call to let them know you're on your way."

As soon as I dropped off Jenkins' suitcase in my room, I headed down to the Student Affairs building. During the short walk over, I asked myself what the urgency was. Probably a misunderstanding or a mix-up of some type, but whatever it was, it better be quick because I had a flight to catch.

When I entered the building, I looked around but the place seemed deserted. Finally, I spotted a lady with an '80s perm to my immediate right sitting at a desk reading a catalogue. I turned toward her to see if she could help.

"Hi, Ma'am, I'm Jack Ca-"

"Jack Carter, right. Dean Baldwin has been expecting you," she said, almost in an accusatory tone. "Please go up the stairs, then second door on your left." Dean Baldwin? The Dean of Students? I'd never met him but knew him by his reputation as the in-house disciplinarian. The bouncer. If you got busted with an open can of beer or smoking a joint, Baldwin was the man you saw. And a meeting with Baldwin never ended well, apparently. As I walked up the stairs, it finally hit me. Did I get busted for cheating?

I didn't have to wait long to find out. When I reached the top of the stairs and opened the second door, there he was. Or there they were. Dean Baldwin. And Professor Saunders. All of a sudden, I felt like one of those guys from the French Revolution who was about to die by guillotine. Except, instead of facing forward, secured in stocks, I could see the razor-sharp blade all the way down.

"Jack Carter?" asked Dean Baldwin, a late middle-aged man with thick glasses, a bow tie, and stern voice.

"Y-yes," I stammered, trying my best to keep it all together. I could feel the sweat already forming in my palms. Good thing he didn't try to shake hands.

"Sit down, please." I did as I was told, quickly glancing at Professor Saunders, who was sitting next to Dean Baldwin, across the table from me. Suddenly Saunders, with a scowl on his ruddy, weather-beaten face, didn't look so clueless.

"Mr. Carter," Dean Baldwin began. "The University of Southern California is one of the most prestigious institutions of higher learning in the country. In addition to our world-class faculty, what makes us a world-class university is our ethics and Code of Academic Honor, to which you and all your classmates took a pledge when you matriculated as first-year students. Mr. Carter, you violated this Code in the most blatant way earlier this month when you knowingly cheated on your US Government final exam, and as such, I have decided to expel you from this institution, effective immediately."

I sat there dumbfounded, shocked and terrified at the prospect of these two old men about to send all my dreams up in flames. I had to act and act fast if I was going to salvage what was left of my future.

In the most polite yet assertive voice I could muster, I began to state my case. "Cheating? I'm sorry I don't know what you're—"

The old hippie Saunders cut me off at once, but he wasn't nearly as eloquent as Dean Baldwin. "Don't be an ass, kid. I've got all the proof in black and white. Several years back, I started noticing that the answers to some finals were looking suspiciously familiar. So, I started photocopying all the submitted finals. I noticed that yours was suspiciously familiar to one that I'd seen before. Then, when I looked up your grades and saw that you'd received a C on the term paper and D on the midterm exam, I knew something was fishy. So, I compared your answers with the ones I'd photocopied last year and two years ago and saw that yours was identical—word for word—with an exam submitted by another student."

Baldwin then chimed in, "Professor Saunders immediately submitted his findings to me, and after an exhaustive review of all the evidence, I have come to share Professor Saunders' assessment that you copied the answers verbatim from another student's test. You may have noticed that you had not yet received your marks for the semester. This was because of the great pains we took to ensure that our review of this situation was thorough, precise, and unbiased.

"If I may add one thing, Mr. Carter," Dean Baldwin concluded. "In arriving at this difficult decision, I read through your file, then spoke with some of your professors and couldn't help but come to the conclusion that you've blown a tremendous opportunity. Although you earned at best mediocre grades in high school, this university chose to award you with a full scholarship because of your prowess on the baseball field. And, yet, even with this golden opportunity, you exerted minimal effort in the classroom, which was evident by the poor grades you earned. In short, despite this university's generosity, you have given little back in return. Good-bye and good riddance, Mr. Carter. Please vacate your dormitory room immediately. A copy of your transcript will be available at the Registrar's Office after the new year."

Stunned, I got up and walked out of the dean's office, down the steps, and exited the building. The breezy December air stung my arms when I got outside, which was a good thing because it helped dissipate the fog that had begun to envelope my brain and enable me to think straight. As dire as my situation was, I figured the one person at USC who would be able to help me was Coach Gillespie. Though my relationship with Gillespie was nothing like the one I'd enjoyed with Coach Orbison in high school, I felt that Gillespie had always appreciated the 100-percent effort I'd given and all I'd done for the team my freshman season. Also, as the longtime coach at one of America's best baseball schools, I hoped Gillespie might have enough influence to be able to convince Dean Baldwin and his cronies not to expel me.

Curving Foul

As luck would have it, as I approached the athletic building, which housed all the coaches' offices, I saw Gillespie exiting the building on the way to his car. We made eye contact immediately and he stopped in his tracks.

"Coach, can I have a minute?"

"Listen, Jack, I know why you're here," Gillespie began, without letting me get a word in. "Dean Baldwin called me earlier today to give me the news. Honestly, I don't know what to tell you except that you've let us all down. We don't want just good ballplayers here, but good citizens, and you proved with your actions that you're not the type of individual we want in the program. Hopefully, you'll take something away from this."

And with that Gillespie continued walking to his car, got in, and drove away. Still bewildered, I started the slow walk to my dorm. With just a couple days to go before Christmas, campus was almost deserted, save for a couple guys throwing a Frisbee and another zipping around on a skateboard. Suddenly, as I approached my dorm, Mandy appeared, and she didn't look happy.

"Jack, what the fuck? I've been trying to reach you all afternoon and left like five messages on your machine. Have you done all the things you were supposed to? Our flight's in a couple of hours."

"Mandy, I just got some really bad news."

"Jesus Christ, Jack! You're not flaking on me, are you?"

"I've just been expelled."

"What? Oh my God! You cannot be serious. What the fuck happened?"

"They caught me cheating on a final. I just came back

from the Dean of Students. I'm done."

Mandy just stood there with her mouth wide open. She was obviously in shock.

"I can't believe this. I just can't fucking believe this. Jack, how could you fuck up like this?"

And with those lovely words, it became evident that Mandy's shock had instantaneously turned into anger. Anger at the fact that she'd wasted an entire semester with a loser who'd just pissed his life away.

"I don't know," I replied quietly, shaking my head as I stared at the ground.

"You don't know? You don't know? What the fuck is wrong with you, Jack? What are you going to do?" Mandy was livid by this point. The happy-go-lucky girl from SoCal I thought I knew so well had suddenly been replaced by a no-nonsense woman who'd quickly come to the conclusion that I'd have nothing to offer her going forward.

"I was hoping you'd be more supportive," I pleaded.

"Supportive? Are you fucking kidding me? I'm not the moron who just got busted and expelled for cheating. I have to go now. I need some time for myself. We'll talk later."

That was the last time I ever saw or heard from Mandy McDougal.

An hour later, night was falling as I sat on a bench outside what was now my former dorm. At my feet were a big gym bag and knapsack with all my possessions. As I sat on the bench, I felt my eyes beginning to well up with tears. Up until this point, I'd had more tough moments than you could shake a stick at, but this took the cake. Losing my father at 10 was horrific, but when he died I at least had the *impression* that my mom and others would look out for me. But now, I was completely on my own with nowhere to go and $47 in my pocket. I tried thinking of people I could call but realized I had no one. I thought of Coach Orbison, but how could I expect him to help me now after I'd let him down like this? I debated whether I should phone the Lapitkas, Rossis, and Finkelmans, and even Anne Honeycutt but was too humiliated to ask for their assistance. I put my head in my hands and started to cry. I cried because I still missed my dad, whom I now needed more than ever. I cried because I'd just had my heart broken by my first girlfriend. I cried because, as Dean Baldwin had said, I'd blown an amazing opportunity. But most of all, I cried because I knew my dream of being a big-league ballplayer had just gone up in smoke.

Just then, I heard someone call out my name. It was a guy's voice but one that was nasal and slightly high-pitched. I turned and there was Brian Goldstein, probably just as stunned to see me as I was to see him.

"Jack, what are you doing here? Wait a minute. Are you crying? What's wrong?"

"I just got expelled?"

"Seriously? What did you do?"

"I cheated on a final and got caught."

"So they expelled you? Did you go talk to Coach Gillespie? I bet he—"

"I tried, but he wanted nothing to do with me."

"Seriously? That sucks. So, what are you going to do? Go home?"

"I don't have a home. I have no idea where I'm going."

"You don't have any parents?"

"My dad died when I was a kid, and I haven't spoken

to my mom since before I came to USC."

Brian just sighed and looked straight ahead. I could tell he was disappointed. Not disappointed in an angry way but disappointed like he genuinely felt bad for me.

"Look, Jack," Brian began. "I have to tell you something. I've loved baseball more than anything for as long as I remember. When I was seven, I could give you the starting lineup for all 26 Major League teams. When I was 11, I got Fernando Valenzuela's autograph and slept with it under my pillow for a whole year. Unfortunately, because of my asthma and the fact I was always the smallest kid on the field, my own career didn't amount to much. Then, when I got into USC, I was so excited, not because of the academics or all the hot chicks running around campus, but because it's the best baseball school in the country. But whenever I tried to befriend or just talk to one of the players, I was either ignored or insulted. Yet, from the time we've met, you've always been super nice to me, even though you didn't have to be. Think about this for a second, Jack. I've made the Dean's List every semester I've been here, got to intern at one of LA's best law firms, and will likely go to a top-20 law school after I graduate, but the most fun I've had at USC is watching you play and talking baseball with you."

"It's been fun talking baseball with you too, Brian. You're a bright guy and I'll bet you'll go far," I said with the utmost sincerity.

"Listen, Jack, what just happened to you really sucks, but life goes on. I'll tell you what, I know you're not Jewish, but why don't you come over to my parents' house for an amazing Shabbos dinner, then we can play Tony La Russa Baseball on the computer. You can sleep over, and in the morning, we'll put our heads together and think of something. How's that sound?"

I was starving and had nowhere else to go, so that sounded great. Although my boyhood friend Justin Finkelman was Jewish, his family was secular and didn't observe any of the religion's customs, making this my first Sabbath dinner. And I was not disappointed! Mrs. Goldstein's brisket and potato pancakes were to die for, while the marble cake made for an excellent dessert. But the most enjoyable part of the evening was the stories Mr. Goldstein, a true Brooklynite, told about the era when the Yankees, Giants, and Dodgers ruled New York and fans of all ages would debate who among Hall of Famers Mickey Mantle, Willie Mays, and Duke Snider was the city's best center fielder. For a brief moment, I even forgot that my life was quickly headed down the tubes.

The following morning, I was awakened by the sound of Brian hastily ruffling through back issues of *Baseball America*, which were strewn all over his bedroom floor. After about 10 more minutes of leafing through about half a dozen issues, he finally exclaimed, "Found it!"

"What's that?" I inquired, still half asleep.

"Your ticket to professional baseball."

It turned out, several months earlier Brian had stumbled across a story on a new independent baseball league, the Western League, that would feature teams in Long Beach, Palm Springs, Salinas, and Sonoma. If he guessed correctly, the caliber of talent would be roughly equal to that of A ball, so not far off from the competition in the Pac-10.

"You've already showed you can hit with wood on the Cape against the best college pitching in the country, so my guess is that you shouldn't have any problems against guys who never made it past Double A. And if you put up decent numbers, there's no doubt in my mind someone will draft you in June," Brian pointed out.

I agreed wholeheartedly with Brian but then thought of something.

"Love your idea, Brian, but this Western League doesn't start for a couple of months. What will I do before then? I can't stay with you guys that long."

"I thought of that, too. My mom's uncle, my great-uncle, Saul Levine, was a B-list movie actor in the '50s, '60s, and '70s and lives in Long Beach. He just came out of the closet to us a couple of years ago. Because he never had a true partner nor kids of his own, he's a lonely guy. My family tries to see him as often as we can, but it's not nearly enough. He's not a huge baseball fan but a nice guy who I'm sure would love your company. Would you be cool with giving it a try?"

Gay, straight, bi, transgender, or whatever, I couldn't care less. Shit, less than 24 hours earlier I was thinking about which bench would be the most comfortable to sleep on.

"Brian, man, how can I thank you?"

"You don't have to. Just make me one promise."

"Anything. Just say it."

"Both my parents have this crazy fantasy that after law school I'm going to get a boring job in tax, real estate, or corporate law, but I have absolutely no desire to do something I'll probably detest for the rest of my life. Obviously, I'm not cut out to make it as a player and after spending tens of thousands to put me through USC, my parents would have a conniption if I started from the ground up working for a Major League team with the intention of one day becoming a general manager. But I really want to do something baseball related. So, how about when you get drafted in June, you make me your agent?"

I had to laugh. In the blink of an eye, I had lost my scholarship, girlfriend, and spot on one of college baseball's best teams, and if that wasn't enough, I was an inch away from joining the ranks of LA's homeless. Yet, Brian seemed to think I was destined for a career in professional baseball.

"Sure," I said with a chuckle. "You're hired."

In today's fast-paced, internet-driven world, the expulsion of a top college baseball player from a premier school would be huge news and warrant headline-grabbing coverage from the likes of ESPN, *Baseball America*, D1Baseball, as well as numerous online college sports message boards. But in the winter of 1994–95, my situation went largely unnoticed. Hence, the difficulty Brian and I encountered trying to convince the Long Beach Barracudas' general manager I was who I said I was—a disgraced former slugger for the USC Trojans just looking for a chance. Finally, after calling the USC Athletics Department to confirm my bona fides, he agreed to add me to the team in its inaugural season.

After USC's Christmas break ended and Brian headed back to school, I moved in with Saul Levine. He came as advertised—extremely nice and happy to have company. So happy, it turned out, that a room with an already made bed and clean sheets was waiting for me when Brian dropped me off.

I quickly got a job as an attendant at On Deck batting cages, which was about a 15-minute walk from Saul's place. The job paid an hourly wage of $4.25, which was California's minimum wage at the time, and I made an extra $10 an hour giving private lessons. But best of all, when I closed up, I was allowed to take as many pitches from the machines as I wanted, provided I collected all the stray balls. It got to the point that I would volunteer to take the late shift just so I'd have the opportunity to take a couple hundred cuts before calling it a night.

Saul couldn't have been a better host, and I'll always suspect Brian gave him a good primer on me before I moved in. In addition to not charging me rent, he gave me all the space I needed and never asked any probing questions about my past or how I'd landed in my current predicament. Instead, when I wasn't working at the cages or running on the nearby beach, I was usually listening to Saul's recollection of what it was like to be a B-list actor back in the day. He told me about Clint Eastwood's early career struggles until hitting pay dirt with *Rawhide*, Steve McQueen's off-the-set exploits during the filming of *Le Mans* in France, and Paul Newman's steadfast opposition to the Vietnam War and his inclusion on President Nixon's "enemies" list. As tough as things were for me at this point, I'll always consider myself blessed to have lived with Anne Honeycutt and Saul Levine, two people who lived life to the fullest and had fascinating stories to tell as a result.

I reported to the Barracudas' "spring training" in early April and was quickly disappointed. Although the team had three ex-Major Leaguers on the roster in infielder Shane Turner, outfielder Tony Scruggs, and pitcher Craig

Curving Foul

Chamberlain, most of my new teammates would have been hard-pressed to make the local beer league softball team. About half the guys looked as if they hadn't touched a bat or ball in years, while the other half could barely complete a set of running drills without passing out. The crazy thing was that all the other teams were in the same predicament.

As a result, it should come as no surprise that several weeks into the new season, I was leading this league of has-beens in batting average, extra-base hits, and RBI. Nor should anyone be shocked that we drew about 40 fans *on a good night*, with most of those in the stands either sympathetic family members or bored senior citizens with nothing else better to do. Panic-stricken over the lack of scouts in the stands, I turned to my agent, Brian, who had dutifully stopped going to USC games so he could more closely monitor the progress of his only client.

"Dude, maybe the Western League wasn't a great idea," I said one day in the car on the way to a game. "Something tells me I haven't exactly become a household name."

"Don't sweat it," Brian answered. "You're tearing the cover off the ball. You'll get noticed soon, trust me." This was the first of many prophetic statements to come out of Brian's mouth.

Not a week later, as I warmed up in the outfield prior to a game against the Palm Springs Suns, I noticed a strange phenomenon taking place in the stands. There were actually people—hundreds of them—taking their seats! And to make things even more interesting, interspersed within the crowd were dozens of scouts, notebooks and radar guns at the ready. I made eye contact with Brian, who was in the first row near the first base dugout talking to a pair of scouts, and he excitedly motioned me over.

"I thought Christmas was in December, not May," I exclaimed.

Brian was so excited he was nearly foaming at the mouth. "No, my friend. Christmas for you is in May this year. So are Hanukkah and Kwanzaa, for that matter. You see the Palm Springs pitcher warming up over there?" Brian motioned toward the opposing bullpen with his hand. "That's Ariel Prieto, the first major Cuban defector to come over in years. He's the real deal, Jack. He's beaten a bunch of US national teams in tournaments over the years, and many scouts think he could pitch in the majors right now. I'd bet that nearly all of the 26 big-league clubs have at least one scout in attendance and wouldn't be shocked if many have sent their scouting directors because Prieto's considered a guy who should go off the board in the first round in next month's draft. Let me put it to you this way: If you do anything off this guy, you will definitely get drafted."

As soon as the game started, I saw what Brian was talking about. This Cuban was good. Not only could this guy hit the mid-90s with his fastball, but he also threw a jackhammer for a curve and knew how to change speeds and paint the corners. After facing slop for the past month, I suddenly had my work cut out for me. I stepped up to the plate in the bottom of the first inning after the first and second hitters had struck out on six pitches. Prieto quickly got ahead of me with a fastball on the outside corner that I took and a changeup that I flailed at. Not good. I was down 0-2. The next pitch was a curve in the dirt that I took, but on the fourth pitch of the at bat, I chased a high fastball for strike three. Damn it!

I came up again in the bottom of the fourth inning after Prieto had retired the first 11 Barracudas in a row, seven via the strikeout. I'd noticed that Prieto had all his pitches working, but he seemed to be relying on his fastball, which wasn't a bad plan since no one on the team had the bat speed necessary to catch up to his cheese. Well, no one except for one guy. Me.

After missing outside with a curveball, the big Cuban challenged me with a fastball. Big mistake. I had started my swing early, caught the pitch with the sweet spot of the bat, and sent a rocket into right-center field. The Suns' center and right fielders, not expecting to have any action with Prieto on the hill, were caught napping by my shot into the gap. By the time the center fielder ran down the ball and fired it into the infield, I was already standing with my hands on my hips at third base smiling at Brian, who was giving me a thumbs-up sign.

By the time I led off the bottom of the seventh, Prieto was out of the game, but luckily several scouts were still in the stands. Were they there to see me take one more at bat? Or was it because of Blair Field's two-for-one hot dog special? Brian later swore it was to see me take another set of hacks, which was a good thing because I didn't disappoint, sending a hard smash up the middle for a single.

During the next several weeks, scouts from several teams showed up at my games, and thankfully, I continued to feast on the subpar pitching I faced. Brian made it a point to talk to each one, and neither of us was shocked when the first thing each scout asked was whether the USC cheating rumor was true. Brian thought it was best to level with them, to tell them I made a horrible mistake but that I was looking forward to a long career in professional baseball.

Brian made a fantastic point a week before the draft when he said, "Cheating or no cheating, you still had a full ride to USC, where you hammered the ball as a freshman. Then you went to the Cape, where you hammered the ball yet again. That means something."

The day of the draft finally arrived. To be honest, it was somewhat of a letdown for me. I always envisioned a big party attended by all my coaches and teammates, past and present, with tables full of food and drink and a DJ spinning loud music. And all this followed by a phone call from an excited scouting director telling me I'd just been drafted in the first or second round. Instead, the guy from Angelo's Pizza dropped off two pies as Brian, his parents, younger sister, Saul, and I awkwardly sat on the Goldsteins' deck and waited for the phone to ring.

Pretty soon, we ran out of pizza, so Brian's mom ran into the house and came back a minute later with several pints of Haagen-Dazs. It wasn't long before those were history and still no phone call. Unlike today, we didn't have smartphones to help take the edge off, so Brian's dad quickly took matters into his own hands by disappearing into the house and magically reappeared with a couple big bottles of hard liquor. Things got a lot more relaxed after that as we all—including 16-year-old Cara Goldstein—began to indulge. Suddenly, the phone rang! Brian and I both looked at each other, our stomachs tied in knots and eyes filled with hope.

"Hand him the phone, Cara!" Brian commanded his younger sister, who was sitting next to the 1987 vintage push-button phone. The bookish high school junior-to-be quickly did as she was told after just two rings, and I took a deep breath before answering.

"This is Jack," I said, hoping to hear the voice of some grizzled scouting director on the other end.

"Jack? I don't know a Jack," began an elderly lady with an obvious Brooklyn accent. "This is Delores. Is Barry there?"

Dejected, disappointed, and disheartened, I handed the phone to Brian's dad. "I think this may be for you, Mr. Goldstein."

As Mr. Goldstein took the phone, he mouthed, "It's my sister" and rolled his eyes. After about a minute, I zoned out their conversation and started to concentrate on my drink, already my third. All of sudden, Mr. Goldstein adopted a sense of urgency and he exclaimed in his native Brooklynese, "Delores! Delores! I have *anotha* call. I have to go." He then clicked over and answered in his best attempt at high English. "Barry Goldstein here. Yes, of course, one moment please. Jack, it's for you!"

"This is Jack."

"Jack, this is Jeff Scott, the scouting director of the Detroit Tigers. It's my pleasure to tell you we've selected you in the 27th round and would be honored if you joined our organization. We know it's been a tough road, but we think you can accomplish great things with us."

And with that I was a professional baseball player.

Bush League

Three days after the draft, I received a contract from the Tigers together with their offer of a $6,500 signing bonus. Don't get me wrong; getting picked as late as the 27th round was a buzzkill, as was a bonus I believed to be not at all reflective of my ability, but after the events of the last six months, I was relieved just to have been given the opportunity to play professional baseball. Plus, Brian gave me some great advice when I lamented that just a year earlier I was well on my way to becoming a first-round pick and likely recipient of a seven-figure signing bonus.

"Jack, reach the big leagues and you'll make it back in spades." Truer words have never been spoken.

Speaking of my bonus, I always get a kick out of hearing how other guys spent theirs. Well, since inquiring minds want to know, I wrote Saul a $2,000 check and practically begged him to let me pay him back for all his generosity over the past five months.

"Absolutely not, Jack," he said. "I'll tell you what. I've

attended countless Oscars and Emmys and gone to more movie premieres than I can remember. But I've never had anyone offer me complimentary tickets to a Major League baseball game. So why don't you be the first and we'll call it even."

Done.

The Tigers assigned me to the Jamestown Jammers, their short-season A ball affiliate in the New York-Penn League. It was in Jamestown that I realized playing in the minor leagues was far different from the romantic image I'd formed in my head. The minors were far less about playing a game I loved with teammates I'd ultimately form strong, lifelong bonds with than they were eight-hour bus rides, eating greasy fast food twice a day, sleeping in fleabag motels, and earning slave's wages. And my teammates weren't really my teammates but instead my competitors against whom I'd be engaged in a bitter battle over a finite number of slots on the big-league roster. Let's not sugarcoat this—the minors sucked. They were a miserable place where I saw dozens of childhood dreams die a miserable death as well as an environment where bickering, backstabbing, and desperation all thrived.

Every minor league team I was on essentially had three main groups of players out of which smaller cliques formed. The first group was composed of the Latinos. These guys had it the worst. Not only were they trying to achieve the same on-field success as their teammates, but they also had to contend with the additional challenges of mastering a new language and learning a brand-new culture and way of life. And mind you, 20 years ago, big-league clubs did far less to ease the integration process than they do now. There were no interpreters, English classes, or Spanish-speaking coaches. Instead, the kids from the Dominican Republic, Venezuela, and wherever else got off the plane and were entirely on their own.

The second group was made up of American kids who signed out of high school. Generally, these kids were either African-American or white kids from predominantly rural areas. Because the New York-Penn League drew largely from the ranks of just-drafted college players and some Latinos deemed not ready for full-season ball, this group was underrepresented in Jamestown but evident at every other stop I made in the minors.

The final group was the American kids drafted out of college. Even though my college days ended prematurely, I always considered myself a member of this group. I always thought that college kids had a huge advantage over the other two groups, especially in the lower rungs of organized ball, because they already had experience being away from home and were used to living without around-the-clock adult supervision

My first roommate and friend in professional baseball was Gabe Kapler, a guy I shared a lot in common with and a good friend to this day. Like me, Gabe was a Southern California kid who had started out at a big-time baseball school, Cal State Fullerton, but didn't last long. A 57th-round pick, Gabe worked harder than anyone I knew. As he moved up the minor league chain, Gabe's numbers got better and better and at every level he defied the naysayers, of which there were many, who couldn't believe that such a late pick could continue to improve as he faced more advanced pitching. But Gabe had more going for him than just baseball. His intense workout regimen left him sculpted like a Greek god, and he was frequently featured on the cover of numerous men's fitness magazines. It's ironic, because regardless of which provincial backwater town we were playing in—Utica, Elmira, or Oneonta—Gabe always managed to find a gym as well as a place that served decent food.

After facing top-tier college pitching a year earlier at USC, then getting over 200 at bats with wood between the Cape and the Western League, I made a seamless transition to pro ball, hitting .318 with an impressive on-base plus slugging percentage (OPS) of exactly .900. However, as well as I had played in my first professional season, I knew that I hadn't legitimately been tested. Most of the college guys drafted out of the major programs bypassed the short-season leagues like the New York-Penn League altogether and jumped straight to full-season leagues. A lot of the pitchers I had faced that first summer were selected out of the weaker conferences and would soon be organizational guys or out of the game entirely. It quickly became obvious to me that my first big test would occur in the following year in A ball.

The Tigers in 1996 assigned me to the Fayetteville Generals in the South Atlantic League, the lowest rung of full-season ball. It wasn't long before I realized that the Sally League, as it was called, was also not going to be much of a challenge. After I went 4 for 5 on opening day with three doubles, my manager, the late Dwight Lowry, even made it a point to tell me to go month-to-month on my apartment lease because he was unsure how long I'd be with the club. I didn't go more than two games in a row without a hit and had three separate games in which

I got at least four hits. Given the success I had, I was with Fayetteville a lot longer than I thought I should have been. When I finally was promoted to Lakeland in the class High-A Florida State League after 92 games, I was hitting .337 with 24 doubles and a robust .961 OPS. Like Gabe, who was also having a banner year but wasn't promoted, I felt that because I was a late draft pick, there was a group of baseball ops people within the Tiger organization who believed I wasn't a true prospect and that at some point in the higher levels, my weaknesses would be exposed.

Lakeland was the first time in my professional career that I felt legitimately challenged. My home park, Joker Marchant Stadium, and most of the stadiums in the FSL were the biggest I'd ever hit in, and balls that were home runs in short-season ball or Low A were now just long outs. The pitching in the FSL was also the best I'd ever faced. It seemed like every night I either faced a pitcher whose fastball could reach the mid-90s or someone who could throw two breaking pitches for strikes at any point in the count. The year 1996 was also my first full season in organized ball, and by the time I was promoted in late July, I had been playing for nearly half a year (including spring training) and was physically and mentally exhausted. By the time the season was over, I had lost almost 10 pounds and weighed less than 180. Nonetheless, my numbers at Lakeland were decent, especially my .387 on-base percentage, though my .418 slugging percentage was the lowest I'd post in any of my minor league stops.

Following the '96 season, the Tigers' brass sent me to the Hawaii Winter League, which was composed of prospects from all the Major League teams as well as young talent from Japan and South Korea. The HWL was a bare-bones operation with only four teams, and the sparse crowds reminded me of my time in the Western League. Still, I faced roughly the same caliber of pitching I had seen in Lakeland and became more adept at hitting off-speed stuff. In 45 games, I hit .347 to lead the league and my eight home runs were good enough for second in the circuit. Off the field, I had a blast. Gabe was also in the league, and the Tigers' brass also sent another prospect from Southern California, Robert Fick, to work on his game in paradise. Never a surfer despite my SoCal roots, I hit the waves hard with those two at least four mornings a week and wasn't bad by the time my stint in Hawaii ended.

The offseason of 1996–97 was the first time I appeared on various publications' top prospect lists. *Baseball America* ranked me the 88th best prospect in the game, five spots ahead of Carlos Beltran but also 16 notches behind the immortal Pat Cline. *Street and Smith's, Athlon Sports,* and several other publications also had me listed among their top 100 prospects. Although I felt like the Major Leagues were still light-years away, I'd be telling a white lie if I said my inclusion on those lists didn't mean anything. In fact, I can still tell you today where each magazine had me ranked.

Despite the big numbers I posted in Fayetteville and Hawaii, I was certain that the Tigers minor-league brass would have me begin 1997 back at Lakeland. After all, I was still only 22 and had less than 200 plate appearances there the prior season. However, Detroit's system those days was paper thin, and I'd hit the tar out of the ball in spring training. Thus, I wasn't all that surprised when Dave Miller, the organization's farm director, approached me on my way to the back fields about a week before we broke camp to let me know the Tigers thought enough of me to push me to the Double A Jacksonville Suns. This was the first time since turning pro that I felt the Tigers' front office no longer viewed me as a suspect taken in the 27th round but instead as a bona fide prospect who would one day be part of a winning team at the big-league level. As cool as being mentioned on all those offseason prospect lists, knowing that the big club believed I would one day be a key player meant the world to me and made me work even harder.

People in baseball circles like to say that Double A is the level that separates the real prospects from the pretenders, and I agree with this 100 percent. From a hitter's perspective, by the time a pitcher makes it to Double A, he's able to command his fastball to both sides of the plate and has enough confidence to throw his off-speed stuff even when he's behind in the count. Essentially, Double A is the first place in organized baseball where a pitcher is supposed to beat you, even if he doesn't have his A game.

Speaking of A game, that's what I brought north with me to begin the 1997 campaign. Lefties or righties, hard stuff or breaking stuff, I was red hot when the season began. Not only do Double A pitchers have better stuff and deeper repertoires than in the lower levels, but there's also something else to consider. The higher the minor league level, the better control pitchers have, meaning hitters are getting more strikes to hit. While I might not have had the physicality of a Gabe Kapler or other highly rated prospects, my approach was as good as anyone's. Even at 22, I knew to stay within myself and to get into hitters' counts where I was most likely to get a pitch to drive. If you were to ask me what the difference is between, say, a top hitter in Low A and one in Double A, it's not strength or bat speed but rather the approach. All top hitting prospects can hit even the best velocity and send line drives screaming into the alleys, and many can crush balls into the stratosphere. But how many have a plan and know how to execute it?

My 1997 season was also the embodiment of how important confidence is to a young player. Prior to the first pitch of the season, I was conscious of how closely front-office evaluators monitor guys' progress in Double A and how vital my success would be in determining whether I would be called up to Detroit. Succeed in Double A, and I'd be just a phone call away from The Show. Struggle, and my standing as a prospect could fall faster than a dotcom after the collapse of the internet bubble.

By early May, my average was sitting comfortably over .300 and I had a half-dozen jacks. More important, I'd faced the best the Southern League had to offer in Kerry Wood, Roy Halladay, and Kelvim Escobar, and I torched them all. Against Halladay, I smashed a bases-clearing double followed by a two-run bomb two innings later. Then rounding third base, I glanced up at the stands and spotted Tigers general manager Randy Smith. Hmmm.

As well as I was playing, my performance paled to that of a teammate. Juan Encarnacion, a skinny Dominican outfielder still just 21, was simply unconscious. I mean, he did it all that year. He hit for average (.323), power (26 home runs and .560 slugging percentage), stole bases (17 steals in just 20 attempts), and covered large swaths of center field while intimidating baserunners with a cannon arm. Encarnacion is the quintessential case study of how volatile young baseball players are. He was at Lakeland the prior year, and I got to see him up close during my 41-game cameo. While it was evident he had some intriguing tools, the guy hit .240 with a sub-.700 OPS and at times looked lost in the field. Then fast-forward to a year later and the guy's a dead ringer for Eric Davis. Go figure.

As the season wound down, I was still comfortably above .300 with the best power numbers of my professional career. Hardly a day went by in which a baseball writer didn't refer to Encarnacion and me as the Tigers' next great hopes. To say my future was bright would be one of the bigger understatements ever. Then, in the second-to-last game of the season, I was certain disaster had struck. We were beating up on the Knoxville Smokies 9-1 in the bottom of the seventh. I'd already collected three hits and was standing on first base after walking with two outs. Encarnacion, who followed me in the order, lofted a fly ball to medium right field that was caught by the Smokies' right fielder. With two outs, I had put my head down and started to run at about half speed, cruising past second base and making my way to third. Suddenly, I noticed a commotion behind me. The Smokies' right fielder, after catching the fly ball, had fired the ball back in to first base. Motherfucker! There was just one out! For the first time in my life, I'd forgotten how many outs there were.

The implications were immediate and severe. Our manager, Dave Anderson, a guy I'd gotten along with all season, threw a tantrum in the dugout and pulled me from the game. Anderson was always a mild-mannered guy, so his blowup hit hard. But I'd be the first to admit I screwed up and deserved a scalding.

After the game, which we'd won 12-2, Anderson wasn't letting up. He called me into his tiny office, where all the other coaches waited.

"Carter, get your stupid ass in here!"

"Skip, I'm rea—"

"Shut the fuck up, Carter! You got fucking balls pulling that bush league routine with me! Just who the fuck do you think you are? Just because you had a good season you think you can loaf it? I got news for you, jackass. You do that in The Show and you'll be riding the pine for weeks!"

Just as Anderson finished, Tim Torricelli, our hitting coach whom I'd grown close with, let out a snort, like he was suppressing a laugh. Next to Torricelli was Rick Bombard, our pitching coach, and he was smiling wryly. Finally, I looked back at Anderson, who was grinning ear to ear. In my life, I'd never been so happy as at that very moment.

"Congratulations, kid," Anderson began. "You're gonna be called up after our last game tomorrow. Just do us a favor when you're up there and don't forget how many outs there are."

Suddenly, someone opened the door to Anderson's office and there were all my teammates, who had already been told of the big news. As I made my way outside the office, each guy took his turn offering congratulations.

As dog-eat-dog as the minors are, I can say with 100 percent certainty that each of my teammates was as happy for me as I was. But as ecstatic as I was, I felt a tinge of sadness and thought how wonderful it would have been if my dad could have shared this amazing moment with me.

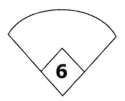

Big League

The first person I met as an official member of the Detroit Tigers was Lynn Henning, the baseball columnist for the *Detroit News*. I had just walked into the visitors' clubhouse in Atlanta's Turner Field, where the Braves would be hosting my Tigers later that night, and was intercepted by a benevolent-looking guy in his mid-40s who was carrying a notebook and wore a press pass around his neck. By this point in my career, I'd been interviewed by dozens of reporters in many of the rinky-dink towns I'd played in but had never spoken to anyone who covered a Major League baseball team.

Right away, it became clear that the pitching wasn't the only thing that was better at the big-league level. This Henning guy knew more about me than any scribe who'd covered me down below and I hadn't even played a day in the majors! With a deliberate Midwestern accent, Henning asked a series of probing questions exploring why I only lasted one season at USC and inquiring whether I had a chip on my shoulder after being picked so low in the '95 draft. As I'd come to learn, Henning never shied away from asking a tough question, but he was always fair and I respected him for that. Tom Gage and John Lowe, two other local reporters who covered the Tigers, didn't ask the same pointed questions as Henning, but they, too, treated me with respect, and I always tried my best to return the favor.

After my brief chat with Henning, I started to meet my new teammates. The first guy to introduce himself was the club's elder statesman, Travis Fryman. Fryman, the club's third baseman since 1990, was the epitome of class and consistency and right away made me feel at home by extending his hand and congratulating me. Next up was first baseman Tony Clark. Clark, a giant at six feet seven, said in that booming voice of his, "Hey, Higgy, come meet the guy who's gonna take your job." Higgy was outfielder Bobby Higginson, who glared at Clark, then glared at me and simply said, "Fuck off. Both of you." Though obviously not the most eloquent human being, Higginson was a guy who always busted it and rang every ounce of talent out of his modest physical skills. I'd be happy to have Higginson, a tough street kid from South Philly, next to me in a foxhole any day.

Finally, bullpen stalwarts Doug Brocail and Todd Jones made their way over to say hello. Brocail was a mountain of a man at six feet five and 240 pounds with a menacing goatee and the persona to match, while Jones, the Tigers' closer, was quick-witted and, as I'd soon find out, an all-around great guy.

A bit later, as clubhouse guy Jim Schmakel was giving me my uniform, someone patted me on the shoulder and said with a chuckle, "Hey, Schmakel, take good care of this

guy. He might be the one who saves our jobs someday."
I turned around and almost had a heart attack. It was
Buddy Bell, my new manager, but an enemy of the state
to any old-school California Angels fan. As a four-time All-
Star and perennial Gold Glove winner with the Rangers,
Bell broke Angels fans' hearts time and time again with
tons of highlight-reel plays at third base and clutch hits.
"What's wrong kid?" he asked. "You look like you've seen
a ghost."

"Worse," I replied. "I still have nightmares about that
grand slam you hit in the ninth inning off Mike Witt to beat
us in 1983."

"Ha! Schmakel, give this kid a good number! At least
someone remembers me from when I was good at my job."

Bell's humor was self-deprecating because I found
him to be great at his job. As I'd soon see, despite a
roster composed of mostly underwhelming talent, the
1997 Tigers were a cohesive unit that overachieved and
played .500 ball until the final week of the season. Bell
had a disarming way about him. He was a commanding
presence able to get the most out of every player but could
also connect to each guy as a human being. I couldn't
have asked for a better first big-league manager.

I didn't play the first night, which was probably a
good thing since we faced Greg Maddux. I didn't play the
next night either, as we were blanked by 20-game winner
Denny Neagle 5-0. Finally, the following day, in the middle
of a 12-4 drubbing of the Braves, Larry Parrish, the bench
coach, sidled up next to me and said I'd be batting for
Melvin Nieves.

Within seconds, my heart was pounding so hard I
thought my chest would explode. "C'mon, man, keep it

together. You've done this thousands of times," I said to myself.

A couple minutes later, as I stood in the on-deck circle, my knees felt like they were made of jelly. Not only that, but I realized I had to take a leak. Too late. Fryman promptly doubled into the left-field alley and I was due up. So, this was it. After all the shit I'd been through, I was seconds from realizing my lifelong dream. As I walked slowly from the on-deck circle to home plate, I heard the Atlanta PA announcer announce my name: *"Now batting for the Detroit Tigers, number 18, Jack Carter."* Holy shit!

As I dug in, I took a deep breath. Pitching for Atlanta was Paul Byrd, a guy I'd never faced. And because of nerves, I'd forgotten to glance at his scouting report when Parrish told me I'd be hitting. Damn it! I had no clue what this guy had. As I waited for Byrd's first pitch in the batter's box, I felt the full bore of 30-something thousand sets of eyes fixed upon me. "A pop up, a ground out, or a fly out," I prayed to myself. "Anything but a strikeout."

Pitching from the stretch, Byrd glanced at Fryman, who was just a few feet off the bag at second, and went into his delivery. The first pitch was a fastball at the knees on the outside corner. It was well placed but was barely 90 miles an hour. Strike one. I stepped out of the box and glanced at third base coach Perry Hill for the sign. But with the score 10-2 in our favor, Hill had nothing. Stepping back into the box, I again concentrated on Byrd. The righty came to his set position and dealt. Another heater, but this one was above the letters. Ball one. From what I saw, Byrd's fastball velocity was below league average. I could definitely tag this guy if I got ahead in the count and forced him to throw another fastball.

A second later, Byrd unleased his third pitch of the at bat, a curveball that broke too late and was above the letters. Ball two. Bird asked the home plate umpire for a new ball, rubbed it with both hands, then got ready to deal. The pitch came in, another mediocre fastball in my wheelhouse. It was a pitch that I'd drilled hundreds of times in my life, but because I was pressing, I was gripping the bat too tight, which robbed me of precious bat speed. The result was a weak foul ball into the left-field stands instead of a line drive somewhere. Son of a bitch! That was my pitch and I missed it.

Javy Lopez, the Braves' great Puerto Rican catcher, must have been thinking the same thing and hissed through his mask, "That was your pitch, *Papi.*"

Angry with myself, I stepped out of the box, took a deep breath, and stepped back in. Byrd peered into Lopez for the sign, set, and threw. From the moment the pitch left Byrd's hand, I could tell from the spin that it was a breaking pitch, but its spin was different from that of Byrd's curve. It had to be a slider, and it had started out of the strike zone but was quickly heading toward it. With two strikes, I was already protecting the plate and had shortened my swing considerably. With my abbreviated swing, the upper third of my bat struck the bottom half of the ball, resulting in a flare out to left field that dropped about five feet shy of Atlanta left fielder Ryan Klesko.

Running on contact with two outs, Fryman scored easily from second base. After rounding first base, I retreated back to the bag, where Atlanta first baseman Randall Simon greeted me with a smile and discreet thumbs-up sign, and first base coach Jerry White enthusiastically slapped me on the back and said, "Nice going, kid, but it's all downhill from here." I just stood there with my heart pounding and tried to savor the moment.

White was right. It was all downhill from there, at least statistically. I played only sparingly that September, posting just a .227 average in 44 at bats over the Tigers' final 25 games. However, I did hit my first Major League home run, a long fly ball that reached the right-field overhang at the old Tiger Stadium, against the Yankees' Hideki Irabu on the final day of the season.

I spent most of that month with the Tigers just watching and listening. My biggest takeaway was how much better the Major League brand of baseball was than in the minors. Not only was the game much faster at the big-league level, but it was played with so much more precision. Pitchers lived for innings at a time on the black, outfielders ran razor-straight routes, and cut-off plays were perfectly choreographed. Clearly, I still had an unbelievable amount to learn before I could be considered a Major Leaguer.

The other thing that struck me that September was how much better life in the Majors was. Let's start with the food. I'll never forget coming into the clubhouse at Turner Field after my first game with the Tigers. Eureka! Fillets of salmon and beef, lasagna, a massive bowl of fresh fruit salad, chilled Heinekens resting comfortably in a gigantic, open cooler—you name it, there it was. I felt like I was at a fancy wedding, not a baseball game. And as we were gorging ourselves on the postgame spread, the clubhouse attendants were scurrying around, simultaneously making sure all our needs were met while keeping the place spic and span. Have a weird craving or need a favor? Then ask a "clubbie." Day or night, they aimed to please.

There was also the issue of travel. Because I'd skipped Triple A, where teams generally fly (albeit commercially and in coach), I had only travelled by bus. Not anymore! As soon as our series with the Braves ended, we boarded a luxury bus for the short ride to Hartsfield Airport, where we met our charter airplane, which was equipped with oversized seats for the comfortable flight back to Detroit. Finally, with my arrival in the Major Leagues, my days of sleeping in cramped, roach-infested motel rooms were a thing of the past. By virtue of the labor contract between the players' union and the owners, each Major League player received his own suite on the road, almost always in a five-star hotel.

As much as I loved the clubhouse spreads, clubbies cleaning up after me, and the first-rate travel arrangements, the biggest difference for me between the majors and minors was the money. At the time I was called up, I was earning only $600 a month at Jacksonville. But the second I put on that Olde English D, my annualized salary jumped to $109,000, the Major League minimum. Put it this way, the $18,166.67 I earned my first month with the Tigers was more than the sum of my signing bonus and every minor league paycheck I'd received. And on top of my much higher salary, I also received $80 a day in meal money when we were on the road. Something told me I wouldn't be seeing the inside of a Denny's for a while.

While we're on the topic of money, I'd be remiss if I didn't mention the following story. A couple weeks after I was called up, we went on a 12-game road trip, the Tigers' last one of the season, that took the team through Seattle, Oakland, New York, and Baltimore. After we landed at Newark Airport and were waiting to board the bus to take us to the team hotel in Manhattan, Todd Jones came up to me and said, "Kid, meet me tomorrow morning at 10 in the hotel lobby." Understanding my place as a rookie, I didn't question Jones. I just nodded and made a mental note to be waiting for him at 9:55.

True to his word, Jones was in the lobby at 10. We took a five-minute cab ride to Barneys, at 60th and Madison, where we got out. When we were about to enter the store, Jones turned toward me and said, "Carter, to be a Major Leaguer, you're gonna have to dress like one."

Within an hour, Jones, who probably was unaware of my very existence just one month earlier, had dropped more than $3,000 on two Hugo Boss suits, three Versace ties, four Zegna shirts, and a pair of shoes. As we left the store en route to Yankee Stadium, I started to thank Jones for his tremendous generosity, but he just shook his head with a wry smile and said, "Welcome to The Show, Jack."

I arrived at the Tigers' 1998 spring training in Lakeland, Florida, curious what the front office's plans for me for the upcoming season were. Shortly after the '97 season ended, I had gone to the Arizona Fall League, a finishing school for the top Double and Triple A prospects, and hit almost .330 with four home runs in under 100 at bats. My performance in the desert helped solidify my prospect status. That offseason, *Baseball America* and *Street and Smith's* ranked me as baseball's 19th and 22nd best prospect, respectively. Because the internet was universally accessible, it was easy to read what the pundits were saying about me. After my big fall in the AFL, most believed I was ready to bypass Triple A altogether and start for the Tigers. Others, and these guys were definitely in the minority, didn't think the

Tigers were ready to contend in '98 and figured there was no harm in having me get at least a couple hundred at bats in Toledo.

The big move the Tigers had made the previous offseason was trading Travis Fryman to the Diamondbacks in exchange for fellow third baseman Joe Randa, my old USC teammate Gabe Alvarez, and a minor league pitcher. With all due respect to Randa, who was a solid player and great teammate, the loss of Fryman was a big blow to the club. Fryman was a near lock for a .280 average, 20 to 25 home runs, and superb defense, and, best of all, at 29 he was still in his prime. I always felt that Fryman's departure was a setback that we never recovered from. We lost our number three hitter and a guy who was the linchpin of our infield defense. Although Dean Palmer would arrive in Detroit a year later and post some big power numbers, he hit for a much lower average than Fryman and wasn't close to Fryman's equal defensively.

Luis Gonzalez was another important acquisition for Detroit in the winter of 1997-98. Though Gonzo didn't put up the big numbers with the Tigers that he would later in his career with Arizona, he was a steady performer and stabilizing force in the clubhouse who took a number of players under his wing, including me.

When camp opened, it became evident that the newly acquired Gonzo would primarily DH, Higginson would be the Tigers' regular left fielder, speedster Brian Hunter would man center field, and Encarnacion and I would battle it out for the right field job. It was an interesting contest. For all his ability, Encarnacion was an enigma. There were days when he'd hit two bombs, steal three bases, or throw out a runner with a seed from 300 feet away and you'd swear he was the next coming of Andruw Jones or Vlad Guerrero. But there were also times where the guy still looked raw and completely overmatched and you wondered if he'd even be able to cut it in Triple A.

I was a much different kind of player than Encarnacion. While I didn't have his ceiling, my floor was much higher. At the plate, I lacked his explosiveness, but I possessed a much better idea of how to attack a pitcher and superior plate discipline. On defense, my arm strength paled in comparison to his, but I was a much more accurate thrower and my more direct routes offset his advantage in foot speed.

As spring training wore on, it looked like neither Encarnacion nor I were ready for prime time. However, while Encarnacion looked lost and was easily exploited by experienced pitchers who frequently enticed him to chase pitches out of the zone, I at least strung together several games' worth of tough at bats and demonstrated to the Tigers' brass that I had a much better chance of contributing to the lineup in the short term.

Midway through the exhibition season, Encarnacion was reassigned to the minor league camp, which unofficially gave me the starting right field job. Although you never want to derive happiness from someone else's misfortune, I treated myself to a massive steak that night and for the first time in my life enjoyed a bottle of French wine. I was big time.

My best friend on the '98 club was Frankie Catalanotto, a second baseman who'd spent most of 1997 in Triple A Toledo and was called up to the Tigers the prior September. Drafted straight out of high school, Frankie was a down-to-earth kid from Long Island with a picturesque left-handed swing. What struck me about Frankie was how well he knew the game for such a young kid. I swear, I learned something new whenever we talked baseball.

Another guy I was close with was left-hander Justin Thompson. A first-round draft pick out of a Texas high school in 1991, Thompson was some talent. His emergence in 1997 was a big reason why the Tigers flirted with .500 for most of the season. A big kid armed with a mid-90s fastball and devastating slider, JT reminded many people of Steve Avery, who had enjoyed a lot of success as a member of Atlanta's vaunted starting rotation earlier in the decade.

It quickly became clear that the Tigers weren't going to sneak up on anyone in '98. By the end of April, we were 12 games under .500 and already seven games out of first place in the A.L. Central. As I already mentioned, the loss of Travis Fryman hurt a ton, as did the departure of right-hander Willie Blair, who had won 16 games a year earlier.

Also, something wasn't right with JT. After throwing nearly 80 innings more in '97 than he ever had, JT's fastball in '98 had lost a couple of ticks and his slider lacked its usual bite. As a result, teams hit JT a lot harder and his ERA was over a run higher than the pristine 3.02 it had been the prior season.

I was another Tiger who bore his fair share of the blame for Detroit's lackluster start in '98. During that horrific first month, I hit a putrid .228 with just one home run and nine RBI. Worse yet was the fact that I was now being benched against left-handers.

With each passing game, I began to press more and more. Always known as a hitter with a good eye and exceptional plate discipline, I gradually began to expand

101

the strike zone and chase bad pitches. Whatever my problems were, they certainly didn't stem from lack of effort. I spent hours taking extra batting practice and reviewing video of my swing with our hitting coach, Larry Herndon. I even tried a new batting stance at his suggestion, getting into more of a crouch so I could see the pitch better. Still, nothing worked. I was failing and miserable.

Something had to give, and it finally did on May 13. Prior to a home game against the Mariners, I was sitting in the clubhouse talking to Frankie and Gonzo when one of our clubbies walked over and said, "Skip wants to see you in his office." There was no question what was about to happen. Both Frankie and Gonzo just looked down at their cleats, unsure of what to say.

Buddy Bell and GM Randy Smith were both waiting for me in Buddy's office. Just from the expression on Buddy's face, I could tell this was not an easy thing for him to do. Even though I'd stunk up the joint, I'd felt that he'd taken a liking toward me, appreciating how hard I'd worked and how much I'd hustled even when things weren't going my way.

"Jack," Buddy began. "It's no secret that the jump from the minors to the majors is the biggest in all of professional sports. And it was even more challenging for you because we had you skip Triple A. We think it would be in your and the club's best interests to go down to Toledo to play every day and get your timing back."

Then Smith chimed in. "Don't think for a second, Jack, that any of us think any less of you now than we did in spring training. If nothing else, we have more respect for you because of how hard you've worked the last couple weeks. So, go down to Toledo, address the parts of your game that need improvement, and you'll be back up here before you know it. We still think you're a big part of what we're trying to build here."

I'm going to level with everyone here. After all the heartbreak I'd been through in my life, getting sent back down to the minors wasn't the end of the world for me. Heck, I was still only 23 and was well aware that I wasn't the only guy to fail in his first trip up to The Show. If nothing else, I was in good company. Mickey Mantle was demoted in just his second month with the Yankees, and it took Jim Thome until his third try to finally stick for good in the majors. And if the Phillies hadn't been a last place team in 1973, Mike Schmidt and his .196 batting average would have surely been shipped out.

Though getting sent back down to the bushes wasn't even close to the worse thing that had happened to me in my life, I certainly wasn't happy about it and went into a funk shortly after reporting to Toledo. Let's face it, I'd gotten used to the good life and wasn't exactly thrilled at the prospect of sleeping in a fleabag motel or subsisting on fast food. I felt like I'd gone to bed with Jessica Biel lying next to me and woke up with Miss Piggy kissing the back of my neck.

In my first four games in dank Toledo, I went 0-13 with six strikeouts. Then in my fifth game with the Mud Hens, I was hit by a Roy Halladay fastball in the knee and had to miss almost two weeks with a bone bruise. Between the injury and getting my timing back, I didn't hit my stride at Toledo until the middle of June. By early July, however, I had hit in 16 straight games to bring my average into the .280s while cutting down my strikeouts.

Curving Foul

Several weeks later, I was getting out of the shower after a three-hit game when the Toledo manager, Gene Roof, shouted from his office, "Carter, get dressed. You're going back up."

The Tiger team I rejoined in late July in Cleveland wasn't much better than the squad I'd left 10 weeks earlier. In fact, at 16 games below .500, it was four games worse. Regardless, I was just happy to be back, and judging from the reception I received, my teammates were just as happy to see me return. Jones, in the middle of a tough season, Frankie, Clark, and Gonzo all made their way over to my old locker to give me a hug, and even Higginson smiled and said, "Good to see you, brother."

I had a big first game back with the parent club, homering and driving in four runs, and thought it would be a harbinger of things to come, but I just couldn't catch fire. For the remainder of the season, I treaded water, usually sandwiching two bad games around a decent one.

When I looked at my numbers after the season ended, I didn't have a lot to be proud of. My batting average was a paltry .239 and my OPS was an equally pathetic .686, thanks in large part to the fact I hit just seven home runs.

As bad as my numbers were, the low point of the season came on September 1. We were playing the Rangers at home that night, and when I walked into the clubhouse prior to batting practice, I could have sworn I entered a funeral parlor. The place was eerily silent with guys in groups of three or four talking in hushed voices. I sidled up to Jones, Brocail, and JT and asked if someone died.

"Nah," responded Jones. He then just said, "Buddy," and followed it up by moving his index finger in a horizontal line across his throat. I wanted to ask if there was a guillotine somewhere in the bowels of Tiger Stadium but knew better.

Although most guys, myself included, liked Larry Parrish, Buddy's replacement, we were all sad to see Buddy go. He was tough but at the same time a player's manager. It wasn't Buddy's fault that JT's arm was throbbing and he wasn't able to go after guys like he had a year earlier. It wasn't Buddy's fault that Brian Hunter, our leadoff hitter, had an on-base percentage under .300. It wasn't Buddy's fault that Randy Smith traded away Travis Fryman. And it sure as hell wasn't Buddy's fault that I had sucked. Although I would eventually learn that managers getting fired were a normal part of baseball, I hadn't yet mastered that lesson in 1998. Still feeling lousy after that night's game against the Rangers, I called Buddy at home to thank him for the opportunity he'd given me and to apologize for not doing more to help the team.

"You've got nothing to be ashamed of, Jack," was the reply from my former skipper. "Keep working hard and you'll have a great career ahead of you."

That winter, in an effort to lay the foundation for what I hoped would be a better year in 1999, I went to Puerto Rico to play winter ball. The highlight of my two months on the Island of Enchantment was sharing the same outfield as Carlos Beltran. Though still just 21 years old, it was obvious to anyone who watched baseball that this guy was going to be a megastar. The kid could simply do it all. Unlike my teammate Juan Encarnacion, who would occasionally show you glimpses of his ability, Beltran's immense talent was on display 24/7. From both sides of the plate, the switch-hitting Beltran could launch rockets to all fields and his blazing speed was an intimidating factor on the basepaths. In center field, Beltran could run down anything between San Juan and the Bay of Pigs, and his arm was a howitzer with laser-like accuracy. Though my numbers that winter were nothing like Beltran's, I still hit over .300 and felt like I'd made decent progress tightening up my swing.

The 1999 Tigers had a revamped look. Gone were Gonzo and Joe Randa, while third baseman Dean Palmer and catcher Brad Ausmus were Randy Smith's major offseason acquisitions. Another who joined us prior to the '99 season, though much to his chagrin I wouldn't characterize him as a "major acquisition," was left-hander C.J. Nitkowski. Like Frankie Catalanotto a year earlier, C.J. and I became good buddies. Sharp as a tack with a great sense of humor, C.J. to this day remains one of my favorite guys in baseball. When C.J.'s playing days ended in 2005, it was no surprise that he embarked on a highly successful career in radio and TV.

One other guy joining me on the '99 Tigers was old friend Gabe Kapler. Since we last played together in Low A ball in 1996, Gabe was always one level below me. In 1998, Gabe had a monster season at Double A, hitting .322 with 28 home runs and driving in a whopping 146 runs. Though not a burner in Hunter's class, the Tigers' front office was convinced that Gabe would have enough defensive chops to serve as Hunter's replacement in center field.

The Tigers' roster wasn't the only place where change was evident. In his first full season as the Tigers' manager, Larry Parrish remodeled the coaching staff and appointed some former Tiger greats to serve as his lieutenants.

Alan Trammell, the former superstar shortstop, became the team's hitting coach, and Lance Parrish, a stalwart behind the plate for nearly a decade, was the new bullpen coach. Though I was a diehard Angel fan back in the day, I fully respected those Tiger teams from the '80s, and Trammell and Lance Parrish were a huge reason why. It was a thrill and privilege to be a part of the same club as those guys, even if they were no longer active players.

Despite these changes, at 69-92, the 1999 Tigers were nearly as bad as the 1998 version. For starters, the team's pitching was awful. Our 5.17 ERA was 12th worst among the 14 American League teams, and of the six guys who had at least 12 starts, only Dave Mlicki had an ERA below 5.00. Particularly disheartening was JT's fall into the abyss. Just two years earlier, JT was frequently mentioned as one of the league's best young starters and now his arm was shot and he was just trying to make it with heart and guile. Our lineup wasn't much better than our pitching. Although our 212 home runs were the fourth highest among A.L. teams, our .261 batting average and .326 on-base percentage ranked 12th and 13th, respectively, and gave us an all-or-nothing offense. Higginson missed more than a third of the season because of injuries, while youngsters like Gabe, Encarnacion, and myself all fell far short of expectations.

For the second year in a row, I just didn't deliver. While my 10 home runs and .255/.331/.391 slash line represented a slight improvement over my 1998 numbers, my production was still far below the norm for a right fielder. Once again, my mediocre performance wasn't for lack of effort. As I did with Larry Herndon a year earlier, I spent countless hours with Trammell working on my swing. We tried a variety of different stances—incorporating more of a leg kick to increase power, reverting back to a crouch to enable me to see the ball longer, moving my feet farther apart to make me quicker to the ball, moving me closer to the plate to better hit the outside pitch—but nothing seemed to work. In reality, after a while all the adjustments we made became counterproductive and I started to overanalyze each at bat. It got so bad that in the throes of a 3-for-47 mid-June skid, the brass decided to send me down to Toledo to clear my head.

My stay in Toledo lasted just three weeks, but during my time there, hitting coach Skeeter Barnes gave me the best batting tip I ever received. After watching my first BP session since being demoted, he had me go back to my original swing and said to rely on the approach that had taken me this far. Barnes made the point that it had taken me almost 20 years to master my current swing and that it would be futile to try to reinvent myself. Sure, minor alterations would be necessary from time to time, but wholesale changes would do nothing but mess with my head.

After that initial talk with Barnes, I went back to my original batting stance and stayed with it for the remainder of my career.

Away from the batter's box, I was loving life as a big-league ballplayer. The Tigers' clubhouse was composed of a great group of guys. Ausmus, a world-class defensive catcher and highly underrated with the bat, replaced Gonzo as my informal mentor. A Dartmouth grad, Ausmus was as even keeled as any person I'd ever met and constantly reminded me of how difficult a game baseball is and not to press. "Look," he'd say, "baseball is the only game that if you fail seven out of every 10 times, they'll erect a statue in your honor and send you to the Hall of Fame. Relax."

Despite my subpar performance and the Tigers' poor record, I loved coming to the ballpark. I became as close with guys like Frankie, C.J., Ausmus, JT, and Gabe as I was with my high school buddies, which was the best compliment I could pay any teammate. Whether it was screwing around in the clubhouse before BP, enjoying a couple of cold ones after a game, or going out to dinner on the road, these guys evolved into more than teammates; they became like family. Many fans don't understand how much time baseball players spend with one another. From the time spring training starts in mid-February until the last pitch of the regular season is thrown on the first Sunday of October, baseball players spend more time with their teammates than they do with their families. Not only do we all share the same clubhouse, but we also travel tens of thousands of miles together. Over the course of a long season, we celebrate together, grieve together, and become an integral part of each other's lives.

My first years in the Major Leagues also exposed me to another facet of big-league life that a lot of players are uncomfortable talking about. As a single, professional athlete with reasonably good looks and a lot of disposable income, I suddenly found myself the center of attention when it came to women. At first, I couldn't think of anything better. I mean, as a young, red-blooded male with sexual wanderlust, I was game for whatever some hot chick wanted to throw at me. Although there were girls who hung around the bars and ballparks in many minor league towns, they were nothing like the creatures of the night who lurked in the shadows once I arrived in the majors.

I first fell prey to one in Seattle shortly after being called up in 1997. Frankie and I had just returned to our hotel after enjoying a steak dinner and were walking through the lobby on the way to the elevator bank. Out of the corner of my eye, I spotted four stunning thirty-somethings sitting unaccompanied at the hotel bar.

"Listen, Frankie. I just got thirsty and think I'm gonna grab a nightcap. Care to join me?"

Frankie, a street-smart kid from New York, knew better. "Nah, you're on your own, Jack. Enjoy."

Seconds later, I was at the bar ordering a Heineken when one of the four sidled up next to me.

"Hi, there," she purred. "You must be new."

"New?" I asked. "New as in what?"

"As in just called up," she clarified.

"Indeed," I agreed with her assessment. "Just called up a couple of weeks ago. Any pearls of wisdom you'd like to share?"

"That remains to be seen. How about telling me about yourself, like your name for starters."

When I told her my name, her eyes lit up. "Ooooh, you're the hot prospect. The one who's going to bring winning back to Detroit. You and that Puerto Rican guy."

"Encarnacion? Actually, he's Dominican."

"Dominican, Puerto Rican, Italian, whatever. I don't sweat the small stuff. Anyway, let's talk about you, Jack. I hear you've got a beautiful swing. A pure hitter, they say."

In the big leagues not even two weeks and I already had my own fan club. And its self-appointed president was smoking hot and ready to play ball.

After a few more minutes of small talk, the feline grabbed the beer out of my hand, rested it on the bar, and said, "Time to get down to business, Jack." And with that, she took my hand and led me out of the bar. As we left, I saw several of my teammates—Brocail, Jones, Blair, Matt Walbeck and Bob Hamelin—some of whom smiled and shook their heads when they saw me. What was that all about, I wondered.

When we arrived at my suite, the cheetah was true to her word—she got down to business in no time. No kissing, no caressing, no pretending. Instead, she flipped off her heels, got down to her knees in the middle of the room, unbuttoned and pulled down my jeans and boxer briefs, and went to work. This chick was a pro—this definitely wasn't her first rodeo, or her second.

After letting her exercise her jaw muscles for a few minutes, I figured it was time to reward her for a job well done. I grabbed her long, brown locks as I removed myself from her mouth, lifted her up, and flung her onto the bed. She was wearing a tight miniskirt, which together with her silk panties and fishnet stockings, were soon lying next to her heels on the carpeted floor. Standing facing the bed, I grabbed her calves, lifted her legs, then entered her lush garden. I'd consumed four beers that night, which spread out over a three-hour interval were not enough to impact my performance. After what had to be five minutes of high-intensity pelvic thrusting, I could feel my abdominal muscles getting sore and beads of perspiration on my forehead. I thought about changing positions, but all of a sudden the kitty started to climax. A loud moan followed by another and yet another. With my good deed for the day in the books, I allowed myself the same pleasure, making sure to spray my venom all over her flat stomach.

Much like when we started, there was no affection.

Curving Foul

She used a scarf from her designer handbag to clean my mess, then got dressed. Before she left, she turned to me and said, "That was fun."

"Definitely," I replied. "It would be cool to see you again. How about dinner some time?"

"Ha, rookie," she said, laughing. "You have a lot to learn." And with that she left.

The next day in the clubhouse, I was tying my spikes before heading out to the field when a veteran, who shall remain nameless, sat down beside me.

"Big night last night, huh?" he half asked.

I just grinned sheepishly.

"Care for some free advice, Jack?"

"Sure."

"Actually, let me begin with a question. Did you even get her name?"

Come to think of it, I hadn't. "No."

"Exactly, and that was by design. Her name's Eva, and if you took a poll of the guys in this clubhouse, at least a dozen would tell you they've fucked her. Then, when we go to Oakland, Baltimore, and New York later on this road trip and you ask guys on those teams, they'd also tell you that they nailed her. You see, Eva loves sleeping with ballplayers. She probably knows the back of your baseball card better than you. But the crazy thing is that Eva is not alone. There must be 30 or 40 like her in every Major League city. Don't get me wrong; they all have their subtle differences. Some have ulterior motives and could destroy your future, while others, like Eva, just want to add a notch to their belt. I guess what I'm trying to say is be careful. And don't fall in love with anyone you meet in a hotel bar or outside the stadium gate. It's not worth it."

That pregame chat ended up being the best personal advice I ever received in a big-league clubhouse. But don't be mistaken—Eva wasn't the last groupie I slept with, yet she was the last one I tried to ask out afterwards.

As I became more familiar with the intricacies of dating in the Major Leagues, I started to realize there are two types of women a ballplayer encounters. The first type is the chick who's only interested in you because of what you do for a living. For some of these chicks, like Eva, it's all about the thrill of being with a professional athlete. For others, it's all the trappings that come with the spot on the Major League roster that's the big draw. Obviously, I'm talking about the gigantic paycheck and all the amazing things it can afford (beautiful homes, luxury cars, shopping sprees in the best stores, meals in five-star restaurants). More often than not, these types of chicks—as hot as they may be—have little or no self-esteem and are often imbeciles. While all groupies fall into this category, a chick doesn't have to be a groupie to be a gold digger.

The second type of girl a player encounters is the kind who couldn't care less about what you do. Almost always, they have careers of their own and would rather have a date that involves an engaging conversation about something other than baseball as opposed to a hiking excursion through a shopping mall or a pit stop in a beauty salon.

Since I'm all about full disclosure on these pages, I'll level with you guys and admit that my first couple years in the big leagues were spent with too many girls who fell under Type A and not enough who I'd classify as Type B. But what would you expect given what you've read so far? For the first time in my life, I was overflowing with both money and self-confidence and wanted to sow my wild oats. Starting in 1998, I had a brand-new Ford Explorer and was renting a spacious condo in the posh Detroit suburb of Birmingham. It felt amazing to be able to go into a bar or any other public place and select the next chick I'd sleep with.

The offseason of 1999–2000 was an interesting one, to say the least. It started with me buying my first place, a one-bedroom condo just minutes away from the water in Santa Monica, California. With the big-league minimum salary set to almost double to $200,000 for the 2000 season, I figured I'd have more than enough money to make the mortgage payments while still having sufficient funds to enjoy my life as a carefree bachelor. Santa Monica was an easy choice. It was within close proximity to my high school buddies, with whom I was still close, as well as all the fun bars and clubs in Hollywood.

That winter, my mom's marriage to Conrad finally ended, though not by choice. The dick had a massive coronary one Saturday morning while working in the garage. By the time my mom found him, he was long gone. Trust me, nobody shed any tears for that prick. At the time of Conrad's death, I hadn't spoken to my mom or sister in years. My mom remained plagued by her alcohol addiction, and my sister Dana dropped out of high school at the age of 16 and moved to San Francisco, where she quickly fell for the leader of a motorcycle gang.

Following Conrad's death, I paid for my mom to attend a substance abuse program, then hired a physical trainer to help her lose the 60 pounds she had gained during her horrible marriage. Though my mom and I remained in touch, I was never able to rekindle the close relationship we had prior to my father's death all those years ago. I also tried to reach out to Dana, and despite polite replies, it was evident that any type of relationship with my mom or me would open old wounds for her, so I just let her be.

I also received a stark reminder of just how much of a business Major League baseball is. On the eve of moving into brand-new Comerica Park, the Tigers traded my buddies JT, Frankie, and Gabe to the Texas Rangers for perennial All-Star Juan Gonzalez. Following a 92-loss campaign in 1999, it was obvious that Detroit was not going to contend in 2000, but with the new stadium set to open, the club felt pressured to add a marquee star who could put fans in the seats. Though the Tigers did draw 2.4 million paying customers in 2000—a 20 percent jump versus the team's last year in ancient Tiger Stadium—the trade was a disaster from a baseball perspective. Gonzalez could never adjust to Comerica's cavernous dimensions and left as a free agent after just one miserable year in Motown. JT, his arm already in taters, threw just one more inning in the majors after the trade; however, Gabe played for another decade as a useful fourth outfielder and won a World Series ring with the 2004 Red Sox, while Frankie notched over 1,100 career hits and batted a respectable .291.

Business and baseball aside, I lost three great teammates, and the Tigers' clubhouse would never be the same for me.

Chemistry Class

It was a couple of hours before our game against the Texas Rangers on Memorial Day, May 29, 2000, a contest we ended up losing 3-2. I was standing outside the cage, waiting to take some batting practice swings, when someone with arms like steel rods snuck up behind me and put me in a chokehold. After a few suffocating seconds, the cyborg released me from his grip and said, "That's all you got, pussy boy?" When I turned around, I was astonished to find out that the guy who had almost decapitated me was Griffin Dengler, the Rangers' third baseman and my teammate from long ago at USC.

However, this wasn't Griffin Dengler, the six-foot-one, 175-pound twig who could barely find the cheap seats when we were in college. No, this was the 220-pound version who looked like he could bench-press a small city. I must have stared at his bulging biceps a second too long because he suddenly blurted out, "You like what you see?"

"Do you lift weights?" was my response. For a second, Dengler—definitely not a brain surgeon, if my memory served me correctly—weighed a response before realizing the joke was on him and simply replied, "Ha, funny guy."

It was almost my turn in the cage, so we parted ways but not before we agreed to meet after the game that night for a bite.

For most of the game, I couldn't stop thinking about Dengler and how much bigger he'd gotten since we last played together at USC. Because he'd been a Padre prior to 2000 and had spring training in Arizona, I hadn't seen him in person since our college days and thus had no idea just how massive he'd become. The guy was enormous! At the risk of being too inquisitive, I planned on later asking him what his secret was. Maybe he could give me a couple tips.

At dinner, I didn't have to wait long to discover Dengler's secret, nor did I even have to ask. The appetizers hadn't even arrived, but Dengler proudly asked me, "So you were surprised at how much bigger I'd gotten, eh?"

Was this guy for real? "Yeah," I replied. "It wasn't exactly how I remembered you."

"Ha-ha," he laughed. "It's not the way I remember me, either. Let me tell you a story."

Dengler spilled his guts. San Diego's 17th-round pick in the 1995 draft, he was surprised he'd been picked even that high after hitting only nine home runs in his three seasons with the Trojans at a time when super-light aluminum bats sparked an offensive explosion throughout college baseball. But the Padres had been impressed with his decent speed, good eye, and ability to play all over the infield and thought he had at least an outside chance of making it to The Show as a utility player.

With nothing to lose, Dengler signed for a $7,000

bonus and reported to A ball. It took him just that first half-season—58 games, to be precise—to come to the realization that unless a miracle happened, the only way he'd make it to the Major Leagues would be as the team's bat boy. That winter, desperate to add strength and increase his bat speed, Dengler met a guy who introduced him to a guy who put him in touch with a guy who knew a guy who was friends with a doctor in Tijuana, Mexico, who had devised a "program" for professional athletes to add significant strength while maintaining most of their agility and speed.

When I interrupted Dengler to ask him about the exact contents of this so-called program, he silenced me with his raised index finger and said with a wry smile and a nod, "I was just about to get to that.

"When I started with the doc's program back in late '95, steroids were still in the primitive stages," Dengler began, impressing me with his advanced vocabulary. "Anabolic steroids, lots of hardcore shit that you had to inject. And the acne on your back fucking sucked. Real ugly cystic shit that hurt like a motherfucker when you popped them. It almost made me quit the program, but I noticed how much bigger and stronger I was getting. I think I put on about 20 pounds that first winter alone. But luckily, I stuck with it. They've made amazing advances in the last year or so. It's all shifted from injectable steroids to creams you just rub on your body and even a solution that you can take orally. And now there's this stuff called HGH, human growth hormone, that really has no bad side effects and just makes everything grow. And I mean EVERYTHING!" Dengler concluded with a wink and shit-eating grin on his face.

By now, the waitress had brought out our entrees, a

rib eye for me and a porterhouse for two for Dengler, who seemed to be growing more animated by the minute.

Dengler attacked his slab of meat with a vengeance, but as he did, he continued his lecture, pausing only to wash the food down with his Diet Pepsi. In between gargantuan pieces, he described how he showed up to his first spring training weighing nearly 200 pounds and saw the fruits of his labor almost immediately. In his first live batting practice, Dengler noticed that balls that would have previously died 15 feet shy of the warning track were now landing 10 rows beyond the fence. The results of Dengler's subsequent batting practices were no different, and before he knew it, this success was carrying over into games.

Soon, Dengler's offensive exploits had transformed him into one of baseball's hottest young prospects. It took just two years before Dengler earned a spot in San Diego's starting lineup. In each of his first two MLB seasons, Dengler belted at least 30 home runs and slugged over .500. He had become so sought after that the Rangers, looking to replace since-departed Dean Palmer, traded for him shortly before New Year's 2000 and signed him to a five-year extension worth over $20 million. If nothing else, Griffin Dengler was proof that in baseball it paid to cheat.

Shortly before our meal ended, I asked Dengler something that had been on my mind since the middle of the meal. Wasn't he afraid of being found out? Of being labelled a cheater and having to wear the proverbial scarlet letter on his head for the remainder of his career?

"Nah," responded Dengler when I posed this question to him. "Let me tell you something," he continued, "I likely never even would have sniffed the bigs if it wasn't for this program and all the stuff I've taken. And do you know what I would be doing right now? Mowing lawns in Brentwood during the day and jerking off into a paper towel at night. So, no I'm not afraid of being labelled as a cheater or anything else. Plus, let me tell you something else. You think I'm the only guy in baseball doing this shit? Look around, man. Look at how big guys have gotten and how inflated the offensive numbers are."

Dengler then proceeded to name names, about a dozen or so, who he knew that were on something. Some of the guys were obvious; they were built like linebackers or tight ends and their names were constantly bandied about as suspected users. Some of the others, however, caught me by surprise. Guys that I never would have suspected of foul play. Granted, they had good numbers, but their bodies looked just like guys who played 20 years ago, before steroids and even weight training became en vogue.

Dengler continued his mini rant. "The cat's out of the bag. (Major League Baseball Commissioner) Selig and all his lackeys in the front offices, they couldn't give two shits. Man, since the strike in '94, they've been desperate for fans to return and they know full well that offense sells. You think Selig cared what McGwire and Sosa were using in '98 when they were hitting all those dingers? Fuck no! The only thing he cared about was the sound of the cash registers. Look, maybe one day there'll be testing, but that day is far, far away. Right now, the game is still too interested in bringing back the fans to be worried about guys using. Plus, if they drug tested, they'd end up nailing half the fucking league!"

Following this monologue, Dengler shifted the

conversation over to me and my precarious situation. It was almost as if he had looked at the back of my baseball card before coming to dinner.

"How about you, Jack? You never used or thought about using? No offense, man, but you're not exactly setting the world on fire. What'd you hit, about 10 jacks, last year? That's not nearly enough, my man. Time is ticking and it's ticking fast. There's money to be made and pussy to be fucked, and believe me, once you're done making the big-league minimum and you're still putting up those shitty numbers, they'll send your ass back down to the minors lickity-split and try their luck with someone else. I see it happen all the time. And when you disappear, you never come back up. Stuck in the bushes. Forever."

By this point, I had too much going through my mind to muster a coherent response to Dengler's last statement. I just stared straight ahead and let him keep talking, realizing he was right on point with what he was saying. Dengler must have seen where my head was because he told me to think things over, and if I wanted to pursue what we had discussed, he'd be happy to introduce me to some people. Then, right before we went our separate ways, he said something that stuck with me.

"Dude, I've never told you this, but I've always respected you. You've had it tough, brother. I remember when all of our moms and dads would come to the games at USC and you were probably the only guy who had no one there in the stands for him. Then, with that whole cheating thing. Man, did you get a raw deal. There wasn't one guy on that whole team who never copied a paper or had the questions and answers to a test before it was given. And yet you were the one fucking guy who got busted. You deserve a break. Let me know if you ever need anything."

I did a lot of soul searching lying in bed that night and was forced to admit that Dengler was right. In over 900 at bats with Detroit, I had just 22 home runs and had posted an equally lethargic .245 batting average. That's fine if you're a slick-fielding middle infielder with a bunch of Gold Gloves in your trophy case or a speed merchant capable of stealing 50 bases but not nearly enough for a corner outfielder. By the end of the following season, I would be arbitration eligible for the first time, which meant that my salary was due to go up significantly. But if I was still putting up bush-league numbers, no Major League team was going to pay me millions of dollars. Dengler was right. I was on borrowed time and needed to get better. Fast.

I then started to doubt myself, something I was doing more of lately. Since picking up a bat for the first time 20 years earlier, I had known nothing but success on a baseball field while overcoming all types of adversity. Little League, high school, college, the Cape, independent ball, and the minors—it didn't matter where I was, I'd always quickly established myself as one of the league's best hitters. Except in the majors, where I'd done nothing but struggle since getting called up over two years earlier. Perhaps all the talk circulating about me was true. Despite my former status as a can't-miss prospect, maybe I was a bust, a "Quadruple A" player who could rake in Triple A but wilted when facing Major League pitching. A guy who simply wasn't good enough to hold down a full-time job in The Show. For the last season and a half, I kept telling myself I'd turn it around, but more than 250 games into my Major League career, I was no closer to figuring it out than I was on my first day with the Tigers.

Up until six hours earlier, I'd never given any serious consideration to taking performance-enhancing drugs, also known as PEDs. But hearing firsthand about Dengler's success and taking inventory of my own pathetic career gave me plenty food for thought. I got out of bed and headed to my laptop, where I pulled up Dengler's player page on ESPN.com. There it was. In 1998 and 1999, the guy had hit .282 with 64 total home runs. And so far this year, he'd already hit 13 jacks. "You've got to be kidding me," I muttered to myself. Griffin Dengler was a nobody in college but was now putting up big numbers and getting all sorts of money thrown at him.

Speaking of money, after having none for years, I'd grown accustomed to a certain lifestyle since arriving in Detroit. It had been easy getting used to driving a cool car, dating as many hot chicks as I'd wanted, living in a nice apartment, and enjoying all the other fringe financial benefits associated with being one of just 750 Major League baseball players. I couldn't imagine how devastated and bitter I'd be if all of it was suddenly taken away from me. I could play dumb, but it was obvious that PEDs had taken over baseball and those not using ran the risk of being left behind. Was I going to keep my head in my ass and likely be out of the Major Leagues in a couple of years or was I at least going to give myself a fighting chance? The answer was too obvious.

There were two things that still concerned me about taking the plunge into the murky world of PEDs. The first issue was the health ramifications. Let's face it, you didn't have to be a doctor to know that steroids and the like had been linked to heart issues, brain tumors, reproductive problems, and a host of other not-so-fun physical maladies. But at 25, I considered myself indestructible and decided I'd cross that bridge if and when I got there.

My second concern was a bit more nebulous. Unlike Dengler, I didn't have a cavalier attitude about getting caught. True, baseball had turned a blind eye toward the likes of Mark McGwire and Sammy Sosa a few years earlier, but the tide was turning. If you recall, by 2000 baseball was starting to get a reputation, even more so than football, as the sport that was the most drug-laden.

As a result, there were rumblings that baseball's next collective bargaining agreement was going to address the game's rampant drug problem. When it did, there were sure to be penalties, as well as a permanent black mark next to the perpetrators' names. Also, although PEDs may not have been formally outlawed within baseball at the time (because MLB had no rules on the books explicitly banning them), they were still illegal in all 50 states and possession of a certain amount would be met with a hefty fine and in some cases a prison term.

As the 2000 All-Star break approached, I was getting more desperate by the day. I finished the first half of the season hitting a tepid .243 with just six home runs and seemed just as helpless at the plate as ever. Luckily for me, though, my Tigers were an equally inept 36-48. Dengler, in the midst of an MVP-caliber season, had pulled his hamstring trying to leg out a triple during the first week of July and was unable to play in the All-Star Game. Still interested at the prospect of jump-starting my career, I gave him a call to see if he was in Southern California and whether he'd be up for a field trip to scenic Tijuana.

It turned out that Dengler was indeed back home and, since he was in the middle of a contentious breakup with his girlfriend, was only too happy to take a quick trip south of the border.

Exhausted after a night of banging two Vietnamese sisters silly, Dengler slept most of the way there. I had been to Tijuana only once in my life—a road trip my freshman year in college with some guys from the baseball team—and had stayed just a couple of hours. The place hadn't changed much—an expansive city filled with gringos looking to do things they wouldn't think of doing back home. I guess I was now one of them.

Dengler knew exactly where we were going. For some reason, I was expecting something resembling a rundown warehouse on the edge of town, but instead Dengler navigated us to a modern-looking two-story building in the middle of the city whose prominent sign read, "Tijuana Wellness Center." Hmmm. Much to my relief, there was free valet parking, and the crisply dressed attendant greeted us in perfect English.

"Good afternoon, gentlemen. Who are you here to see?"

"Dr. E," Dengler responded proudly.

"Excelente. First floor, third room on the right."

It turned out that "Dr. E" was as Mexican as I was. Dr. Ali Esfandiary was Iranian. Probably left or got kicked out at about the same time the Ayatollah and his boys sent the Shah packing. One of the benefits of growing up in Southern California in the '80s was that you could easily tell the difference between a Persian and a Mexican and you got a crash course in modern Iranian history.

Maybe it was the starched white lab coat, but Esfandiary seemed decent enough. Sixtyish with close-cropped salt-and-pepper hair and a thin moustache, he too spoke excellent English, though deliberately chose his words as he spoke.

"Griffin, as always a pleasure to see you. How's the season going so far?"

Interesting, I told myself. You had to figure that Dengler, judging by the before-and-after photos, was one of Esfandiary's best customers and yet, this Persian had no idea how his poster boy was doing. Even the most casual fan knew that until getting hurt, Dengler was having a monster 2000 and was in the running for MVP. This told me that Esfandiary was completely disconnected from baseball, meaning he had absolutely no idea who I was, which would only help to preserve my shell of anonymity concerning the web of deceit I was contemplating getting involved in. Sensing this, I quickly went on the offensive, introducing myself to the good doctor with a throwaway alias.

"Dr. Esfandiary," I blurted out, "my name is Dave Johnson. And it's a pleasure to meet you. My friend here has told me about all the wonderful work you do here at the clinic and I'm looking forward to learning more."

Surprisingly, my man Dengler didn't miss a beat. "Yep, Doc. I've told him of all the great things you've done for me and my career. Dave here is interested in getting involved with the program."

"That's wonderful," Esfandiary countered. "I assume you are looking for the same results as your colleague?"

"Oh, yeah," I exclaimed. "I just have a couple of

questions related to the actual regimen and possible side effects."

"Not a problem," offered Esfandiary. "Why don't we go next door into the examination room for a couple of minutes."

We had been sitting in the doctor's plush office and migrated next door. Upon Dr. Esfandiary's request, I sat up on the examination table and took off my shirt. Dengler plopped down in a chair in the corner and quickly closed his eyes. Those Vietnamese sisters must have been something else.

After checking my blood pressure, breathing, and heartbeat, which were all normal, Esfandiary asked me a couple of routine medical questions. Had I or anyone in my immediate family ever suffered from high blood pressure or cholesterol, heart disease, or liver ailments? When I answered in the negative, Esfandiary got down to the nuts and bolts of his recommended program.

Because I don't want to put anyone to sleep, I'll try to keep the pharmacology lesson simple. It turned out that Dengler was right. Gone were the days of old-school steroids that were injected into the buttocks and carried with them horrific side effects. In their place were far more efficient and safe forms of treatment. These included tetrahydrogestrinone (THG) and HGH, both of which Esfandiary highly recommended. The best thing about both THG and HGH was that they were taken orally, HGH in pill form and THG via drops placed under the tongue. Also, neither therapy could be detected by any type of standard urine-based drug test.

While these drugs alone would not enable me to hit a baseball farther or put good wood on the ball with a greater frequency, they would allow me to work out longer and harder while shortening the recovery time my body needed. This would enhance my lean muscle mass and overall strength, which would, in turn, increase my bat speed. All this for only $20,000 per year, payable in quarterly installments and cash only.

The side effects of this regimen were negligible, according to Esfandiary. HGH users ran the risk of contracting nerve, muscle, or joint pain, carpal tunnel syndrome, numbness, and high cholesterol. THG increased patients' risk of high blood pressure, infertility, acne, liver disorders, and immunosuppression; however, the risk of incurring these side effects was far more negligible compared with PEDs of the past.

Esfandiary then told me about the strict usage protocols for both THG and HGH but assured me he would send the precise instructions with each shipment and added that he'd be available via cell phone 24/7 should I have any specific questions or concerns. He then gave me his business card, which was professional looking.

Finally, I told Esfandiary of my privacy concerns. Although Mexico did not have the same HIPAA laws as the United States, he promised that discretion was of paramount importance not only to him but also to the entire facility. He added that the facility employed trained runners, guys who were adept at reliably delivering the product to U.S. customers free of charge.

Esfandiary's last statement bothered the crap out of me and was the reason for my abrupt ending of the meeting. I needed some Mexican drug runners knowing my name and address like I needed yet another trip to the minors. There had to be another way, I said to myself. Until then, this plan was on ice.

The ride home was not a fun one, with Dengler stewing in the passenger seat.

"Dude," he said, "I take time out of my break to go down to Mexico with you to introduce you to my guy and you get cold feet! What the fuck? You make me look like an asshole!"

"Don't worry," I assured him, "your Vietnamese sisters will be waiting for you. All rested and ready for more fun. You up to the task big guy?"

"Goddammit! Shut the fuck up, Jack. I'm sick of your shit. You're gonna be back in the bushes in a year."

Dengler's temper tantrum aside, the day went according to plan. I got all the information I needed. The place looked reputable, the doctor seemed competent, and the regimen was undetectable. Also, Dengler had no idea that my interest in taking the PEDs was as strong as ever. I just needed a way to get my hands on the drugs with no one ever knowing—a tall task since I was in faraway Detroit more than half the year. Then, somewhere just north of San Diego, it hit me. I needed my own guy to transport the drugs for me. Someone I could trust. I needed a mule.

As I later found out, the call came way too early on a weekday morning. After hearing the voice on the other end for a few seconds, it all came back to him. The initial eye contact at Prescott's Bar, the awkward pick-up line, the four rounds that emptied his wallet, and, finally, the all-night fuckfest that went down without a condom. It was that last part that caused the hairs on the back of his neck to stand up straight and his stomach to drop 10 stories when she told him that she was two months pregnant and was planning on keeping the baby. Kenny Lapitka's life had taken yet another turn for the worse.

Though not on the scale of my misadventures, my buddy Kenny had embarked on an ill-fated journey of his own after we parted ways following our graduation from high school in 1993. Never much of a student (especially in sex ed), Kenny had graced three different colleges with his presence in a span of less than three years before deciding that a framed degree in a box in his parents' attic was not worth the trouble. Luckily, he had the foresight to get his Cisco Certification, which paved the way for him to become a computer network engineer. This was huge in the late '90s when the internet was starting to take off and companies were desperate to hire qualified people to build and service their networks.

Despite Kenny's lack of a college degree, he was pulling in six figures a year before turning 25. Unfortunately, however, a former coworker talked Kenny into investing his life savings into an internet startup that went up in flames not long after the dot-com bubble burst in early 2000.

And we haven't even gotten into Kenny's personal life, which was also a mess. You see, Kenny's escapades following his patronage at Prescott's weren't the first time he had decided to get it wet while flying solo, which resulted in him being the not-so-proud papa of Jenna Christina Donaldson, a cute two-year-old with Kenny's eyes and her mother's hair. This first foray into fatherhood cost Kenny about $1,200 a month in child support, which, given his current financial situation, had him teetering on the financial abyss. Then throw in Kenny's father's hefty medical bills—Mr. Lapitka had lost his health insurance when he was laid off from the General Electric plant four years earlier, six months before he was diagnosed with advanced-stage multiple sclerosis—and you've got a guy ready to jump off a cliff.

Suffice to say, the walls around Kenny's life were closing in fast by the time he and I met for an early afternoon lunch on a California swing of an 11-game road trip the Tigers took that August. Although baseball had taken me far from Fullerton, Kenny and I had done our best to stay in touch over the years, and the proliferation of email had made it a lot easier. Still, given my hectic life and his relatively new "family commitments," I didn't get to hang out with him as much as I'd wanted, so I considered encounters such as this one a big deal.

Kenny, deep bags under his eyes, wasted no time getting down to business after the customary man-hug and handshake.

"Dude, I'm fucked," was his eloquent opening remark as we both sat down.

"What now?" I asked, fully aware I could have a long afternoon ahead of me.

"I got a chick pregnant," he offered.

"Again?!"

"Yes, we both got loaded one night at Prescott's and I took her home and—"

"Amateur," I interrupted.

"H-how w-was I supposed to know she hadn't been on birth control?" he stammered.

"Morning-after pills, my man," I opined. "You should always have one handy. Hell, I keep a stack in a drawer in my nightstand. Vital for us men of leisure."

"Yeah, well, those things cost money, of which I have

131

none right now," lamented Kenny. "I can only imagine what my nut is gonna be once this episode is all said and done. And I still can't get a steady job to save my life. I have no idea how—dude, you listening?"

Actually, I wasn't listening. I was staring into space, congratulating myself on my sudden good fortune. I had found my mule.

From the beginning, Kenny and I had the perfect partnership. Not only did we have the utmost trust in one another that had been cultivated during our 20-year friendship, but there was also a mutual dependence that essentially guaranteed the arrangement was going to work out. He was flat broke with a growing mountain of financial obligations. And I was a mediocre ballplayer—albeit one with a $205,000 salary—desperate to do anything to hang on.

Our operation was going to be simple. Four times a year, Kenny was going to drive down to Tijuana and pick up the HGH and THG. A clean-cut white guy with a nondescript 1998 Volkswagen Jetta, he wasn't going to arouse any suspicion on either side of the border. In the offseason, Kenny would just drop the drugs off at my Santa Monica condo after returning from Mexico. During the season, he would just drive to Detroit or wherever the Tigers were playing—whichever was closer to the Mexican border. The driving would be a bit of a pain in the ass, but it was a lot less risky than Kenny flying commercial with a quarter-year's worth of drugs in his bag. I, on the other hand, wasn't worried about travelling with the stuff. The Tigers flew charter, and, as far as I knew, there was never any security.

Kenny was only too happy to hear and then accept my

offer of employment. For his trouble, I'd give him $5,000 cash for each trip to Tijuana. I'd also give him $300 per trip for all automobile-related expenses. In addition, I loaned him $10,000, which he could pay me back whenever he got back on his feet. Was this a lot of money? Sure, but it was nothing compared with what I could be making someday if this all worked out.

Kenny was going to be more than just my mule. He was going to be my eyes and ears when it came to Dr. Esfandiary and the clinic. If there was ever going to be any change in my regimen, it was Kenny who would convey the pertinent information from Esfandiary's mouth to my ears. And if I had any questions, Kenny was the person who would communicate them to the good doctor and get back to me with the answer. Under no circumstances was Kenny to ever give my name to Esfandiary or anyone at the clinic.

Big Muscles, Big Numbers

My 2000 season ended prematurely on August 27 after I sprained my ankle making a sliding catch on a line drive off the bat of Minnesota's David Ortiz (yes, that David Ortiz). I recovered in enough time to come back the final two weeks of the season, but there was no point me trying to return to play in just a handful of games. After an 18-10 record in August to bring us within spitting distance of the A.L. wild-card lead on Labor Day, we went 12-17 in September to finish the season 79-83. Definitely an improvement over our 69-92 record from a year earlier but a long way from being a legitimate contender.

As for Jack Carter, the 2000 season was one to forget. Not only did I hit a measly .251 with just 11 long balls on the way to an embarrassing .389 slugging percentage, but also there was growing talk that after almost 1,200 big-league at bats I was a bust.

Against that backdrop, you can imagine my relief in early December when I found out that the Tigers had decided to tender me a Major League contract for 2001.

I didn't need anyone to tell me it was going to be a make or break year.

If there was a silver lining to the just-completed season, it was that my injury allowed me to get a one-month head start in preparing for '01. About a week after our fateful lunch, Kenny called Esfandiary to tell him that he represented a baseball player interested in beginning an HGH and THG regimen and that he had $5,000 for a three-month supply of the drugs. When Esfandiary inquired about the identity of this mystery athlete, Kenny simply said that the athlete wished to remain anonymous and reminded the doctor of the 50 crisp $100 bills he had with him. Esfandiary, as I expected, was thrilled at the prospect of earning an additional $5,000 every three months and couldn't care less that he had no idea where his clinic's powerful drugs were going. Ah, capitalism at its finest.

Many teams insist that injured players stay with the team as they rehab minor injuries, which my sprained ankle surely was. But because the Tigers in those years were such a poorly run organization and it was so late in the season, I was able to head home to California several weeks early. I had been taking the PEDs for only a couple of weeks at the time of my injury, but since I spent just a minimal amount of time in the gym during the season, I didn't expect to notice any tangible results.

That all changed when I got home to Santa Monica. The first thing I did after putting down my bags was to call my buddy Rocco Tomassini. Rocco, a transplant from Clifton, New Jersey, was a physical trainer who had been on me for years to work out harder. Well, he was about to get his wish.

Curving Foul

I guess you could say I was partially honest with Rocco. While I did tell him that I was coming off a miserable season and that D-Day was a year away if I didn't work out like a madman and make myself into a lean, mean hitting machine, I didn't tell him that these workouts would be chemically enhanced. Regardless, Rocco was going to have his work cut out for him.

Rocco was up for the challenge. The best thing about him, other than his animated personality and seemingly boundless energy, was he knew the game inside out as well as the nuances of training for it because he'd already worked with so many Major Leaguers. So, when I hired him and said I needed my workouts to give me more explosiveness and increase my bat speed, he knew exactly what needed to be done.

Rocco was a fireplug of a guy. At about five-seven and 200 pounds, all muscle, he had olive skin and dark, spiked hair. The third of five kids from a close-knit Italian family, the guy combined tremendous people skills with a relentless work ethic and oozed optimism. This was just what I needed after shitting the bed in 2000. If anyone could bring me out of the funk I'd been in since getting called up to the Major Leagues, it was Rocco.

Rocco and I agreed that we'd work together four days a week and each session would last between two and two and a half hours. In addition to having me do the customary weight work and plyometrics to boost my quick-twitch muscle fibers and add explosiveness, Rocco also insisted on Incorporating speed drills into the mix because he was convinced I still had enough in the tank to make me a faster runner.

When coming up with my plan of attack for that winter,

I kept Dengler in the back of my mind. His great numbers notwithstanding, I did not want to bulk up to the extent that he had. Looking into my proverbial crystal ball, I saw Dengler as a guy, who, because of his excess bulk, was going to be highly susceptible to muscle strains and tears as he aged, and I wanted to avoid this at all costs. I also wanted to avoid all the steroid rumors that would haunt me if I showed up at camp 30 pounds heavier.

As a result, in addition to my work with Rocco, I decided to incorporate a healthy dose of yoga and distance running into my training regimen. Two days a week, I'd take a hot yoga class (yes, with about 30 hot 20-something chicks wearing next to nothing), and on alternating days, I'd run between three and four miles. I figured both activities would keep me flexible and lean despite all the strength I was hoping to add. Finally, as was the case every offseason, I'd hit the batting cages on Monday, Wednesday, and Friday.

If you add it all up, I was going to be spending a fortune in the winter of 2000–01 to transform myself into what I hoped was a legitimate Major League hitter. On top of all the money I was giving Esfandiary for the PEDs and Kenny's "commission," Rocco was costing me a cool $100 an hour and each hot yoga class ran $50. I'd been to Vegas a bunch of times, but this was the most expensive bet I'd ever made.

Rocco and I started the offseason like we meant business. I showed up at his gym every morning at 8 a.m., water bottle in hand and ready to roll. First, I'd ride the bike for between 10 and 15 minutes to get the blood flowing (several weeks later, after my ankle was fully healed, I'd occasionally start my mornings by jumping rope). Then it was on to free weights. One day we'd work the chest and triceps muscles, another day we'd concentrate on the shoulders and biceps, then we'd do the back and glutes, and we'd finish the week by working legs. We generally used free weights for the first hour and after a short break, it was on to plyometrics for about an hour. While I originally thought it would be increased work with free weights that would enable me to add power, it was the plyometrics that got me into unbelievable shape.

Rocco devised "circuits" for each body part, which consisted of about eight different exercises, and we'd commonly repeat each circuit four or five times, each time with a lower amount of repetitions. For example, on days we worked my lower body, the circuit contained eight to 10 exercises, including 90-degree jump squat twists, alien squats, bench jumps and sprints, and box jumps and skips. The first time around the circuit, I'd complete 15 repetitions of each exercise, the second time 12 reps, the third time 10 reps, then eight reps, then finally five. And, remember, this was all after doing six sets each of conventional squats, split squats, calf raises, and a host of other fun-filled free-weight exercises. By the time we were finished, I almost had to crawl to the whirlpool and sauna, where I'd go for the last half hour to let my body regroup.

Usually, I'd leave the gym just before 11 and head straight to the beach, where I'd perpetrate a tan and read for a couple hours. Around 3 or 4 in the afternoon, I'd make my way back to my apartment, where I'd take a quick nap, then head out for a run, go to a hot yoga class, or get in a couple hundred swings at the batting cages.

After that, I'd return home so I could eat dinner, then either read or watch TV before going to bed no later than 10:30. By the time my head hit the pillow, I was exhausted. I was always a good sleeper, but that offseason I led the league in shut-eye.

In case you're wondering, no, I didn't have much of a social life that winter. Don't get me wrong, I dipped it in the ink when I had the urge and would occasionally have a couple of cold ones or smoke a joint here and there, but for the most part, I lived the life of a monk. I figured since I was spending so much coin on the PEDs, Rocco, and the hot yoga classes, it would be sheer stupidity if I offset all the progress I'd made by partying. If I had a good 2001 and signed a multimillion-dollar deal, I'd have the rest of my life to go crazy.

In addition to working out like Arnold Schwarzenegger circa 1980, I paid close attention to my diet for the first time in my life. Since childhood, I'd always been skinny, so I never had to worry about what I put into my mouth. Big Macs, cheese fries, buffalo wings, ice cream, movie popcorn, and Coca-Cola had all been staples, but that suddenly changed in the winter of 2000–01. While I didn't go vegan and start eating kale, I did add structure to my diet and made a conscientious effort to eat more high-protein and less fatty foods. I'd usually have a fruit smoothie, several links of turkey sausage, and a handful of roasted almonds for breakfast, a protein shake as I was leaving the gym, a simple sandwich for lunch, and either grilled chicken, salmon, or steak for dinner. Also, I cut out fried foods and sweets and made it a point to drink at least three liters of water a day.

Like a lot of guys who've used PEDs, I felt that the

biggest benefit I derived was not the increased strength or size per se but rather the much shorter recovery time between workouts that enabled me to go all out every day without worrying about muscle fatigue. Tiring between workouts was what plagued me earlier in my career and was the main reason why I was never able to adhere to a strict regimen. Once in college and twice in the minors, I had suffered muscle strains from working out too hard and had to take a long break from the gym. However, after I began taking the PEDs, it seemed the more I pushed myself, the better I felt.

I reported to spring training in mid-February 2001 certain that I was going to have a big year and with good reason. My hard work with Rocco enabled me to put on 14 pounds of solid muscle and tip the scales at 213 pounds, easily the most I'd ever weighed. More important, though, I didn't feel that I had bulked up or lost any flexibility. Rocco was also right about me being able to add more speed this late into my career through plyometrics and sprint work. Previously, I had done the 60-yard dash in 6.9 seconds, which scouts rate as average, but when I showed up at camp, I was down to 6.6 seconds, a time that gave me "plus" speed in the eyes of evaluators.

When I got to Florida, I was a bit dismayed that the competition for an outfield slot would be a bit stiffer than I had imagined. In addition to the perpetually underachieving Encarnacion and Higginson, who was coming off a career year, you also had newly arrived speedster Roger Cedeno. Higginson, the closest thing Detroit had to a star, was a lock. Encarnacion had teased the Tigers' brass for years with his power/speed combo, and it was obvious that all the front office guys and coaches were committed to giving him yet another opportunity to unlock his vast potential. In Cedeno, Detroit had a guy who had stolen almost 70 bases two years earlier and was still only 26.

Camp started off swimmingly when, in the fourth game of the exhibition season, Encarnacion got hit on the wrist by a Brian Boehringer fastball and would be out until mid-May. Then, about a week later, Cedeno hurt his shoulder diving for a ball in center field, and suddenly Higginson and I found ourselves alternating in center field. Talk about weird, I hadn't played center since an intrasquad game at USC. That didn't stop me from making a couple of highlight-reel plays with my new wheels.

In one game, Mike Piazza of the Mets hit an absolute rocket to right-center field. The instant Piazza made contact, I could tell that the ball was going to be trouble and started sprinting in the direction of deep right center. Because Piazza had hit the ball with such top spin, it was curving toward right field and sinking quick. It didn't matter because I had gotten an excellent jump and had good closing speed as I dove to where I thought the ball would hit the ground. At the same time, however, our right fielder, Wendell Magee, who was built like a running back, had also started his dive from the opposite direction. I was so fixated on making the catch that I didn't see Magee, which was probably for the best. We ended up crisscrossing each other in midair, and as we did, I stretched out my glove and made what was probably the best catch I've ever made. That night, the grab made ESPN SportsCenter's Top 10 Plays of the Day.

Curving Foul

At the plate, I wasn't having as much success. My timing was off, and I'd been getting caught too much on my front foot, especially against soft breaking stuff. But because we'd been plagued by injuries to key guys, I still felt that my starting job was secure and never pressed. Finally, during the last two weeks of the spring, I finally came around and started to hit the ball on the screws.

The Tigers began 2001 at home against the Minnesota Twins. It was a typical Tigers' home opener—barely above freezing temperatures, an annoying wind, and, of course, a Tigers loss (we'd go on to lose seven of the first 10 games on the way to a 66-96 season). But something happened in that game that would be a sign of what was to come. In the seventh inning, I stepped in to face Brad Radke, a guy I always felt was one of the most underrated pitchers of my generation. He had four quality pitches and all he did was throw strikes. Anyway, Radke was just dealing that day, changing speeds and painting the black like the pitching maestro he was. When I stepped up to the plate in the bottom of the seventh inning, I was greeted by freezing rain and a howling wind blowing in. Not exactly ideal conditions for a kid from the OC, to say the least.

With me quickly down in the count 0-2, Radke fired a fastball on the inside corner that was designed to induce a called third strike or jam me if I swung. With two strikes, I was swinging, and because of Radke's impeccable control, I was unable to get any barrel on the ball. I lofted what a year earlier would have been a lazy fly ball to medium right field. But that was then and this was now. And now I was a new man with ice in my veins and PEDs in my muscles.

As I trotted out of the box to first base, I noticed that the ball kept going. And going. Though it finally landed in Twins right fielder Matt Lawton's glove just shy of the fence, I was dumbstruck by how far the ball went in such adverse conditions. Damn, I said to myself, just wait till the weather warms up and the wind dies down.

I was prophetic, it turned out. For the next month, I treaded water as the weather in Detroit and most other American League cities hovered near Arctic levels. Then it warmed up, and I got hot. On May 8, we began a six-game homestand against the Texas Rangers as the temperature throughout the Midwest began to break. It must have been in the mid-70s when we took the field for batting practice, and as I limbered up before stepping into the cage, I felt loose for the first time all season.

I was never a guy who put a lot of stock in batting practice because it's a lot easier to hit a coach's 70-mph soft tosses than it is a Major League pitcher's best stuff. Off the top of my head, I can tell you about the dozen times I hit the crap out of the ball in BP only to be drowning in my sorrows with a postgame beer four hours later wondering how I took an oh-for-four with three strikeouts. But this night was different. I must have hit nine straight balls out at one point, and two or three made it to at least Lansing. Even guys on the Rangers, including my old buddy Dengler, stopped what they were doing to watch me pound the baseball. Usually, when you have a good BP, you hope the success carries over to game time. But on this night, I *knew* it would.

Right-hander Rick Helling was pitching for Texas. Helling was a guy I'd always had success against because he didn't hide the ball well and his stuff lacked movement. In the bottom of the second inning, I came up to the plate with two guys on. I knew that Helling could bring the heat, and with two runners aboard, he wasn't going to fool around.

I couldn't have been more right. He tried to sneak a 95-mph fastball by me on the inner third of the plate, about waist high. Bad move, Rick. With my newfound bat speed, I whipped my Louisville Slugger around and connected right on the sweet spot. Some 421 feet later, a kid in Kaline's Corner had himself a souvenir and I had my fourth home run of the year. In the bottom of the fifth inning, with the score tied 3-3, I came to the plate for the second time, and once more Helling tried to blow one by me and again I took the former Stanford star deep. 4-3. After walking in the seventh inning, I stepped up to the plate with nobody on and the game tied four apiece in the bottom of the ninth. Rangers skipper Johnny Oates had brought in southpaw Mike Venafro to face me, thinking a lefty-on-lefty matchup would work in Texas' favor. Not quite. Venafro threw me a show-me curve ball and I showed the Rangers once again where Kaline's Corner was to give Detroit a 5-4 victory. It was my first-ever walk-off homer, my first three-homer game, and the first of many curtain calls.

But I didn't stop there. Two nights later, I hit another walk-off to beat the Rangers. This one was a moonshot off Rangers closer Jeff Zimmerman with two outs in the bottom of the ninth to give us a come-from-behind 6-5 win. My hot streak continued for the rest of May and through June as I had the type of games I thought were only possible on Atari. For example, on June 19, we faced the Yankees, who had firmly established themselves as the team to beat in the American League. It didn't matter. I launched an opposite-field three-run home run in the first inning off Yankees starter Randy Keisler, then hit a solo shot out to right in the second inning. In the fourth, I tripled into the right-center field gap and followed this up by doubling down the right-field line in the sixth. Finally, in the bottom of the eighth, I singled into the hole past a diving Derek Jeter to complete the cycle. When all was said and done, we won 7-1, and I was five-for-five with six RBI. More important, my big day had put me over .300.

With the All-Star Game in Seattle rapidly approaching, I was anxious to see if I'd be selected to the A.L. squad. Ichiro Suzuki, Juan Gonzalez, and Manny Ramirez had been voted in by the fans as the starters, but I was hopeful to be named as a reserve. While I definitely could have used the four days to recharge my batteries, I thought back to how far I'd come in the last year and that a trip to Seattle would be a tremendous reward for all the hard work I'd put in. After all, it was exactly one year earlier that Dengler and I had taken our field trip south of the border.

It turned out that I was selected as a reserve and even got a pinch-hit single in the bottom of the sixth off the Cubs' Jon Lieber. But the highlight of the entire experience was just being in the same dugout as guys I had always revered and considered to be the best of the best. Titans of the game like Roger Clemens, Cal Ripken Jr., Alex Rodriguez, Pudge Rodriguez, and Juan Gonzalez. And now these guys were all my teammates, even if just for one night.

The other cool thing was being a part of Ripken's 19th and final All-Star Game. I admit, I got chills in the top of the second inning when A-Rod, who started the game as the A.L. shortstop, moved over to third base in deference to Ripken. And it got even better an inning later when Ripken hit one out against Chan Ho Park. I was never one for sentimentality, but after the game I made it a point to ask Ripken to sign a ball for me. In addition to signing his name, Ripken wrote, "To Jack, this will be the first of many."

With the first half in the books, I took a look at my numbers. I'd already hit 18 home runs and driven in 57 runs, both career highs, and my batting average of .309 was more than 60 points higher than what it had been coming into the season. The only thing better than my stats was how I was feeling, which was amazing. Though I wasn't working out with the frequency or intensity I had during the offseason, I was on a plan drawn up by Rocco that allowed me to maintain most of the gains we had made during the offseason.

Often, you'll hear of guys struggling once the season hits the dog days of July and August. In most of North America, it's hot and muggy, and though baseball isn't an aerobic sport like basketball, hockey, or soccer, it's still a grind. Then throw in the crazy travel schedule—one that allows 162 games to be played in just 180 days—and it's no surprise that some guys' production takes a huge nosedive, while others get injured. Luckily, the PEDs enabled me to follow Rocco's plan to a T, which, in turn, helped me keep up the pace I'd been on prior to the All-Star break.

While we're on the topic of full disclosure, I'll let you in on a secret that's not such a secret anymore. Even if you're just a casual baseball fan, you probably know all about the huge impact amphetamines had on the game before they were banned several years ago. Let me tell you, none of this was an exaggeration. Nearly all players were on something. You had to be.

During my career, so many people not in the game would give me a hard time when I complained about how crazy our travel schedule was. "Come on," they'd say, "you guys travel charter and don't even carry your own bags." Big deal.

Each season the average Major League team travels over 20,000 miles in the air, and most of these flights are at the most inconvenient times. Come to think of it, I don't ever remember a time during the season when I was completely well rested and my biological clock was normal. Red-eyes were the worst.

Imagine this scenario: You finish a long night game in Anaheim, Oakland, or Seattle around 11:30 p.m., grab a quick postgame bite, followed by a shower and a talk with the beat writers. If you're lucky, the team bus leaves for the airport at around 1 a.m., meaning the flight back east won't take off a minute before 1:30 but probably closer to 2 a.m. Factoring in the time change, you land at 9:30, meaning you likely don't get home until almost 10:30 a.m. Long story short, you were lucky if you got a total of five hours of sleep that night but more likely you got only three or four. Then try to go out the following night and hit a Randy Johnson fastball, a Rogers Clemens splitter, or a Pedro Martinez curve. It's no wonder amphetamines, or greenies as they were commonly called, were so pervasive throughout baseball. I even played on a team that put them in the coffee pots brewing in the clubhouse.

As the second half of 2001 began, I continued taking PEDs (and greenies) and kept hammering the ball. I enjoyed a monster August, and by the start of September,

Curving Foul

I was up to 30 home runs and nearly 90 RBI. Then shit happened.

After singling in the first inning of an 11-0 loss against the Blue Jays' Esteban Loaiza, I broke for second on an attempted steal. Of the thousands of times I slid into bases during my career, I could probably count the number of times on both hands that I went in head first. Not only do you not get to the base any quicker, but also if you go in feet first you can get up sooner in the event the ball gets by the fielder. Oh, and if you go in head first, you run the risk of jamming your fingers like I did on this occasion.

I was lucky because the trainer initially thought I'd torn a ligament in my hand and would miss the remainder of the season, but fortunately the MRI came back negative. Not wanting to let anything get in the way of my hot streak, I was in the lineup the next day even though my hand was completely swollen. I could barely grip the bat, let alone swing it. I tried to tough it out another several weeks before I told manager Phil Garner that I was done.

Despite the injury-induced slump that put a damper on my final numbers, I'd had a season to be proud of. I hit .296 with 31 dingers, though I barely missed out on 100 RBI with 96. For you *Moneyball* fans out there, my 79 walks (versus only 77 strikeouts) gave me a .384 on-base percentage, which, combined with my .545 slugging percentage, gave me a sterling OPS of .929, good for ninth in the American League, right behind feared slugger Carlos Delgado of the Blue Jays.

My breakout season earned me recognition from numerous publications. From *USA Today's Baseball Weekly* to *Sports Illustrated* to *ESPN The Magazine*, I appeared on more magazine covers than I could count. Guys like old buddy Lynn Henning and Jim Callis from Baseball America, who had predicted stardom for me years earlier, looked like geniuses, while Peter Gammons, who had remarked just a year ago that my bat was too slow to ever become a productive Major Leaguer, was forced to eat crow.

The craziest thing about the 2001 season was that no one had a clue my improved numbers were the result of the PEDs. I mean, here I was hitting the ball harder and farther than ever and not one teammate, writer, or opposing player or manager even hinted that my sudden rise from a borderline big leaguer to one of the top 10 hitters in the American League might at least be partially attributable to nonnatural means.

There were several reasons for this. First and foremost, this was supposed to happen to me. Remember, I wasn't some guy who came out of nowhere to catapult himself into the upper echelon of the game's best hitters. Instead, I was a former top prospect who took longer than most to put it all together. So, when I finally did emerge, it was just a matter of me fulfilling my "vast potential" as opposed to foul play.

Second, my decision to incorporate hot yoga and long-distance running into my workout regimen combined with my naturally somewhat-lanky build meant I didn't look like a juicer. At almost six-three, the 14 pounds I gained during the six-month offseason were evenly distributed on my long frame. This modest weight gain was a stark contrast to the 30 to 40 pounds admitted, suspected, or proven PED users like Jose Canseco and Barry Bonds had gained in prior offseasons. Even Rocco, who was an outspoken critic of steroid use and had trained big leaguers for over a decade before we worked together, had no idea what I was doing.

The final reason why my cheating was able to fly under the radar was that in the late 1990s and early 2000s, PEDs were all the rage and every year a bunch of guys were seeing massive spikes in their production. In other words, I was just another face in the crowd.

My big numbers notwithstanding, 2001 was yet another hot mess for the Tigers. At 66-96, we finished below .500 for the eighth season in a row and our attendance in the second year of Comerica Park dropped by over half a million. Shortly after the season ended, the organization hired Dave Dombrowski as CEO and President. Clearly, the Illitch family, which owned the team, was not happy with Randy Smith, who had posted six straight losing seasons since taking over general manager duties after the 1995 season. Dombrowski had built winning teams in Montreal and Florida (including a World Series champion in 1997) and was known as a guy who didn't consider anyone untradeable. Obviously, he was coming in with the mandate to rebuild the organization and transform it into a perennial winner.

It would be interesting to see how my situation would evolve going forward. Because I was still just 26 and three years away from free agency, I was the ideal guy to build a winning club around, but I was also the team's most marketable player and could probably fetch two or three top prospects in a trade.

Financially speaking, there are two seminal moments in a Major League baseball player's career. The most important one occurs after a player has accrued six years of service time. At this juncture, the player is no longer bound to his team and is free to negotiate a contract with any one of the 30 clubs. For almost all guys, free agency means a huge jump in salary as well as the security of a guaranteed multiyear contract.

The other key point generally occurs three years earlier when players and their organizations are permitted to determine the players' salary through the arbitration process. With arbitration, the player (always through his representation) and the team present an independent arbitration panel with each's desired salary figure for the upcoming season. Each side then presents its argument as to why its figure is the more appropriate one and the arbitration panel decides in favor of either number. The panel makes its decision based on a number of factors, including the player's statistical performance and salaries of comparable players.

Because an arbitration hearing can get contentious, the two sides usually settle on a number before the start of the hearing. Although arbitration-eligible players don't experience the salary spike that free agents do, they still enjoy a hefty increase in their paychecks because during the first three years of a guy's career, teams are allowed to renew contracts for any amount at least equal to the big-league minimum.

Because I was arbitration eligible for the first time, my salary was going to increase significantly from the $225,000 I had made in 2001. The only question was how significantly. In the early 1990s, the Cleveland Indians started the trend of teams locking up their best players through their arbitration years, and in some cases even bought out some of these guys' free agent years. This was a hot-button issue because on the one hand a lot of players longed for the security of a multiyear deal, while the powerful players' union believed that long-term deals artificially held salaries down and preferred that players—especially stars—establish their values on the open market.

Given my past, I would have been happy to take a below-market deal because it would have offered me the financial security I'd never had in my life. My agent, Brian, had a far bolder view. To his credit, he was convinced that 2001 was my coming-out party and a harbinger of great things to come.

In early November, Randy Smith reached out to Brian and proposed a four-year deal worth a total of $20.5 million followed by club options worth $10 million each for 2006 and 2007. I couldn't sign on the dotted line fast enough, but Brian was not convinced.

"You can wipe your ass with this contract," my agent declared.

"Seriously?" I responded. "Obviously, you have a short memory. Wasn't too long ago I was couch-surfing and dining on ramen and Mars bars. And now these cats want to give me 20 mill and possibly as much as 40. I'll be set for life—and so will you, Bri. We have to take this."

"Are you nuts? Why don't you ask them to throw in some KY while you're at it because these shysters are trying to bone you in the ass," Brian said. "With this piece of shit deal, you'll be making well below market during your arb years and forget about the free-agent year covered in the contract. And if the numbers you put up in the future even remotely resemble this past season, they'll be certain to exercise the 2006 and 2007 options, which will make you the biggest laughingstock in all of baseball. Get this. If you go year-to-year then opt for free agency after '04, I'll probably be able to get you at least

50 percent more than what this moron is offering you."

That did it. Brian convinced me to reject Smith's offer of financial security for me and likely several generations of still-unborn Carters.

After several weeks of back-and-forth haggling, Brian and Smith agreed on a 2002 contract worth $3 million, which was more than a 12-fold increase from what I had earned in 2001 and half a million more than what I would have taken home had I signed the long-term deal Smith had proposed.

THREE MILLION DOLLARS! Damn! This was more money than I had ever imagined I could make in my entire life, let alone in just one year. I was just about moved to tears when I thought of all the tough times I had to endure to get to this point. Having my stepfather punch me in the mouth because I asked him for a few bucks, being scared out of my mind and having just $47 to my name after being thrown out of USC, subsisting on greasy food and sleeping on roach-infested beds in the minors, and, up until just a year earlier, worrying if I was good enough to even stay in the majors. Did I even—just for a second—think about PEDs and their role in getting me to this point? Hell, no. Life was good. Finally.

9

Love

Life wasn't just good on the baseball field. Early in the 2001 season, before a Sunday afternoon home game, I was at the Home Depot in Birmingham to buy air filters for my air conditioner. It was just starting to warm up and I was afraid that my place would soon resemble a sauna if I didn't replace the filter.

In a desperate rush to get to the park in enough time to suit up for batting practice, I wasn't thrilled when the cash register malfunctioned with me next on line. Neither was the cute auburn-haired chick in spandex behind me. After about two minutes of additional waiting, I'd finally had enough and delivered the greatest pick-up line of all time.

"Listen, I've got someplace I have to be. Do you think you can buy these for me and drop them off at my place? It's just down the road."

"Oh, and like I have nothing else to do on a Sunday but provide air-filter delivery service for a total stranger," came the unfriendly reply.

"Good point," I said. "How about I throw in tickets for

today's Tiger game and dinner afterwards?"

"Don't the Tigers suck?" she asked.

Fortunately, the check-out girl miraculously fixed what was ailing her register and finally rang me up. As I was paying, the conversation ended.

"Actually, my friend and I are going for a run and then I've got plans. But thanks for the offer. I'm sure there are plenty of guys in here who'd love to see the game with you, though the dinner part may be questionable. My name's Jennifer, by the way."

I was about to correct her by saying that if she did go to the game she'd be watching me instead of watching with me but didn't deem it worth the trouble. As I already explained, for a ballplayer, there are two types of girls, those who liked you because you're a ballplayer and those who couldn't care less. I had a strong suspicion this chick was firmly entrenched in the latter camp. Plus, I was already tagging two chicks. Who had time for a third?

As I walked away, I said, "Well, it was great to meet you, Jennifer. Have a great run. And my name is Jack."

For some reason, I was a tad disappointed as I left the store. As a professional athlete, I'd gotten so used to using the "do you know who I am" card to pick up girls—almost always with success—but this time the only card I'd used was my American Express to pay for the air filters. That said, there was something about this Jennifer that told me even if I had done that, she wouldn't have taken the bait. After several years of horsing around with chicks enamored solely by my baseball career and all the trappings that came along with it, I realized I longed for a girl like Jennifer.

Almost a month later, we were back home against

the Milwaukee Brewers. I'd been red hot for weeks and my confidence was at an all-time high. On this particular night, a 9-4 victory for the Tigers, I'd hit a home run off of Paul Rigdon and almost hit another off of Mike DeJean but had to settle for a triple when it hit high off the wall in right-center. Usually, after a Friday night game, I would have been walking out of the players' entrance with the likes of Jeff Weaver, Rob Fick, and a couple of other guys on our way to cause some trouble. But since I'd been battling an annoying cold that wouldn't go away, I decided to head home and get some much-needed rest.

While bending down to sign a kid's jersey (something I never would have done had I been jetting out of there with Weaver and Fick), I heard a semi-familiar voice call my name. Looking up, I was shocked to see Jennifer, though unfortunately wearing jeans instead of spandex. Still, she looked amazing.

"Nice game, Jack."

"So, Jennifer, I guess we didn't suck tonight."

"Not at all. How are the air filters working out?"

This chick was good. Definitely a cut above the groupies I was quickly growing accustomed to. "Too well and I have the cold to prove it."

"Sorry to hear you're sick because I was going to take you up on that dinner offer."

"I said it's a cold, not cancer."

So much for a restful evening at home.

What followed was the best first date I've ever been on. We hung out at a quiet bistro called Jean Luc's just off the strip in Birmingham for nearly four hours and closed the place down. We hit on a variety of topics—our upbringing, religion, politics, pop culture—except baseball.

It was almost surreal. All the "dates" I'd been on since I'd made it to the majors had the same feel—mere formalities before the real show in the bedroom (or in some cases the backseat) began. But on this night, we hung on every word that came out of each other's mouth. The best part of the evening had to be Jennifer's recollection of how she learned I was a Major Leaguer and why she decided to stalk me by the players' entrance.

Right after we met that fateful Sunday morning, Jennifer told her friend about the cute guy named Jack who tried to give her Tigers tickets and ask her out. Her friend, a huge Tigers fan, inquired whether Jack meant Jack Carter, as in the Tigers right fielder who was (finally) hitting. Jennifer replied that this Jack couldn't have been a professional athlete because if he was indeed a Tigers player, he certainly would have told her to seal the deal.

Upon seeing a photo of me online and making a positive ID, Jennifer was intrigued about this baseball player who didn't leverage his status to get in the sack with her. Finally, after some deliberation, Jennifer and several friends decided to go to a game. When the other girls took off for Hockey Town after the last out, Jennifer made her way to the other side of Comerica Park to try her luck. I was happy she did.

We went our separate ways after that first date, as well as after the second, third, fourth, and, well, let's just say she made me earn it. Which, as you can imagine, made me like her even more. It was so bizarre. For the past five years, practically every girl that I'd hung out with couldn't wait to sleep with me, but Jennifer made it clear she wasn't in a rush. Yet, I knew she was into me.

Before long, we were inseparable. It helped that we

lived only several minutes from one another and that as a schoolteacher she had the summer off, but chemistry is chemistry and we had that in spades. A U Mich grad, she was intelligent, and as captain of her high school lacrosse and tennis teams, she was probably a better athlete than I was. The other amazing thing about our relationship was that it started just as I was beginning to hit my stride, which meant that I was in a clear, relaxed state of mind.

Before I continue with the story, I feel obliged to give some free advice to all the ladies in a budding relationship with a professional athlete. The best way to gauge whether your man has long-term plans for you is to see whether he invites you on the road, because as we've seen, on the road trouble lurks around every corner. With Jennifer, I realized I had big plans for her early on when I dropped all my other distractions and started taking her on the Tigers' road trips. By the end of the summer, she rarely missed a trip. Most of the Tigers I hung with at the time like Weaver and Fick were bachelors, so I took some heat in the clubhouse, but I didn't care.

It was a blast having Jennifer as a travel buddy. We went to the Rock & Roll Hall of Fame in Cleveland, the Texas Book Depository in Dallas, the Space Needle in Seattle, and the CN Tower in Toronto. We even visited the World Trade Center barely a month before it came crashing down on 9/11. I met Jennifer's parents when they came to Detroit from their home outside Cleveland. They seemed like good people who took a lot of pride in raising their amazing daughter. Modest and conservative, they were nothing like my parents prior to my father's death, though after spending time with them, I was sadly reminded of what might have been.

In those first several months Jennifer and I dated, I learned more about dating and relationships than I had during the past 26 years. I came to the conclusion that all I knew about healthy relationships came from observing my mom and dad from early childhood until the age of 10. After my dad died, the closest thing I came to experiencing a strong relationship was by watching Mike and Carol Brady interact with one another on *Brady Bunch* reruns. Words like trust, unselfishness, empathy, and commitment were all foreign to me.

It didn't take Jennifer long to realize that my background wasn't conducive to what she was looking for, yet she was sympathetic with my hardscrabble past. When I didn't call at the time I promised or I'd show up late to her place after having an extra beer with the guys in the clubhouse, she'd just laugh it off and pretend it didn't bother her. But I'm sure it did.

Just a couple months after we started dating, we had plans to do dinner and then attend an outdoor concert with some college friends of hers. But it was pouring and I'd showed up later than expected after an extra-inning game, so we decided to just stay in. It ended up being a memorable date—you know, one of those times when you're doing nothing elaborate yet still enjoying one another's company to the fullest. We started off playing a couple board games, then suddenly Jennifer had another idea.

"Jack," she said. "Tell me something no one knows about you."

This was too easy, I thought. I'd been agonizing for weeks whether I should tell her about my PED usage and thought me not telling her was the same as lying. Also, I'd been wanting to tell her as a way of demonstrating to her how much she meant to me. I started to talk but suddenly stopped a second later. She threw me a confused look. So, instead, I said something else I'd been meaning to tell her.

"I love you, Jennifer. More than you could ever imagine."

She broke into a huge smile, then brought her beautiful face right up to mine.

"Jack, you stole my line! I was going to say that!"

"Well, then. I'm waiting."

First came her infectious laugh. Then, the best line ever.

"Jack, I love, love, love, love you! So much!"

Like I said, chemistry is chemistry.

Jennifer and I were hit with a dose of reality in early October when the season ended. By then, she had been teaching for six weeks and my season was about to end. I contemplated not returning home to California and staying in Detroit during the offseason, but we were both afraid that if we moved in together we'd be rushing things. Also, I remembered all the hard work I'd put in with Rocco during the prior winter and felt it was in my best interests to keep my offseason routine intact.

On top of that, I had no desire whatsoever to endure a winter full of subarctic temperatures on the Michigan tundra. It was a tough decision, one made even more complicated by the fact I was madly in love with this amazing girl. That said, on the morning of Sunday October 14, 2001, I kissed a crying Jennifer Swanson good-bye before I boarded a plane bound for home. There was work to be done.

Having a steady girlfriend I was nuts about was the best thing that could have happened to me that offseason because it enabled me to keep all the unnecessary distractions at bay and concentrate on my work with Rocco.

The grind of a six-month, 162-game baseball season is not conducive to staying in peak shape, and while I worked out as much as I could, it was inevitable that as the season progressed I would lose some strength and muscle mass. I was afraid that if I lifted too much before games, I'd be tight and not able to catch up to good fastballs during the nine innings that followed, but after games I was simply too exhausted to make any headway. By midseason, I had figured out that the best approach was waking up super early twice a week to go heavy and then two other days I would work out with light weights before games. Though I had dropped about five pounds by the end of the season, I still felt strong and I had retained most of my bat speed.

The PEDs had been a godsend. In prior years, between the grind of all the travel and taking thousands and thousands of swings, I was dead by the time the last pitch of the season crossed the plate. While I didn't feel as good as new in early October, I certainly felt like I still had something left in the tank.

It also seemed like I had been spared all the side effects of the HGH and TGH I was using. Several times a week, I took a mental and physical inventory of my body and bodily functions to make sure there weren't any problems, and, thankfully, each time I came away relieved. Still pissing and crapping OK? Check. No chest or abdominal pains or headaches? Check. Balls still normal size? Check. No bacne? Check.

Curving Foul

Rocco and I kept the same schedule from the prior winter except for a couple minor changes. Once again, I supplemented my work in the gym with a good deal of running and yoga, a healthy diet, and plenty of sleep and beach time. By late November, I'd regained the weight I'd lost during the season and actually felt stronger than I had the prior March. The only interruptions to my routine occurred when Jennifer and I saw each other, which was for a week around Thanksgiving, almost two weeks during Christmas and New Year's when we went to the Caribbean, and two long weekends in January. Trust me, it wasn't easy, but somehow we made it work that winter.

I reported to Lakeland for spring training 2002 in the best shape of my life at 218 pounds. What a difference a year made. The previous spring, I was fighting for a job and treating every at bat like it could be my last with the big-league club. This spring, on the other hand, I was a regular with job security and acted like it. I worked at my own pace and made sure not to go out too hard or do anything stupid that would put me on the shelf. In fact, I didn't get four at bats in an exhibition game until the middle of March. No sweat. Once again by last two weeks of the Grapefruit League, I had my timing down and was tagging line drives all over the yard. The season couldn't start soon enough.

Unfortunately, I was making a habit out of starting slow. As of May 15, I was hitting just .204 with only two home runs and a whopping 11 RBI. It wasn't long before a slew of writers started spouting their venom, claiming that the league had caught up with me and that I was nothing more than a one-year wonder. If nothing else, the tough stretch I endured in the opening weeks of the 2002 season showed me how much I'd matured as a player. Once upon a time, I would have pressed, my slump would have snowballed, and I would have ended up sleeping on someone's rollout couch in Toledo. But after having the season I'd had in 2001 and proving to all my critics—and, most important, myself—what I was capable of, I couldn't care less what a bunch of columnists wrote about me. Even after striking out four times against Jarrod Washburn and the Angels on May 7 and being moved from third to sixth in the lineup the following game, I wasn't the least bit phased. My time would come.

I didn't have long to wait. On May 17, with the Tigers having lost seven straight games, I exploded against the Texas Rangers' Dave Burba. In the third inning, I hit a mammoth three-run homer off the Kaline's Corner façade for the longest dinger I'd hit up until that point in my career. I followed it up with a solo shot two innings later. Before I knew it, I had embarked on a 31-game hitting streak and was breathing down the back of Boston's Manny Ramirez, who was leading the American League in hitting. Furthermore, starting in early June, I had a stretch of 12 straight games in which I tallied at least one extra-base hit.

With a .338 average, 18 homers, and .592 slugging percentage during the season's first half, you would have thought that I'd be a shoo-in to start the All-Star Game in Milwaukee's Miller Park. But I finished a distant fourth behind Ichiro, Manny, and Torii Hunter and had to be content with coming off the bench for the second year in a row. And for the second year in a row, I came through with a pinch-hit single.

But the real story was the game's final score, a 7-7 tie! I'll never forget the bewildered look on Bud Selig's face when, at the end of 11 innings, the powers that be realized they had run out of players and had to stop play. What a joke! Not only were the thousands of fans who were soundly booing Selig completely pissed, but nearly all the players were seething as well. It's important for fans to understand that save for the first-time All-Stars and guys playing in front of their hometown fans, the All-Star Game is about as much fun as a case of hemorrhoids. With all the traveling we do, the thought of having four days off in the middle of July to veg on the couch, connect with our families, fish, or do whatever is huge. So, having to take yet another road trip for a game that doesn't count is not exactly high on the players' to-do list. Just saying . . .

With the exception of a three-week slump in August, my second half of 2002 was about as good as my first. Though I hit the same 31 home runs I did the year before, my .316 average and .567 slugging percentage were both good for sixth in the junior circuit, the latter catapulting me ahead of future Hall of Famer Frank Thomas. I also drove in over 100 runs for the first time in my career, and my 20 steals were evidence that all my speed work with Rocco had paid off. Suffice to say, Brian and I were looking forward to upcoming contract negotiations with the Tigers' brass.

Speaking of the Tigers' brass, 2002 was a watershed year for the organization's front office. After starting the season 0-6 en route to a horrific 55-106 campaign that landed the team in last place, team president Dave Dombrowski fired not only the manager, Phil Garner, but also Randy Smith. I had mixed feelings about these

164

moves. I liked Garner a lot, both as a manager and as a person. I found him to be a straight shooter who didn't play games and was always appreciative of his empathy and support when I had been struggling. I always believed that the way Garner treated me was the result of his own lengthy playing career and that he realized how hard of a game baseball is.

On the other hand, Smith, as nice a guy as he was, made a lot of moves that caused me to scratch my head. Many fans don't realize that most players are not students of the game and barely follow it when they're not playing. In other words, when the game is over and guys shower and head home, the last thing they want to do is watch another game, let alone talk about it or analyze it.

However, I always considered myself the exception. I never had a problem talking to complete strangers about the minute details of a game or the minor transactions a team's front office made. That said, I've never been shy about discussing the job I thought my team's manager and general manager were doing. In that vein, I believed Smith's firing was justified. The guy was in Detroit for six consecutive losing seasons, during which time the Tigers were a combined 155 games under .500. Sometimes you just have to pull the plug.

The guy pulling the plug was Dombrowski. In time, Dombrowski would gain notoriety for his ability to turn around bad clubs, as well as his large selection of turtleneck shirts that matched his even larger assortment of checkered blazers. Dombrowski's reputation was earned by his willingness to trade anyone, and I mean anyone. Hell, the guy even traded a young Randy Johnson as GM of the Montreal Expos! Taking all this into consideration, when Brian received a cool reception from Dombrowski in mid-October after approaching him to discuss a contract extension, he assessed that my days in Detroit would soon be coming to an end.

From a baseball perspective, I wouldn't be leaving much behind if the Tigers traded me. The organization remained the armpit of the A.L., if not all of baseball, and the still-barren farm system made sure that wouldn't be changing anytime soon. In addition, Comerica Park was one of the worst stadiums in the league for hitters. Despite my gaudy overall numbers during the past two seasons, I hated hitting there. The place was cavernous, with the deepest power alleys in the A.L., and had robbed me of at least 15 home runs in 2001–02 alone. When you combine that with polar temperatures for April and most of May, you're talking about conditions that would likely cost me tens of millions in the long run.

The other negative about my time in Detroit was the poisonous clubhouse culture that by the end of 2002 had turned every day into a painful grind. Ask any big leaguer and he'll tell you that the clubhouse is supposed to be a refuge, a place where you can escape the problems of the "common man" like a bad marriage, sick parents, or nagging children. Instead, the Tigers' clubhouse in the early 2000s resembled a sorority house with nothing but bitching and cattiness. Obviously, if you put 25 different guys in a confined space over the course of over six months, cliques will form and disagreements will occur, but the Tigers of the early 2000s took the term dysfunctional to a whole new level.

Because we were so bad, nearly every player was afraid of losing his roster spot, which led to a lot of me-first bullshit, which, in turn, resulted in excessive bickering, backstabbing, and even physical altercations. Over time, various clubhouse factions formed, and guys in different cliques often wouldn't even talk with one another. This type of environment made it next to impossible to form lasting friendships.

By the time 2002 was over, I realized I had no true friends left in the clubhouse. No one I could grab a quick beer with or invite over to my place to shoot the breeze. Old mentors like Brad Ausmus and Luis Gonzalez had been dealt years earlier, as had old running buddies Frankie Catalanotto, Gabe Kapler, C.J. Nitkowski, and Justin Thompson. Bobby Higginson was still around, but he was a lone wolf who didn't let anyone get close. Right-hander Jeff Weaver and outfielder Robert Fick were also guys approximately my age whom I'd hung out with in prior seasons, but they were prickly dudes whose worldview was a lot different from mine. Dombrowski had traded Weaver midseason, while Fick and I were no longer on speaking terms.

While discord reigned supreme in the Tigers' clubhouse, things were chugging along on the home front. Jennifer and I had been together for almost one and a half years, and it became obvious that marriage was inevitable, despite the fact neither of us was 30. Jennifer, who'd grown up in a stable family and had already been in a long-term relationship, was totally down with the idea. I, on the other hand, had reservations. On the one hand, Jennifer was the most beautiful, sweetest, and coolest chick I'd ever known and I loved her to death. However, having just come into my own as a Major Leaguer and likely just months away from earning out-of-this-world money, I wondered what the rush was.

I was also becoming increasingly restless. And curious. The thing that scared me the most was the idea of spending the rest of my life with just one girl when there was so much fun to be had. Whether it was the chick in skintight leather pants and stiletto heels gallivanting through LAX, the vixen in the short, leopard miniskirt and thigh-high boots at the lounge in Chicago, or the mermaid in the thong bikini at the hotel pool in Miami, I came to the painful conclusion that a certain corn-fed girl from the Midwest might not be enough to satisfy the impulses of a highly virile professional athlete about to become independently wealthy.

We all have only one life to live, and I intended to live mine. To the fullest.

New York, New York

If you polled all the Major Leaguers who've been traded, an overwhelming majority would tell you that the first time they were dealt came as a complete shock. I'm in the minority. Between Brian playing hardball with Detroit's long-term offer during the 2001–02 offseason and new GM Dave Dombrowski's reputation as a shrewd wheeler-dealer, I fully expected the Tigers to trade me. Dombrowski had already traded Jeff Weaver, Detroit's best pitcher who had less than four full years of service time, during the middle of 2002, and Brian and I were convinced I'd be the next one out the door. Also, Brian and the front office didn't even exchange contract offers after the 2002 season.

At first, Brian and I thought I was headed to either the Anaheim Angels or Toronto Blue Jays. The Angels had just won the World Series, but their right fielder, Tim Salmon, was past his prime, and they'd made some noise about wanting to transition "Kingfish" (one of my favorite baseball nicknames, by the way) to full-time DH.

Obviously, I was ecstatic at the mere thought of going home to play for my boyhood team and begged Brian to do whatever he could to steer me to Anaheim.

The other team we thought would make a serious play for me was the Toronto Blue Jays. Raul Mondesi and Jose Cruz Jr. had shared right-field duties for the Jays in 2002 and neither would be back in '03. Reed Johnson was viewed as the most likely candidate to man the position going forward, but several scouts told Brian that Johnson profiled more as a fourth outfielder because of his lack of power.

I wasn't thrilled at the prospect of playing in Toronto for a variety of reasons. First, in the post-September 11 world, travelling to and from Canada had become a bitch. Second, back in 2003, SkyDome still had an AstroTurf surface, which had wreaked havoc on many outfielders' knees. And, finally, in the early 2000s, the Blue Jays, despite the large Toronto market, had become an also-ran in the competitive A.L. East with a reduced payroll and chronically mediocre teams. After spending the first part of my career with the lowly Tigers, I longed for a winner.

One night in early December, I glanced at my cell phone as I was leaving a movie theater and noticed that Brian had called four times from the winter meetings in Nashville. "Uh-oh," I thought. I didn't think my agent was calling to give a weather update. I quickly called Brian back, and when he answered, all I could hear was Frank Sinatra singing "New York, New York."

"So, you've decided to become a DJ?" I asked my agent.

"No," he responded. "Get used to hearing this song multiple times per day. You're now a Yankee."

Motherfucker. I couldn't believe it. The Yankees! I just stood there with my mouth wide open.

"Jack? Jack? Are you there? Talk to me!"

Despite making the All-Star team the past two seasons, knowing that the Yankees traded for me was the ultimate confirmation that I'd fulfilled my vast potential and become a star. In the eight seasons from 1995 to 2002, New York never missed a trip to the postseason, winning four World Series and appearing in another. With a lineup stacked with stars like Derek Jeter, Bernie Williams, Alfonso Soriano, and Jason Giambi and stalwarts like Mike Mussina, Andy Pettitte, and Roger Clemens in the rotation, the Bronx Bombers were more than just a great team. They were a team for the ages.

When I finally regained consciousness and discussed the situation with Brian, we agreed that the Yankees acquiring me made perfect sense. Paul O'Neill had done a marvelous job manning right field for New York from 1993 to 2001, but the position had become an area of weakness for the team. Raul Mondesi was the primary right fielder after New York acquired him in the middle of 2002, and he had hit only .241 while playing shoddy defense.

There were many reasons why I was thrilled to be a Yankee. While the opportunity to win the World Series every year was at the top of my list, as a baseball historian, I considered it an honor to play for an organization that had boasted legends like Babe Ruth, Joe DiMaggio, Mickey Mantle, and Reggie Jackson.

I was also excited to move from spacious Comerica Park to Yankee Stadium, one of the best home run parks in the league, especially for left-handed hitters. I salivated trying to guess how many home runs I could hit in a stadium with a right-field porch just 314 feet away while being surrounded in the lineup by the likes of Jeter, Williams, and Giambi.

Finally, I had come to love New York during visits as a member of the Tigers. There was just something about the city that separated it from the rest of the pack, this intensity that would grip me from the minute I arrived until the second I left. Just walking down the street, I always felt this incredible energy that made me not want to leave.

When Brian and I arrived in New York about a week before Christmas for my introductory press conference, I could tell instantly that New York, the Yankees, and I would be a match made in heaven. The Yankees showed me right away what kind of first-rate organization they were by putting me up in a penthouse suite at the Peninsula Hotel, which is just five blocks from Central Park, probably my favorite place in Manhattan. After the press conference, which was held at Yankee Stadium, and a celebratory dinner with the Yankees' front office in a private room at Strip House, Brian and I made our way back to the bar at the Peninsula for a nightcap. As we sat off to a corner sipping our drinks and spotting one supermodel-caliber chick after another, I thought to myself that this could all be mine for the taking. At that moment, I made the most difficult decision of my life.

Jennifer picked up the phone after the third ring. "Jack," she said groggily. "Do you know what time it is? Are you OK?"

"Yeah," I lied. "I just wanted to talk." The words exited

my mouth in quick, staccato-like fashion. My armpits were already drenched. This was going to be tough.

"What is it?" There was genuine concern in Jennifer's voice.

"Listen, Jennifer, I think we need to talk—"

"At almost one in the morning? I have work tomorrow. This can't wait?"

"It's just that I have some things on my mind."

"Like what, Jack? What's going on? You're being really weird." The concern was now being augmented with annoyance and a touch of panic.

"Like what we're going to do now that we're in separate cities. I don't think it's fair to both of us that we have to be apart like this."

"I thought we discussed this before you left for New York." She was clearly pissed. Pissed that I was waking her up in the middle of the night but even more pissed that I was calling into question her master plan. "Just let me finish the school year, then I'll come out to New York with you. I already spoke to my mom's friend out there. There are plenty of schools in Westchester that will be looking for an English teacher after June. I don't understand what the problem is."

"Yeah, but what'll we do before then? That's still a half-year away."

Suddenly, Jennifer figured out what was happening and the sharp, measured tone of voice she'd been using quickly gave way to hysterics. "Oh my God. Are you fucking kidding me, Jack? Are you trying to break up with me?" She was crying and yelling at the same time. There was no worse sound in the world.

"No," I replied, grasping for the right way to get myself

173

out of this situation. I felt my back. It was soaked as well.

"Then why THE FUCK are you saying these things? You've been such a flake lately! The last two times you were supposed to come out to Detroit you cancelled, and whenever we speak on the phone, you seem like you can't wait to hang up. What's wrong with you?"

"I don't know, Jennifer. It's just that the distance thing has been getting to me lately. Plus, I need some space. Maybe it would be a good idea to take a break."

"Oh . . . my . . . God." Jennifer could barely get the words out between angry sobs. She was now in DEFCON 1. "You are making no sense! First, you're saying that the distance between us is a problem, then you want to take a break. What's going on with you?"

"Look, it's late and you're tired. I know I shouldn't have called you—"

"FUCK YOU, Jack! Don't you dare put this on me. You've been acting like an asshole for weeks, then you call me out of the blue after midnight with this? Are you kidding?"

"I just think we should take a break, that's all." I couldn't believe I was saying this. What was I thinking?

"NO BREAKS! We've been together for a year and a half, and before this phone call, I wanted to spend the rest of my life with you. But if you don't want this, just tell me and I'll move on. It'll be the worst thing I've ever dealt with, but I'll get through it."

"OK, then I think we should end it."

"You are such a pathetic excuse for a man, Jack. Go fuck yourself."

And with that, the love of my life hung up.

My first spring training with the Yankees in Tampa confirmed what my December trip to New York had suggested: Top to bottom, the Yankees were a first-class organization, and my experience in New York would be nothing like it was in Detroit. After I left Detroit, Mike Illitch asserted himself as not just a model owner by acquiring and locking up star talents like Miguel Cabrera, Victor Martinez, Justin Verlander, and Magglio Ordonez, but he also became a huge advocate for his hometown, especially when he let the automakers advertise for free at Comerica Park in the wake of the substantial financial losses. However, during my time in Detroit from 1997–2002, Illitch maintained a low profile and rarely opened his wallet.

The words "low profile" were never in Yankees owner George Steinbrenner's vocabulary. Though I didn't meet The Boss at my introductory press conference in New York, I met him the day after I arrived in Tampa. I met President Obama at the White House after the Yankees won the World Series in 2009, and the President, despite being the leader of the free world, didn't have the gravitas of Mr. Steinbrenner when the latter showed up in the Legends Field clubhouse on that February morning. Later in the decade Mr. Steinbrenner suffered from some health issues that severely hindered his speech and motor skills, but he was still full of piss and vinegar the day we met.

I remember how several minutes before Mr. Steinbrenner entered the clubhouse, a bunch of clubbies immediately shifted into panic mode. "The Boss is coming! The Boss is coming!" they kept yelling. And when Mr. Steinbrenner did enter, it was with his lieutenants, Yankees president Randy Levine and GM Brian Cashman, at his side. Mr. Steinbrenner walked up and down the rows of lockers, eyeing us players like he was reviewing a battalion of soldiers. Certain guys, such as Jeter, Clemens, and Pettitte, he would acknowledge; otherwise, he just kept walking.

When they approached my locker, Cashman turned to Mr. Steinbrenner and said, "This is Jack Carter from the Tigers who'll be taking over in right field."

Since this was the guy who would be signing my paychecks, I thought it would be a good idea to shake the The Boss' hand. I stuck out my hand and said something like, "It's a pleasure to meet you, sir. I'm thrilled to be here." But all Mr. Steinbrenner did was look me up and down, nod, and proceed down the row of lockers. Something I said?

I could go on and on about the differences between the Yankees and Tigers, but the one thing that struck me the most—other than the obvious discrepancy in talent levels between the two clubs—was the difference in media coverage. In Detroit, the Tigers were mainly covered by the two Detroit rags, *The Detroit News* and *The Free Press*, as well as several smaller, suburban newspapers such as the *Toledo Blaze* and *Battle Creek Enquirer*. Also, because the team was so bad when I was there, we almost never had someone from ESPN or another national outlet following us. That all changed when I got to the Yankees. In New York, *The New York Times*, *New York Post*, *Daily News*, and *Newsday* were the four primary papers that reported on the Yankees, and each dwarfed their Detroit counterparts. There were also about 10 suburban or regional newspapers that covered the team, and each had a readership that far exceeded the suburban Detroit papers. Also, because the Yankees were one of baseball's marquee teams, national reporters were always present. And I haven't even gotten to YES, the Yankees' very own TV station, or the Spanish-speaking and other foreign media members who also wanted a piece of the action. Suffice to say, New York was not a place for shy ballplayers!

As friendly as I was with the press during my playing days and as much as I wanted more recognition, after seeing the sheer magnitude of the media presence in first my Yankees' camp, I began to question whether I was cut out for the microscope I would now be living under. But that's where the Yankees' cult of personality came in. I may have been a two-time All-Star when I got to the Bronx, but I wasn't even close to being the marquee name in my own clubhouse. I was just another tree in the forest. As I soon found out, unless I had a near-career day or laid a complete egg—I'm talking oh-for-five with four strikeouts and two errors—the press after every game would much rather talk to a Jeter, a Clemens, or even a Giambi. I could definitely live with that.

My original thought that I'd enjoy hitting in cozy Yankee Stadium and in a lineup full of sluggers proved correct. I hit two moonshots off Minnesota's Joe Mays in our home opener and never looked back. For most of the year, I hit second, sandwiched between Jeter and Alfonso Soriano, meaning I saw a steady diet of fastballs. Although I had always prided myself in being an accomplished opposite-field hitter, I became adept at pulling balls on the inner half of the plate to take advantage of Yankee Stadium's short right-field porch.

Curving Foul

My final numbers were better than I could have ever imagined. With the exception of triples, I set a career high in every offensive category, and my .339 batting average was 13 points higher than Boston's Bill Mueller to lead the league. I would have won the Triple Crown, but my 44 home runs were second only to Alex Rodriguez's 47 and my 128 RBI fell 17 short of league leader Carlos Delgado. A-Rod also edged me out in the running for A.L. MVP, beating me by just three votes. In 2003, the concept of "Moneyball" was still in its nascent stages, and fans and reporters weren't as fixated on OPS as they were now, because if they were, they would have seen that my 1.082 dwarfed Delgado's 1.019. Who knows, had Moneyball been more prevalent in the early 2000s, maybe I wouldn't have had to wait until I was blue in the face to win my first MVP.

With the Yankees posting an A.L.-best 101-61 record, I wasn't the only guy on the team who enjoyed a banner season. Try this on for size: Among the 14 American League teams, we finished in the top five in offensive categories including home runs, steals, batting average, on-base percentage, and slugging percentage, while placing in the top five in ERA, strikeouts, and least walks allowed on the pitching side. Our 101-61 record was six games better than the second-place Red Sox. The one guy who caught my eye that year was Soriano, whose 38 home runs and 35 stolen bases went underappreciated because of the immense talent we had in the clubhouse.

For the Yankees in the 2000s, the regular season was just a dress rehearsal for the American League playoffs, which, when you boiled it down, was just another chapter in the Yankees–Red Sox jihad. Although our season series was hotly contested, with us winning 10 of the 19 games, it was nothing compared with the hysteria of the best-of-seven American League Championship Series that saw every game but one decided by three runs or fewer and us putting up a combined 30 runs to their 29.

From the first pitch, the raw emotion and intensity of that ALCS was unreal. Every guy on that field knew how thin the margin for error was and that just the slightest mistake could change the complexion of the entire series. And it was that tension that led to the fireworks of Game 3, which saw Boston slugger Manny Ramirez overreact to a high Roger Clemens fastball, Red Sox starter Pedro Martinez pile-drive 72-year-old Yankees coach Don Zimmer, and New York reliever Jeff Nelson almost come to blows with a Fenway Park groundskeeper in the bullpen.

The guy who started the dumpster fire was Martinez. As good as Pedro had been that year, he was beginning to feel the effects of more than 2,000 Major League innings. By the time we faced him, his stuff wasn't nearly as electric as it had been, and he felt he had to become an enforcer to remain effective. Hence, he beaned Karim Garcia, which got the tempers flaring in both clubhouses and ultimately led to the subsequent fireworks.

My theory of Pedro not being at the top of his game picked up more steam in Game 7. Though he had eight strikeouts, his stuff was a far cry from what it had been during his prime in the late '90s and even earlier in the '03 season. His fastball, which once sat at 97 to 98 was now at 91 to 93 with far less movement, and his curveball wasn't nearly as devastating as I remembered. Then throw in the fact that he was running on fumes at over 120 pitches, and it's not hard to see why we were able to touch him up for three runs in the bottom of the eighth inning, setting the stage for my old USC teammate Aaron Boone hitting one of the biggest dingers in Yankee history in the 11th inning to win the game and series for us.

For a lot of us, those seven games against the Red Sox felt like the World Series, but we still had to face the Marlins, a young, Cinderella team many prognosticators believed would be outclassed by the more experienced, talent-laden Yankees. I had my doubts. That series against Boston had taken a lot out of us.

Two things scared me going into the Fall Classic. First, the Marlins were a lot younger than we were. Florida's oldest starting pitcher was just 29, while the four guys who started for us were all over 30. And, speaking of starting pitchers, in Josh Beckett, Brad Penny, and Carl Pavano, the Marlins boasted a trio of flamethrowers who had the potential to neutralize even the most dynamic offenses.

Unfortunately, I proved prophetic. We lost the World Series four games to two to a Florida team that was just younger and faster and played with more energy than we did. The two things from that defeat I remember the most vividly were Miguel Cabrera's home run off Roger Clemens during a seven-pitch at bat in Game 4 and Josh Beckett just stuffing it down our throats in Game 6.

Cabrera came up to the Marlins in midseason 2003 and took the league by storm as a 20-year-old. Although I didn't participate in the pitching meetings prior to the games, I was aware that Cabrera, despite his youth and inexperience, was the guy our pitchers were going to not let beat them. I only played with Clemens in 2003 and again in 2007, when he came out of semi-retirement in the middle of the season to pitch for us, but one thing I learned about the guy was that he was one mean son of a bitch. Until the day he finally did retire, Clemens could dial it up into the mid-90s and had no qualms about using the pitch as a weapon to move guys off the plate.

In 2001, my first big year with Detroit, I took Clemens deep in the first inning and was forced to quickly jump out of the way of a high, hard one when I came up again in the third. I never charged the mound in my career, but that was probably the closest I came to doing so. Many people don't remember this, but early in that at bat against Cabrera, Clemens went up and in to try to intimidate the young Venezuelan slugger. Only this had the opposite effect, totally pissing the kid off. To Cabrera's credit, he bore down, fouling off a couple of tough pitches before taking a Clemens fastball out to right field. That home run set the tone for the rest of the series. We had been up two games to one with arguably the best pitcher of the latter half of the 20th century on the mound, but the Marlins rode Cabrera's coattails to win Game 4, then used the momentum from that big victory to prevail in the next two games.

Josh Beckett was an absolute stud for Florida in Game 6 and made Marlins manager Jack McKeon look like a genius for pitching him on three days' rest. Beckett was dominant that day, using excellent command of a high-90s fastball and knee-buckling curveball to strike out nine Yankees (including me three times) en route to a five-hit shutout. While Andy Pettitte was his usual rock-solid self that day, giving up just one earned run, he wasn't in the same stratosphere as Beckett.

After hitting a combined .317 (13 for 41) with three

long balls in the ALDS against the Twins and ALCS versus Boston, I disappeared against the Marlins, hitting just .158 (3 for 19) with no extra-base knocks. The New York papers, which were out for blood following our unexpected loss, blamed my poor performance on me wilting under the pressure in my first Fall Classic. That was complete nonsense. The fact of the matter was that the troika of Beckett, Penny, and Pavano, joined by Dontrelle Willis and his blistering fastball and herky-jerky delivery in the bullpen, pitched their asses off and just had my number. Plain and simple.

Many fans remember the 2003–04 offseason as one that was dominated by the Yankees' acquisition of Alex Rodriguez, which was set in motion when Aaron Boone tore his anterior cruciate ligament in a pickup basketball game in January 2004. What these fans don't remember—or more accurately put, didn't even know in the first place—is that I was the guy responsible for Boone's injury.

After the Yankees' acquisition of my old USC buddy at the July 2003 trading deadline, we rekindled our friendship. Because Booney lived so close to me in Newport Beach, we hung out a lot that offseason with the thought we'd be teammates again. In addition to hitting the SoCal bar scene and getting some swings in at the cages, we'd play a game of hoops with a bunch of USC guys like Jenkins and Alvarez. I was probably the worst of the bunch and strictly did it as something that complemented my running. Booney, however, was a baller on the court and took it a lot more seriously than I did.

During the game in question, Booney and I were on opposite teams and I drove to the hoop against him.

Miraculously, I blew by him and sank the layup. Knowing how seriously Booney took pickup hoops, I couldn't resist and started talking some smack. Of course, that got Booney all fired up, and on his team's next possession, he tried returning the favor. As he accelerated past me, I thought I'd be cute and stuck out my foot. Unfortunately, Booney didn't see it and went crashing down onto the parquet. Uh-oh.

"God damn it, Jack!" he yelled out, grabbing his knee.

"Ah, dude. Sorry," I said. "I was just kidding. I thought you saw my foot."

"Jack, man, you've got to be the biggest idiot we've ever played with," Jenkins chimed in.

Believe it or not, Booney got up and tried to resume playing. But after a couple minutes of limping around the court, he said enough was enough and left to get ice. Next thing I knew, I'm getting a call from Jenkins.

"Dude, you are not gonna believe this. Booney tore his ligament," Jenkins said.

"How?" was my boneheaded response.

"Seriously?"

Oh, shit.

And it got even worse. It turned out that Booney had a clause in his contract forbidding him from playing hoops.

Brian Cashman, realizing that Booney's injury was severe enough to force him to miss the '04 season, immediately released him, citing breach of contract, costing my buddy his $5.75 million salary. Beside myself, I called Booney and must have said, "Man, I'm sorry" about 15 times. But Booney, the stand-up guy that he was, took it all in stride and merely said, "Jack, do us all a favor and stick to baseball."

183

Curving Foul

The reverberations of Booney's injury were swift and severe. Within weeks, rumors started circulating that the Yankees would be obtaining A-Rod from the Rangers and that he'd be shifting from his natural shortstop position to third base to replace Booney. Then, in mid-February, as I was preparing to head to Tampa for my second spring training with the Yankees, Brian called me.

"Forget about Jeter, Rivera, or Giambi," he began. "You are probably the most valuable Yankee. Not only did your exploits on the baseball field enable the team to reach the World Series last year, but your hoops prowess prompted them to trade for A-Rod."

"Fuck you, Brian."

As horrible as I felt about what happened to Booney, I was intrigued to see what A-Rod's arrival would bring with it. Talk all you want about Jeter, Clemens, and Giambi, A-Rod was hands down the best player in baseball at the time we acquired him. Still just 28, A-Rod had already won a batting title, an MVP (and finished in the top five on three other occasions), two Gold Gloves, and seven Silver Sluggers, while being named to seven All-Star teams. In other words, he'd done everything. Everything, that is, except win a World Series.

The next nine years I spent as A-Rod's teammate would be quite a ride that, if nothing else, kept life from getting boring. I was there when A-Rod unselfishly moved off shortstop just so he could come to New York in his pursuit for a title. I also witnessed the guy's 400th, 500th, and 600th home runs as he seemingly closed in on what we all thought was his assault on Barry Bonds' coveted record. However, I was also a bystander when A-Rod choked in repeated postseasons and was at one point moved down to eighth in the order. Then there was A-Rod's reported trysts with numerous call girls, charges of marital infidelity, and, of course, accusations of PED usage and his eventual mea culpa. All while we were trying to win a World Series. Like I said, never a dull moment.

When I arrived in camp in 2004, the circus surrounding A-Rod's arrival obscured the drama that was enveloping Jason Giambi's life. A high-profile free agent signing, Giambi got to New York a year before I did in 2002 as a replacement for fan favorite Tino Martinez. Even when he was still in Oakland, there were rumors about Giambi's supposed use of PEDs. Through his brother, Jeremy, who was a year ahead of me and attended high school in West Covina, then college at Cal State Fullerton, I loosely knew Jason Giambi.

What always caught my attention with Jason was how big he got. When he was still in college at Long Beach State, he couldn't have been much bigger than six-two and 190 pounds and was certainly not viewed as a power threat. But by the time he reached his prime, he had bulked up to about 240 pounds and was a legitimate 40-home run guy. In Giambi's first two years in New York, he gave the Yankees their money's worth, belting 41 dingers each season while posting an on-base percentage over .400. However, Giambi came to spring training in 2004 noticeably lighter than in recent years, crediting removal of fast food from his diet as the cause of this weight loss.

No one bought this explanation, which sparked a new set of rumored PED use. The accusations became even louder when Giambi started to break down—first a knee injury, then discovery of a benign tumor in his pituitary

185

gland—and his performance suffered. By July, Giambi was mired in a deep slump and his average was languishing in the .220s.

Given my situation, I paid particularly close attention to what was happening with Giambi. On the one hand, I felt horrible for the guy. I didn't have a better teammate on the Yankees. When a guy hit a three-run bomb to win a game, Giambi, along with Jeter, was always the first to offer congratulations. And when a guy made an error in a key point of the game, Giambi was always the first to put his arm around the guy's shoulder.

But on the other hand, Giambi was running interference for me as the face of PED use on the Yankees. As long as the omnipresent New York press was concentrating on Giambi's alleged PED use, I figured I was safe. With photos of a menacing, bulked-up Giambi appearing alongside articles tracing the history of his alleged steroid use, attention would be diverted from my sins. After all, despite my continued PED use, compared with Giambi I looked smallish and I had become adept at attributing the spike in my own power numbers to "hard work, adding loft to my swing, knowing the pitchers better, and the benefit of hitting in a much smaller stadium."

Things got worse for Giambi before they got better. After returning to the club following treatment for the tumor, Giambi never regained his timing at the plate and was left off the Yankees' postseason roster.

Then in December 2004, someone leaked testimony Giambi had given in 2003 to a grand jury investigating BALCO, a California-based company linked with the distribution of steroids to Barry Bonds, Jeremy Giambi, football star Bill Romanowski, and numerous other athletes across a wide spectrum of sports. In his testimony, Giambi admitted to using several different steroids during the offseasons from 2001–03 and injecting himself with HGH during the 2003 season.

When he kicked off the 2005 season by hitting .231 with just four home runs through May, there were calls throughout baseball for the Yankees to invoke his grand jury testimony as evidence of his steroid use and void his contract. Fortunately for both parties, Giambi got red hot in July and he stayed put.

I'll say this in closing about Giambi: He's one tough hombre. Even when the fans and media were skewering him and it was obvious that Brian Cashman was looking for a way to rid the Yankees of the remainder of Giambi's expensive contract, Giambi didn't budge an inch. He remained the same fun-loving guy and amazing teammate. And that was why, even after he later came clean about his PED use, he never lost the respect of all his teammates and won back the admiration of the fans.

In addition to the Giambi saga, the other story that piqued my attention in the spring of 2004 was that after years of burying its head in the sand, MLB was finally getting vigilant with PED use. By virtue of the collective bargaining agreement signed in 2002, over five percent of players whose urine samples were taken in an anonymous test tested positive for banned steroids, triggering random urine tests starting in 2004. Those who failed the random tests going forward faced not only suspensions and fines but also the humiliation of wearing the figurative scarlet letter on their heads for the rest of their careers. As the number of guys busted after 2004 demonstrated, the rewards for cheating outweighed the penalties for getting caught, so as time progressed, MLB made the penalties stiffer.

When the testing was first announced, I freaked out. Because the results of that initial survey were anonymous (though over time, the names of many of those who tested positive surfaced), I had no idea whether I was one of the players who had initially tested positive. I was petrified that once the official testing began, I'd be outed and my run as one of baseball's best hitters would come to an abrupt end. I even contemplated not using the PEDs anymore. But when Kenny made his next run down to Dr. Esfandiary in March 2004, I made him ask Esfandiary whether MLB's newly mandated drug tests would spell my doom.

Kenny came back with good news. According to Esfandiary, he was years ahead of MLB's testing protocol and the THG and HGH I'd been taking would go undetected. I didn't have long to wait before the good doctor was proven right. In mid-March, some guy showed up at my locker after a game with a cup and followed me into a bathroom, where he literally watched me hoist it out and take a leak. A week later, I received word that I was clean. Halleluiah.

Despite Giambi's injury-wracked year, we ran roughshod over the rest of baseball and cruised to the A.L. East title with a 101-61 record. With A-Rod and Gary Sheffield now in the mix, our 242 home runs paced the A.L. and offset our surprisingly pedestrian pitching staff, which posted a 4.69 ERA. I enjoyed another big year, tying Manny Ramirez for the league lead in home runs with 43 and finishing tied for fourth in batting average with a .334 mark. Yet, for the second straight year, I got screwed for the A.L. MVP. This time, the culprit was Anaheim's Vladimir Guerrero, a fantastic player, but whose .989 OPS paled to the 1.049 I had posted. My day would come.

The Red Sox' day came in 2004, that's for sure. By now, Boston's comeback after being down to us in the ALCS three games to none has been well chronicled in countless books and various NESN and MLB Network programing, so I won't beat a dead horse by giving a detailed recap of the series.

However, I will challenge all those people out there who accused us of choking. In the seven-game series, our offense put up an .860 OPS, a mark that far eclipsed the .811 that we posted during the regular season, against a pitching staff that had the A.L.'s third-best ERA. Although our pitchers had been roughed up, we had pitching issues all season and our series ERA of 5.17 was just a half-run higher than during the regular season and was far better than Boston's 5.87. The series came down to just a select number of plays, particularly Dave Roberts' ninth-inning steal of second base against Mariano Rivera in Game 4, and the Red Sox never failed to execute. But to call our loss in the '04 ALCS a choke job is a stretch.

Since those fateful seven games, I've frequently been asked when I thought we were in trouble, and my response has always been after Game 5. Because in Game 6 Boston had Curt Schilling going, and, bloody sock notwithstanding, I knew that there was no way that Schilling, the best money pitcher of my generation, was going to lose that one. Then we would be down to a one-game series, where in baseball anything can happen.

Game 7 pitted Derek Lowe against Kevin Brown, two highly unpredictable pitchers. Lowe had a miserable 2004 season but threw well against us in Game 4, and though Brown had far gaudier career numbers of the two, he was running on fumes by 2004 and prone to the big inning. Lowe was in top form that night, allowing just one run on short rest, while Brown gave up crooked numbers in the first two innings. It was a gap we couldn't bridge, and before we knew it, we were watching the Red Sox celebrate.

The major story for me during the offseason leading up to 2005 was my pending free agency, or that time in a player's career when he goes from being merely rich to mega rich. While I was just as big a capitalist as every other Major Leaguer, from early on in the 2003 season, I had been happy as a Yankee and perfectly willing to sign a long-term, below-market deal to keep me in New York.

On several occasions in 2003 and 2004, Brian approached Yankees GM Brian Cashman with the intention of starting talks on a multiyear contract and each time he was rebuked by Cashman, who claimed it was Yankee policy not to negotiate long-term deals with players who were still arbitration eligible.

Shortly after I arrived in New York in December 2002, Brian and the Yankees avoided arbitration with a one-year, $5.8 million contract. A year later, on the heels of my first batting title, Brian and the team agreed on a one-year, $9.5 million deal. Whatever my new contract was going to be, both Brian and I knew it would be worth multiples of the approximately $20 million I'd already earned in my career and put me in the upper echelon of highest-paid players.

Once we realized I was headed toward free agency,

Brian and I agreed that I should move deliberately and wait until the market cleared. While my first choice was to remain a Yankee, I didn't want to shortchange myself.

The player Brian targeted as a suitable comp for me was Carlos Beltran, who was also a first-time free agent. Although Beltran was two years younger and considered a superior outfielder, my offensive numbers had his beat by a wide margin. It brought me a lot of satisfaction to think back to that winter in Puerto Rico when Beltran wowed me with all his tools, and yet now I was hoping to land a deal that would top his.

I was granted free agency in late October 2004, and unfortunately the market was slow to develop that offseason. The winter meetings, the traditional venue for offseason trades and free agent signings, came and went as did Christmas and New Year's. In the interim, J.D. Drew, a physically gifted yet chronically injured outfielder, signed a five-year, $55 million contract with the Dodgers.

Brian and I wouldn't have paid close attention to the deal except for the fact that because the Angels had inked Vladimir Guerrero the year before, the Dodgers had been my primary fallback option should something go awry with the Yankees. Drew's signing in Los Angeles left the Mariners, who were willing to move Ichiro from right field to center to accommodate me, as my only Plan B, and I sure as hell didn't want to go to Seattle. Not only was Safeco Field the worst A.L. park to hit in, but also Seattle was isolated in the Pacific Northwest and the Mariners always led the majors in miles travelled while enjoying the fewest days off.

Finally, in early January, the Yankees floated a five-year, $85 million offer, which I was ready to pounce on, if for nothing else than to end the drama and bring some certainty back into my life. But here's where Brian earned his commission. He then shopped the deal to the Mariners, who in an effort to rebound from a 99-loss campaign in 2004, floated a six-year, $108 million contract and indicated a willingness to go even higher.

A day later, the dam broke when the Mets announced they would be signing Beltran for seven years at $119 million. Within minutes, Brian Cashman's number appeared on Brian's cellphone, and an hour later I had an eight-year, $144 million offer.

You would have thought that with the fourth-largest contract in baseball at the time (behind only A-Rod, Jeter, and Manny Ramirez), I would have been jumping through hoops, but the reality was that I was exhausted and felt less gratified with this monster deal than I was with the $3 million contract I signed with the Tigers prior to the 2002 season. That was my first multi-million-dollar deal, and in my mind, it validated my status as a legitimate big leaguer. By the time I signed the $144 million contract, I was already set for life with millions in the bank. At the end of the day, the 144,000,000 was just a number.

Much like 2004, my spring training in 2005 was dominated by talk of PEDs. This time the source of my agita was Jose Canseco's new book *Juiced*. Canseco was one of my boyhood heroes, a 240-pound beast who could hit balls a mile and run like a gazelle. At the tender age of 24, Canseco posted baseball's first 40-home run/40-steal season and appeared headed toward immortality until injuries derailed his career. Although steroid rumors had dogged Canseco since the late 1980s, these rumors remained hearsay until *Juiced* showed up on the shelves.

Then all hell broke loose. Canseco, livid because he believed he had been blackballed within the sport, didn't just admit to using steroids for his own gain but also threw every user he knew under the bus. Mark McGwire, Rafael Palmeiro, Pudge Rodriguez, Sammy Sosa—no one was spared. But the crazy thing was that the wave of expected libel lawsuits aimed at Canseco never materialized. Instead, all the accusations Canseco made in his literary masterpiece became gospel.

The reverberations from Canseco's fucking book were felt all over baseball and even outside the game. Even Congress stopped what it was doing and held hearings for a day to get to the bottom of baseball's PED problem.

Ultimately, Bud Selig and his cohorts on Park Avenue were forced to tighten penalties for PED usage because the initial penalties were deemed not severe enough. Worse, however, was the witch-hunt mentality that infiltrated the sport. Each guy who experienced a boost in his numbers was then subject to the "eye test." "Man, Player X hit 11 more home runs this year than last year and looks a lot bigger. Is he using?" became the refrain of every fan and sportswriter in America.

Because I was never teammates, friends, or even acquaintances with Canseco (I'd briefly met him once at a club in South Beach) and my own PED usage was a secret I shared only with my buddy Kenny, I was never afraid of Canseco ratting me out. However, the witch-hunt mentality scared the crap out of me. As the internet was gaining more prominence, what was to stop some young blogger working out of his parents' attic from determining that my sudden spike in numbers from 2000 to 2001 was PED-induced and call me out publicly?

Curving Foul

At this point, you're probably asking yourself why this schmuck, after getting all his money, didn't just stop the PED usage cold turkey. Man, it's not that simple. Although the PEDs themselves are not addictive, the success and the accolades that accompany them certainly are. While I initially got involved with PEDs to help me just stay in the big leagues, over time, as I established myself as one of the best hitters in baseball, that was no longer my primary concern. Instead, I became obsessed with cementing my legacy. After two near misses, I longed for an MVP, though not as much as I wanted a World Series trophy. And the only way to get either, or so I thought, was to keep taking the PEDs.

My pursuit of an MVP and World Series trophy looked like they both might finally be fulfilled in 2005. Hitting in the middle of what I always believed was the best all-round Yankees lineup I was a part of, I enjoyed the most prolific season of my career. I won my second batting title with a .341 average, and my 401 total bases, which included 46 home runs, also paced the A.L. These counting stats translated into a .649 slugging percentage, which, along with my .444 on-base percentage, enabled me to capture my second "slash triple crown" in the past three years. And, if this wasn't enough, my 30 stolen bases made me just the third Yankee to join the coveted 30-30 club. Yet, I once again finished second in MVP voting to A-Rod, whose sterling offense and defense made him the most complete player in all of baseball.

Much like my MVP aspirations, my dreams of getting that elusive World Series title were also crushed. This time the culprits were the Angels, who beat us in five games in the ALDS. Unlike in 2004 against the Red Sox, there was no key, series-changing moment like Dave Roberts' stolen base or Curt Schilling's bloody sock. Instead, we were just flat. If there was a silver lining to the cloud, it was my *mano a mano* duel versus Angels closer Francisco "K-Rod" Rodriguez with two outs in the bottom of the ninth inning in Game 4. It was an at bat that would eventually go down in the annals of baseball history.

The K-Rod who closed for the Angels early in his career was a fire-breathing savage and much different from the guy who relied exclusively on heart and guile as a member of the Brewers and Tigers later on. The K-Rod I faced that night was anywhere from 97 to 100 with his heater, while his slider was the most vicious in baseball.

We were down 2-1 to begin the bottom of the ninth, and Angels manager Mike Scioscia had brought in K-Rod to put the proverbial final nail in our coffin. Jeter led off, and on the first pitch Jeter did Jeter things by grounding a single in the hole between third and short. I could have played in the bigs for 40 years, and I never would have played with a guy better in the big moments than Jeter.

Next up was A-Rod, who was in the middle of a brutal series. Despite his MVP regular season, A-Rod all but disappeared against the Angels, hitting .133 with five strikeouts in 15 at bats. This at bat was one of those strikeouts. A-Rod took a fastball down Broadway, then chased an outside heater to fall behind 0-2. Then, he went fishing against one of K-Rod's venomous sliders for our first out.

People often asked me what the difference between Jeter and A-Rod was, and this sequence was the perfect illustration. Jeter, despite having the inferior talent, had the uncanny ability to bear down in tight situations and make big things happen. A-Rod, on the other hand, frequently pressed in the same situations, putting unbelievable pressure on himself and often failing to deliver.

Giambi followed A-Rod. Compared with 2004, Giambi enjoyed a serene season in 2005 and it showed in his numbers. His 32 home runs were 20 more than he'd hit a year earlier and his .975 OPS dwarfed the .720 mark he'd posted in '04. Giambi had carried his success during the regular season into the series with the Angels, hitting .421. However, Giambi relied on brute strength much more than bat speed, a weakness K-Rod exploited to the fullest extent. Throwing a fastball that registered 98 miles per hour on the Yankee Stadium scoreboard, K-Rod went into Giambi's kitchen twice, and both times Giambi was late. He then tried an 89-mph backdoor slider, but Giambi's discerning eye allowed him to spit on the pitch. K-Rod then blew a high, hard one past Giambi, and I was all that stood between an early winter and a Game 5.

My plan against K-Rod was simple. I rarely got a good swing against his slider. The pitch had too much movement, and it was often directed at the back foot of left-handed hitters. As a result, I'd try to sit on a fastball, not an easy task when the pitch is near the century mark.

K-Rod started me off with a slider that broke inside. Ball one. Ahead in the count, I thought he'd come in with a fastball. But the Venezuelan wasn't budging. Another slider, but this one caught a sliver of the outside corner. Strike one. On the third pitch, K-Rod finally went with the cheese—99 mph according to the Stadium gun—but it was high. Ball two. K-Rod threw an outside slider for the fourth pitch of the at bat, which I fouled into the left-field seats. Strike two. With two strikes, I'd be shortening up my swing but was confident that even with an abbreviated swing, the velocity on K-Rod's pitches would still enable me to hit one a long way if I connected.

K-Rod came in with the gas on the next pitch, and with my shortened swing I fouled it straight back, a surefire sign I was on him. K-Rod was no dummy and tried a slider on the next pitch. Ninety-nine times out of 100 K-Rod's slider was one of the best pitches in baseball, but this time it wasn't. He hung it, and at 90 mph it was the same speed as an average Major League fastball. I jumped all over the pitch and sent a moonshot down the right-field line. I'd definitely hit it hard enough, but because I was expecting something harder, I offered a second too early.

As the hometown crowd followed the ball's trajectory, the roar got louder and louder, coming to a crescendo as the ball found its way into the upper deck. I raised my arms in victory and began my march around the bases. Suddenly, umpire Derryl Cousins, who was covering the right-field line, signaled that my home run was not a home run but a foul ball. And because instant replay review on close calls wasn't yet permitted, Cousins' call stood.

On my way back to the batter's box, a thought came to me. That hanging slider probably scared the crap out of K-Rod and his catcher Bengie Molina enough to ensure that the next pitch would be a fastball. I had to sit fastball.

I got back to the box, picked up my bat, and took a couple practice swings. I was ready. With Jeter dancing off first, K-Rod peered in to pick up the sign and nodded. Had to be the cheese, I told myself.

From the stretch, K-Rod delivered the pitch. It was indeed a fastball and a thigh-high one at that. With a slight uppercut swing, I made contact with the sweet part of the bat, and the result was a loud, authoritative *crack*, one of the prettiest yet most violent sounds I've ever heard. Years later, a season-ticket holder who was sitting about 12 rows up behind the plate swore it sounded like an artillery shell.

As a player, I always did my best to never show up an opponent, but I did a lousy job this time. After my follow-through, I remained in the batter's box and admired the path of my latest handiwork. This homer would end up being one of the farthest I'd ever hit, reaching the final row of the right-field bleachers 492 feet away, and I admired the beautiful arc of the ball's flight. Only once the ball landed did I begin my trot around the bases, this time for real.

When I rounded first base, our normally stoic coach, Roy White, was laughing hysterically. As I continued on to second and third, I noticed that most of the Angels had already exited the field. Had they started running in before my home run had even landed? Crossing third base, I spotted Luis Sojo with a beaming smile on his face and his outstretched hand waiting for acknowledgment. I complied with the most vicious hand slap of my life. *"Maricon!"* was his reply. Rounding third, I saw the welcoming committee waiting for me, with Jeter and Giambi at the front. As I got closer and closer to home plate, the madness started as I was jumped by a posse of at least 20. Soon, I was on the bottom of the dogpile, my face getting mutilated by the bottom of someone's spikes while I struggled for oxygen. And I was loving every second of it.

Despite our early exit from the 2005 postseason, we entered 2006 with plenty of optimism and with good reason. Longtime nemesis Johnny Damon was brought in from Boston to add some speed and explosiveness to the top of our already potent lineup, and a full year of youngster Robby Cano would give us one of the best all-around second basemen in all of baseball.

Throughout my career, I stayed true to my Southern California roots, usually not heating up at the plate until the weather warmed up. This wasn't ideal given that I played my entire career in cold-weather states. But '06 was an anomaly. I hit .330 in April with seven home runs and never cooled off.

From late May until early July, I embarked on a 41-game hit streak, the longest of my career. I don't know what it was like in Joe DiMaggio's day when he crushed it for 56 straight games, but, man, once I got to 30 games, the coverage was more exhausting than the streak itself.

Wherever I went, the streak was all people wanted to talk about. "So, do you think you'll break DiMaggio's record?" had to be the most frequently asked question in the United States in July 2006. It also affected my play. I'm convinced it caused me to press and took me out of my game. On several occasions, I'd be out in right field thinking more about extending the streak than what I would do if the ball was hit to me. Or I'd be in the on-deck circle obsessing about what would happen if I didn't get a hit as opposed to thinking what the pitcher threw.

The worst thing about the streak, however, was the way it finally ended. Against old buddy Paul Byrd (yes, that Paul Byrd), I hit the ball on the screws twice but was robbed both times by highlight-reel plays courtesy of Indians center fielder Grady Sizemore. Then I was walked three straight times by the Cleveland bullpen! Then, as if on cue, I hit in eight straight games after my streak ended.

The end to my hit streak notwithstanding, I had nothing to complain about during the '06 season. My .329 average was tied for fifth best in the A.L., and my 42 home runs and 127 RBI were also firmly entrenched among the league leaders. However, I was convinced that Jeter, Boston's David Ortiz, or Minnesota's Joe Mauer, who'd won the A.L. batting title, would walk away with the A.L. MVP. At any rate, I was more concerned with winning a World Series trophy.

The Yankees' path to a world championship would go through Detroit of all places. Since my departure from the Motor City, GM Dave Dombrowski had used the Illitch empire's pizza and casino money to restock the club with talent, bringing in the likes of Pudge Rodriguez, Magglio Ordonez, and Carlos Guillen. These acquisitions, together with the big-league debut of young flamethrowers Justin Verlander and Joel Zumaya, enabled the Tigers to shock the baseball world and make the playoffs in 2006, where they would meet us in the ALDS.

From the beginning, I had a queasy feeling about this matchup. Not only did I feel that we as a team underestimated Detroit coming into the series, but also the Tigers' young power arms of Verlander, Zumaya, Jeremy Bonderman, and Nate Robertson could pose a serious threat to all the veterans in our lineup who were well into their 30s and whose bats had slowed as the season wore on. Sheffield (37 years old), Williams (37), Giambi (35), and catcher Jorge Posada (34) were all a little long in the tooth and had looked vulnerable against hard stuff in the season. Then throw in A-Rod's postseason foibles, and you had a recipe for disaster.

The series started off according to plan when we beat Detroit 8-4 in Game 1 in Yankee Stadium, with Jeter getting five hits, including a homer and two doubles. However, the next day, Verlander and his 98-mile-per-hour heat held us at bay until the sixth inning, when the Tigers' bullpen took over. Jamie Walker, Zumaya, and Todd Jones, back for his second tour in Detroit, gave up only one hit in three and two-thirds innings of work.

The turning point of the entire series occurred in the eighth inning when Zumaya blew 101-mile-per-hour gas by Giambi and then A-Rod. In the nine years of playing with A-Rod, I had never seen him humiliated like he was in that at bat against Zumaya. Watching the carnage from the dugout, I turned to Damon and said if we didn't get an early lead on these guys we'd be finished.

What happened in New York was just a preview of the horror show that occurred over the weekend in Detroit. Forty-one-year-old Kenny Rogers started Game 3 for the Tigers and shocked all of us by ditching his crafty lefty routine in exchange for a 94-mph fastball and power slider. Guys—myself included—were so stymied by Rogers' sudden transformation that we couldn't touch him.

By the time we realized what had hit us, we were down 6-0 in the late innings with no hope against Detroit's vaunted bullpen. Game 3 of the ALDS was the most humiliated I had been on a baseball field in years. Rogers made mincemeat out of me, striking me out twice and inducing two weak ground ball outs my other two trips to the plate.

What happened prior to Game 4 was probably unprecedented in the history of baseball. Our manager, Joe Torre, in a last-ditch attempt to shake up the club, took matters into his own hands by radically remaking our batting order. His major alteration, and a move that was intensely debated from the time it appeared on the lineup card, was dropping A-Rod from fourth to eighth in the lineup. To this day, I thought that was a dumb move on Torre's part. Regardless of how poorly A-Rod was hitting going into the game and how dubious his postseason history was, you don't humiliate the best player of his generation by hitting him eighth. Lead him off, bat him fifth or sixth, bench him even, but don't put him eighth.

By hitting A-Rod that low in the lineup, Torre was just screwing with A-Rod's head and effectively taking him out of the game before the first pitch was even thrown.

All Torre's bonehead move did was create a distraction at the worst possible time, which made our already near-impossible task of taming the Tigers even more difficult. With A-Rod neutered and the rest of the team in a seemingly inescapable funk, we were embarrassed yet again by the upstart Tigers, 8-3, and were left sitting in the visitors' dugout as Magglio Ordonez and company climbed into the stands to spray champagne on the fans in what was the best victory celebration I've ever witnessed. I contributed to the fiasco by hitting just .214 in the series with no extra-base knocks.

When we landed back in New York, I think I set the world record for quickest time ever to clean out a locker. After another early playoff exit, I just wanted to leave New York and forget about the season.

Without telling a soul about my impromptu travel plans, I hit London, Paris, Berlin, Prague, and Rome for almost a month before jetting off to the Caribbean for another week to "relax."

When I finally landed at Miami Airport in mid-November and checked my texts, I was shocked to see hundreds of messages in my inbox, and my voicemail was full. *Oh, man, did somebody die?* I asked myself. Then, once I began checking my texts, it hit me. In my haste to get out of Dodge and leave the bad taste from our latest playoff ouster behind, I had completely forgotten about the MVP voting. Which I had won!

Leave it to me. For years, winning the A.L. MVP, along with a World Series, had been my primary goal. Then, when I finally did win the award, I was nowhere to be found and was instead sipping a Pilsner Urquell with some leggy Czech model in a Prague tavern. What would I do for my next act?

My next act, I hoped, would finally be winning a World Series. Unfortunately, however, it was not meant to be. The Yankees, after winning nine straight A.L. East titles, were finally starting to show chinks in the armor.

In 2007, we failed to win the division for the first time since 1998, coming in second to the hated Red Sox and relying on the wild card to enable us to sneak into the playoffs. Although our lineup was once again an offensive juggernaut, leading the league in home runs, batting average, on-base percentage, and slugging percentage, our pitching was arguably the worst it had been since I had been with the club. Not even Roger Clemens parachuting in during the middle of the season could help us as our ERA of 4.49 was just eighth best in the A.L.

Our suddenly mediocre pitching caught up to us in the ALDS against the Indians as Clemens and Chien-Ming Wang got bombed in their starts and Cleveland beat us in four games. My .333 average and two home runs in the series didn't come close to easing the pain of getting booted out of the playoffs yet again, but they did complement yet another strong season.

In most years, I would have thought that my .336 average, 45 home runs, and 133 RBI would at least give me a fighting chance to capture my second consecutive MVP. But 2007 wasn't most years, thanks to A-Rod going bananas to the tune of 54 home runs, 156 RBI, and a career-best 1.067 OPS. As if to celebrate the fact that I knew no one would miss me on the day of the MVP voting, I travelled to Brazil, Argentina, and Uruguay for most of October and November. Still, I couldn't avoid the fact that there would once again be a surprise waiting for me once I passed through customs: Joe Torre would no longer be my manager.

One of the best things about wearing the pinstripes for as many seasons as I did was the privilege to play for Joe Torre for five of those years. By the time I'd gotten to New York in 2003, Joe had won his four World Series rings and established himself as the sole Yankees manager who could withstand George Steinbrenner's impulses and tantrums. This allowed him to function more like a senior executive or elder statesman and leave a lot of the clubhouse discipline and other dirty work to his *consigliere* like Don Mattingly, Joe Girardi, Willie Randolph, and Larry Bowa. Also, because we were largely a veteran team, a lot of the policing was done by the players themselves, further allowing Joe to stay above the fray.

None of this should take away from Torre's accomplishments as the Yankees manager, however. Just dealing with the enormous demands of the New York and national media was a tall task that required a delicate mix of diplomacy and toughness, and Joe handled this part of the job with aplomb. Over the years, he ran a lot of interference for his players, allowing us to avoid unnecessary distractions and concentrate on what we had to do on the field.

Joe was also an excellent communicator. If he was going to give you an off day, you would know a week in advance. Or if he was thinking of using you in a role you weren't accustomed to, he would invite you into his office and explain his decision. I was a low-maintenance player who kept interactions with the manager at a minimum, but I had an excellent relationship with Joe and always felt we had a high level of mutual respect. While a lot of Joe's detractors often cited the Yankees' gigantic payroll as the main reason for his managerial success, the guy repeatedly proved himself as being the ideal guy to manage the Yankees. Regardless of how qualified Joe's successor was, Joe's calm demeanor and steady hand would surely be missed.

During the 2007–08 offseason, baseball was rocked by yet another PED-related event, the release of the Mitchell Report. The Mitchell Report was the culmination of a 20-month investigation by former Maine Senator George Mitchell that closely examined the history of the use of illegal performance-enhancing substances by Major League players and the effectiveness of the MLB Joint Drug Prevention and Treatment Program.

In addition, the report named 89 MLB players alleged to have used steroids or other performance-enhancing drugs. While a number of household names like Barry Bonds, Jason Giambi, Gary Sheffield, Matt Williams, and Troy Glaus appeared in the Mitchell Report, it was obvious from the moment the report was released that Roger Clemens was the guy squarely in the crosshairs. Many of the other big names, like Bonds, Giambi, and Sheffield, had been in one way or another linked to PEDs for years, but Clemens had largely enjoyed a pristine reputation when it came to steroid or HGH use.

With the tenacity that he had displayed on the mound, Clemens fought off all the PED-use allegations, even testifying before Congress that his accuser, former personal trainer Brian McNamee, had "misremembered." Before Clemens knew it, he was the defendant in a perjury trial, which he ultimately won due in large part to inconsistencies in McNamee's testimony. More important, however, was the fact that Clemens never again wore a Major League uniform and his name and long list of accomplishments were forever tarnished.

The Mitchell Report emboldened me. Canseco's book, the A-Rod fiasco, and now the Mitchell Report had exposed the dirty little secret of some of baseball's biggest stars, but one Jack Michael Carter remained unscathed. I breathed a huge sigh of relief—the extreme caution I had exercised from the beginning of my "relationship" with Dr. Esfandiary, including using Kenny as my mule and leaving no paper trail, had paid off.

Barring a calamity, I was positive that I'd continue to fly under the radar. As thorough as Senator Mitchell and his lackeys may have been, no one from the investigation ever contacted me, nor did my name come up in anyone's statement. As was the case with Canseco's book, the public's infatuation with Clemens and the other big names mentioned in the Mitchell Report allowed me the luxury to continue to cheat in peace.

Joe Girardi outdueled Don Mattingly in the quest to become Joe Torre's successor as Yankees manager. I knew Girardi well from when he was the Yankees bench coach in 2005. Although Girardi wore his emotions more on his sleeve than his predecessor, he still offered a calming presence and knew how to run a clubhouse. In addition, as a former catcher and Northwestern graduate with an engineering degree, he not only knew the game and how to run a pitching staff inside out, but he was also sharp as a tack and fully grasped the sabermetric wave that had by 2007 established a strong foothold on the MLB beachhead.

Despite all of Girardi's qualifications, 2008 was not a good year for the Yankees, as we failed to reach the postseason for the first time since 1993 in our last season before moving into the "new" Yankee Stadium. Our third-place finish came as no surprise, as our pitching staff continued to underperform and injuries and old age plagued our lineup. My .295 average marked the first time I'd been unable to crack the .300 mark since 2001 and the 36 home runs I'd clubbed were the lowest I'd hit since coming to New York. At 33, I was confronted with the question of whether Father Time was knocking on the door.

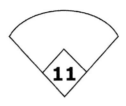

Good Times, Good Times

I didn't realize it at the time, but when I broke up with Jennifer, I thrust myself into the upper echelon of New York City's most eligible bachelors. Think about it: I was about to turn 28 with millions in the bank, tens of millions more on the way, and my own personal abode in Yankee Stadium's right field. Who wouldn't want to meet me?

The problem was, however, that I knew nothing about New York and how it operated. Though I worked in the Bronx, I intended to live and play in Manhattan, a 23-square-mile island with 1.6 million people that had its own unique set of social mores. As far as I was concerned, I was still a country bumpkin susceptible to being eaten alive by the city's bright lights.

Here's where Brian and his connections became invaluable. Because both of Brian's parents were originally from New York, he had several cousins in the city. One of these cousins was Sara, a 29-year-old, attractive, up-and-coming ad executive with tons of interesting, successful, well-plugged-in friends who knew how to enjoy life. Three of these friends, Eric, Travis, and Anthony, were take-no-prisoners investment bankers who, when they weren't working their asses off, were always up for a good time. I hit it off with these guys from the beginning, and they became the gateway to a lot of the fun I had my first few years in the Big Apple.

It's a good thing I met and became friendly with ETA, as I soon called them, because the Yankees' clubhouse ended up being far different from what I was used to in Detroit. The Tigers' clubhouse, at least in my early years with the team, was a fun-loving place with guys like Frankie, Kapler, C.J., and myself all savoring our time in the big leagues. We busted it on the field but also had the time of our lives off it not knowing when we'd wake up and realize it was all just a dream.

The situation in New York was completely different. For starters, the Yankees were a much more seasoned squad filled with guys who had long grown accustomed to big-league life. That, combined with the Yankees' traditional buttoned-up culture, made the Bombers' clubhouse a reserved, almost somber place. With the exception of Jason Giambi and a few others, I figured out early on that if I was going to get the most out of New York socially, it was going to be with a crew not affiliated with my day job.

Before my first spring training with the Yankees, ETA hooked me up with a realtor who helped me buy a place. After looking on the Upper East Side, Upper West Side, and Financial District, I settled on a just-converted loft in SoHo. The place was exactly what I needed. It was near all the great bars and restaurants downtown, was nearly 2,000 square feet, and had its own garage. The only problem was that it was a bitch getting up to the stadium.

The other big "investment" I made occurred the following offseason. I'd been growing sick of California and was ready to try something new. As a freshly minted New Yorker, that "new" meant South Beach, Florida. I bought a decent-sized condo to serve as my part-time winter home just off Collins. The problem was, however, I didn't want to leave Rocco, whose dedication (along with my medicinal endeavors) had helped transform me into a superstar. So, I did what any athlete making an exorbitant amount of money does: I took Rocco with me. That's right, in exchange for his promise to keep kicking my ass, I paid his travel expenses, four months' rent on a luxury, beachfront apartment, health insurance, and a $75,000 salary. At least Rocco wasn't married with kids. Imagine how much that would have cost!

I didn't get into the full swing of the New York social scene until May of my first season in New York. When we were in town, I would generally go out with ETA after Friday night and Saturday afternoon games. Because the Friday night games ended so late, I would just meet up with ETA at the club or bar of their choice. On Saturdays, because our games were usually done by 4 p.m., I would meet them at a steakhouse or upscale sushi place for dinner, then we'd tear it up afterwards.

Despite all the partying, I had some hard and fast rules. First, I wouldn't do any drugs during the season. Second, I wouldn't have more than four drinks in a night during the season. And, finally, I had to make it to a bed (not necessarily my own) in enough time to get at least seven hours of sleep if I had a game the following day.

No matter how much fun there was to be had in New York, I never lost sight of how important my career was and how many guys there were on the bench and in the minors who would do anything just to have a crack at my job.

ETA and I hit all the best places and left plenty of destruction in our wake as money was never an issue. Regardless of whether it was Marquee in Chelsea, Employees Only in the West Village, Café Noir in SoHo, or Level V or the Gansevoort Rooftop in the Meatpacking District, the alcohol flowed like the Nile during the rainy season and the girls were drawn to us like moths to a bright light. We had the pick of the litter.

We'd buy bottles of champagne for gaggles of girls, then each pick the one we thought would be the most fun on that particular night and take her home. We weren't bachelors but instead parasites who extracted every ounce of pleasure from each girl we bedded before moving on to the next.

As crazy as it may sound, after a while I got bored of sleeping with what appeared to be the same girl: 24 to 30, tall, stunningly beautiful, dressed to the nines, not an eyelash out of place, eating disorder, and at least three gym memberships. So, I diversified my portfolio and eventually indulged in all the food groups. First came the Russian and Eastern European models, and when I got sick of them, I added Latinas to the mix. When that novelty wore off, I moved on to Asians, who were followed by ebony princesses. Later on, I hit the cougar crowd, then finally I dabbled with multiples.

Each demographic had its pluses and minuses. The Warsaw Pact chicks were superhot and their generally poor English skills meant you didn't have to even bother with small talk, but, shit, they sure knew how to spend your money.

The Latinas were always game for anything, but when you pulled a disappearing act, their hot tempers meant you ran the risk of castration if they ever found you. And believe me, they looked. The Asians would let you do whatever you wanted but never wanted to leave the next morning. The black girls also knew no limits, but you had to be careful because they were notorious for showing up nine months later with a care package. The cougars had been in the game a long time so they knew all the tricks, but STDs were always a concern. Finally, multiples were always a dream scenario of mine, but even as a high-profile professional athlete, the chances of a ménage-à-trois or more happening that did not involve prostitutes were slim to none. Until one night, that is.

It was the winter of 2006–07 and I'd already become a fixture in the New York social scene, having dated numerous models, actresses, and other A-listers and was well into my "experimentation" phase. For about three months, I'd been dating this Russian chick, Svetlana, who worked as an extra in those Dos Equis commercials and did God-knows-what-else on the side.

One night, I agreed to meet her and some of her friends at Pravda, a Soviet-themed cocktail lounge not far from my apartment. Svetlana wasn't the first Russian I'd dated, so I knew the drill: Lavish her with as much Louis Vuitton, Gucci, Prada, and expensive champagne as possible and let her tongue do the rest. There wasn't any real chemistry or meaningful dialogue, but I could think of worse ways to spend an evening. Anyway, when I walked into the bar, I quickly saw Svetlana with two of her friends at a table toward the back. Svetlana was wearing a black, skintight jumpsuit that had to be made out of spandex and five-inch stilettos. Her two comrades were clad in tight, black leather from head to toe. From the get-go, I had a feeling that things were about to get interesting.

Two bottles of Moët & Chandon Bicentenary Cuvée Dry Imperial 1943 later, the four of us were yucking it up on an oversized couch toward the back of the lounge. Unlike the other chicks I'd dated from east of the Elbe, Svetlana spoke good English, as did her friends, Katarina and Anna. Their language skills were so good that instead of conversing in Russian in front of me, they did so in English. At one point of the evening, Svetlana proudly showed her friends the $2,000 Prada handbag I'd bought her the day before. Katarina then turned to me and inquired, "Jack, why don't you buy me a bag like that."

Nine times out of 10 I just would have smiled or shrugged my shoulders, but on this night, there was a little *perestroika* in the air, so I replied, "I'd be happy to, Katarina, but you'll have to earn it."

Almost all the chicks I've dated would have gone bananas when they heard what had just come out of my mouth, but Svetlana—along with Katarina and Anna—just giggled. Anna then blurted out, "Don't forget about me, Jack. You know, I'd LOVE to have the Gucci bag I saw in Saks today."

Emboldened by what was transpiring, I asked, "But what's in it for me, Anna?" More giggling.

Was all this the champagne talking or was I about to do more to enhance U.S.-Russian relations than anyone since Kissinger?

As the evening wore on, I kept getting inviting vibes

from Anna and Katarina. On a couple of occasions, Anna, who after returning from a trip to the ladies' room was sitting to my immediate left on the couch, used her heel to massage my ankle and lower leg, while Katarina, who was sitting on the other side of Svetlana on my right, threw fuck-me eyes at me at least twice. But the key was Svetlana. Would she allow Katarina and Anna to rub her genie's lamp?

It was getting close to midnight and I was itching for some action. Normally, patience was my most-trusted ally. My status as a wealthy, professional athlete allowed me to sit back and wait for the action to gravitate toward me, but this was different. This was the fulfillment of every straight male's fantasy, three gorgeous women lusting after the opportunity to satisfy all of my sexual desires.

As a result, I was about to go completely out of character and take a stab at a likely awkward-sounding invite for the party to move back to my place, but as if she were reading my mind, Svetlana turned to her friends and for the first time that night said something in Russian. The response was overwhelmingly positive, with both girls smiling and nodding enthusiastically. Svetlana then looked at me and matter-of-factly said, "We're going back to your place. This is going to cost you."

When we arrived back at my loft, I quickly took off my coat and headed to the kitchen to get some drinks and make sure my guests didn't get thirsty. I grabbed the best bottle of wine I could find, an Argentine Malbec, and some glasses and headed to my living room where I expected the girls would be but found no one. Sheesh, I hope they didn't get cold feet and leave, I told myself.

Just then, the door to the master bathroom opened

and one by one each chick emerged. Svetlana was first. She had on the same stilettos but had stripped to her undergarments, a black underwire bra and matching thong panties that were see-through. Katarina and Anna were dressed similarly, though Anna's ensemble was leopard-skin.

Svetlana walked right up to me so that just inches separated our faces. She, like both her friends, was five-ten or five-eleven, which meant with her heels on we were looking into one another's eyes. Suddenly, she grabbed my crotch and squeezed. "Give me your credit card," she demanded.

"What? You're nuts!" I shot back.

My retort was met instantly by a hard slap to the face that stung like a bitch. Svetlana didn't let up. Her open palm hit the same cheek again and then she said, "You think we're going to do this for free? Anna wants the Gucci bag, Katarina wants the Prada one, and I want a pair of David Yurman earrings."

As Svetlana was shaking me down, Katarina had positioned herself behind me and started slowly running her fingers through my hair. Anna had entered the fray and affectionately kissed the side of my neck. Realizing I wouldn't be able to hold out much longer, I scooped my wallet out of my pocket and handed it to Svetlana, who took out my Platinum AMEX and placed it in her bag. The transaction complete, the fun began.

The action moved into the master bedroom, where there was more room and more toys. Svetlana pushed me onto the bed so that I was lying on my back. As she took off my shoes and my socks, Katarina and Anna began slowly unbuttoning my shirt. When the shirt was completely unbuttoned, both Katarina and Anna started kissing me gently, Katarina up in my chest area and Anna around my navel. As this was happening, Svetlana unbuckled my belt, undid my button, and unzipped the zipper of my pants. She then slid my pants off me so that I was just now in my boxer briefs. She gave a shit-eating grin when she noticed the elevation she and her comrades had caused.

As much as I was enjoying this, I wanted more. I sat up and removed my unbuttoned shirt. Then I looked toward Anna and gave her a long, passionate kiss as Svetlana and Katarina looked on. The kiss concluded, I ran my fingers through Anna's thick, long hair several times. Then, out of nowhere, I seized the bottom of her mane and pulled. The fact that it hurt was made evident by the "Oooouuu!" that left her mouth. In a stern voice, I commanded the hot *tovarish* to kiss Katarina. This was met with a smile from both girls. Anna leaned over, and she and Katarina enjoyed a carbon copy of the kiss Anna and I had just had, with plenty of tongue. Just when I thought the kiss was wrapping up, they started again and then again. Clearly into this, or at least a top-notch job pretending they were, Anna maneuvered Katarina onto her back, then got on top of her and the two girls resumed the hot kissing.

I then turned to Svetlana, who had been sitting on my bed watching her friends get intimate, and said, "I don't want you to feel neglected, Baby."

"What are you going to do to me, Jack?" Svetlana inquired.

I leaned over the bed toward my nightstand, opened the drawer, and pulled out a pair of handcuffs. Anna and

Katarina, who had been taking their friendship to a whole new level, stopped making out and wanted to see what my intentions were.

"Handcuff her," I told Katarina with a glance at Svetlana. Katarina didn't need to be told twice. She took the cuffs from me, then seized Svetlana's arms, pulled them behind her back, and bound her wrists. Interestingly enough, Svetlana seemed none too pleased.

Anna, interest piqued at the sight of the handcuffs, wondered out loud, "What else do you have in that drawer?"

"Why don't you find out?" I replied.

Anna complied and appeared intrigued when she saw the vibrator, duct tape, erotic massage oil, blindfold, and other goodies. Katarina, also longing for a piece of the action, said with a laugh, "Think of the things we can do to her with this stuff!"

Svetlana, obviously not happy in her current predicament, then blurted out something in Russian. Just by the tone of her voice, I could tell that something was about to go awry with my sociology experiment.

"Did she call us dykes?" Anna asked.

"What a bitch!" Katarina exclaimed. "Give me that tape."

Just then Svetlana said something else in her mother tongue, once again with a sharp tone.

Katarina took off her panties, revealing a beautifully manicured fertile patch, then tore off a healthy sized piece of the duct tape Anna had given her. Yet again, Svetlana threw out some sort of warning in Russian, but Katarina was having none of it and mid-sentence stuck her moist panties in Svetlana's mouth, then covered it with the duct tape. "Mmmmmm!" was all Svetlana could muster.

Anna, clearly enjoying the moment, went into her bag a pulled out her makeup kit, which included an eyeliner, and wrote "DYKE" over the duct tape. She then added to Svetlana's humiliation by using the mirror on the flap of her makeup case to show Svetlana her handiwork. Svetlana responded with another sound that was muzzled with the gag, evoking even more laughter from Anna and Katarina.

"You know," I said to Svetlana's tormenters, "she always complains that I don't go down on her enough."

"Well, then," Anna added, "we have to fix that, don't we, Katarina?"

"Absolutely," responded Katarina. And with that, Katarina positioned Svetlana to be flat on her back, then started kissing Svetlana's belly button. Slowly but surely, she started working her way down. Svetlana was no longer combative and instead was emitting sounds of pleasure from behind the gag. Simultaneously, Anna took off her own panties and positioned herself on all fours over Svetlana's upper torso, with her world in Svetlana's face. She then leaned forward, undid Svetlana's bra, which had a clip in the front, and gently started teasing Svetlana's nipples with her tongue. Svetlana's moaning grew louder.

Katarina had made her way down to the top of Svetlana's panties, but instead of continuing her downward path, she diverted and began lightly kissing and licking the inside of Svetlana's upper legs. Svetlana, her eyes closed, was in a universe of ecstasy. She repeatedly tried to say something, but her gag wouldn't let her. Finally, after enough teasing, Katarina pulled Svetlana's panties down to her ankles and went in for the kill. First, Katarina kissed Svetlana, who was completely bald, lightly. Then she worked her way up and down, albeit softly and deliberately. Then she worked her way inside, expertly locating and locking in on her target. Say what you want about the Russians, but they are well trained.

Anna, looking to spice things up, removed Svetlana's gag, then greeted her newly liberated mouth with a long kiss. She then propped herself up so that her jewels were within inches of Svetlana's mouth and said, "Lick me. Both places."

Svetlana enthusiastically obeyed her friend's command, shifting her tongue from locale to locale at will. Svetlana and Anna's cries of pleasure filled the room and added to the ambience the four of us had created.

Acknowledging that Katarina was the only one of my three houseguests not being serviced, I decided it was high time for me to be a better host. Already aroused from the excitement of the past 20 minutes, I got up and walked over to the side of the bed where Svetlana was pleasuring Anna. Svetlana stopped tending to Anna and took me inside her mouth. Then it was Anna's turn to taste me. Satisfied, I took up position behind Katarina as she continued to rock Svetlana's world. I entered Katarina from behind and started thrusting. Katarina moaned loudly when I penetrated her domain. This made her tongue go deeper into Svetlana, who couldn't care less that I was inside her friend.

The debauchery continued for several more minutes. All of us were sweating, moaning, and occasionally grunting. Svetlana was the first domino to fall, as she let out a long scream. I'm no gynecologist, but I assume the sounds vibrating up and through Anna's valley of love had a special effect on her because she was next to climax. She was followed immediately by Katarina, whose arrival at the zenith was accompanied by a Russian war chant. Finally, less than two minutes later, I let myself go with such a vengeance that Katarina enjoyed a daily double.

Though I never enjoyed another night like that one, I continued to enjoy all that New York's prettiest had to offer. But gradually things began to change. In the fall of 2007, Anthony got engaged to the girl he'd been dating for a year and a half, and the following summer, Travis and his girlfriend decided it was time to get hitched. And not three months later, Eric and his sweetheart decided to take the plunge. With my crew severely depleted, going out wasn't as fun as it once was, and to be blunt, all the chick-hopping didn't give me the satisfaction that it once had. As I approached my mid-30s, I wondered if the changes in my attitude were signs that I should find someone and settle down myself.

It was also around this time that I began to think about Jennifer. For years, I was so preoccupied with checking every box on my sexual fantasy and desire list that I barely thought about the one woman in my life I had truly loved. But as the years ticked by, bedding the supermodel, pop star, or famous actress didn't bring with it the excitement that it once did, and I slowly began to realize how unfulfilled I was on an emotional and mental level. I recalled being a kid in Detroit and being so uninspired by the chicks I'd dated; much to my chagrin, I noticed I'd come full circle. I hated admitting this, but after so long, I finally missed Jennifer.

More than once, I started to google Jennifer's name

but stopped myself, knowing that if I saw something online that indicated she was married or in a serious relationship how devastated I would be. So, I decided not to cry over spilled milk and decided to get on with my life.

Enter Kirsten, a tall, blonde, sophisticated attorney I'd met through a marketing agency during the 2009 season. On a scale of 1 to 10, Kirsten was a 15. A Princeton grad who got her JD at Georgetown, Kirsten grew up in posh Greenwich, Connecticut, the only child of a heart surgeon and investment banker. She was gorgeous, witty, and intelligent. And after years of dating chicks who were drawn to my uniform number or my account number, it was refreshing that Kirsten didn't give a damn about either.

Things moved slowly when we started dating for several reasons. First, as a second-year associate at a big-time Manhattan law firm, Kirsten regularly put in 80-hour work weeks as she was evaluated on how many hours she billed her corporate clients. Second, after playing the field for years, it was a tough adjustment for me to quit the world's best dating scene cold turkey and concentrate on just one girl.

While our relationship was far from perfect—there were times when I missed the crazy nights like the one I enjoyed with Svetlana & Co., Kirsten's job had her constantly stressed out, and I got the impression that she took some heat from her highly educated parents and friends for dating a guy who didn't have a college diploma on his wall—we were able to circumvent the inevitable roadblocks that appeared and enjoyed spending time with one another.

I realize that as you're reading this, you might

be saying to yourself that Kirsten was just a proxy for Jennifer, the girl I should have ended up with and didn't. You're not the only one. I often thought of that as well but had learned years earlier that comparing your current partner to an ex was never a good thing, so I tried my best to avoid it. Still, the occasional comparisons in my mind were inevitable, and unfortunately, Kirsten always came out on the short end of the stick. Her glamorous looks and pedigree notwithstanding, there was just a certain "it" Kirsten was missing that Jennifer had in spades.

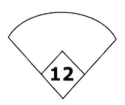

World Champions

With the Yankees set to move into their sparkling, new stadium in 2009, ownership went all out during the prior offseason, signing sluggers Mark Teixeira and Nick Swisher, as well as established starting pitchers C.C. Sabathia and A.J. Burnett. The arrival of Teixeira and Swisher gave our lineup two switch hitters in the middle of their primes capable of working the count, while in Sabathia and Burnett, we now had two power pitchers capable of missing bats and logging over 200 innings a year.

With not even two weeks to go until the start of spring training, MLB and the Yankees, in particular, were dealt a severe blow when a *Sports Illustrated* article revealed that A-Rod was on a list of 104 Major League players who tested positive for banned substances in 2003 during MLB's initial survey. But rather than challenge *SI*'s story, A-Rod came clean. Well, sort of. In an exclusive interview with legendary baseball reporter Peter Gammons held just days after the *SI* article broke, A-Rod admitted to using steroids during the "loosey-goosey" years of 2001–

03 while he was with the Rangers yet maintained he had not used any PEDs since. A-Rod blamed the pressure associated with the record-breaking $252 million contract he signed with the Rangers after the 2000 season as the main reason why he turned to steroids. You might recall that A-Rod ended up being full of it. As his involvement in the Biogenesis scandal years later indicated, A-Rod was still juicing long after leaving the Rangers.

A-Rod is the most complex individual I've ever known, let alone played baseball with. In over 30 years of playing the game, I'd never seen anyone as talented or insecure as A-Rod. Looking back, I'm surprised A-Rod and I weren't closer. After all, we shared a lot in common—humble beginnings, spending most of our childhoods without a father, no significant time spent on a college campus, deep love and appreciation of the history of baseball—but for some reason we rarely spoke with one another and never hung out.

From the moment A-Rod joined the Yankees, he emitted a weird vibe. There was something a little bit off about him, something that just didn't make sense. The guy was always looking to please everybody, right down to the clubhouse guys. I'm no certified psychologist, but I'm convinced A-Rod's insecurity was the sole driver of his PED use. While I used because I knew my days as a Major League ballplayer were numbered if I didn't do something drastic, A-Rod indulged because he never felt he was good enough. That all said, I will say this about A-Rod: I never saw him not hustle, and he was the most prepared teammate I ever had. If there was a kid just up from the minors pitching against us, A-Rod knew what he threw and how good his pick-off move was.

Any conversation about A-Rod's days as a Yankee would be incomplete without the mention of Derek Jeter. You could probably write a book longer than this one about the dynamics of that relationship. Jeter and A-Rod were best friends up until a 2001 *Esquire* article was published in which A-Rod dissed Jeter, and by the time A-Rod joined us in New York prior to the '04 season, he and Jeter were barely on speaking terms. Jeter was a consummate team player who always gave 100 percent and was, as I explained earlier, lethal in the clutch. Whether it was making that shovel pass relay to nail Jeremy Giambi of the A's in the playoffs, diving into the stands and nearly mutilating his face to snare that pop-up against the Red Sox, or driving in the winning run in his last Yankee Stadium at bat, *Il Capitano* always had a flair for the dramatic. No one I ever played with rose to the occasion better.

But there was another side to Jeter, a side that the public didn't see. Jeter was an intensely private person who demanded complete loyalty from those around him. And if you didn't display that loyalty, you were finished, plain and simple. Just ask A-Rod about that.

There were numerous occasions after A-Rod came to New York where it was obvious to the rest of us that A-Rod resented Jeter for what Jeter had become—the face of the Yankees and the poster boy for all of baseball. In A-Rod's mind, he was a far superior player to Jeter, just as good looking, and therefore just as deserving of all the attention and accolades as the guy to his left. I also think A-Rod felt that he never received the credit he deserved for moving from shortstop to third base in deference to Jeter after joining the Yankees.

While I never witnessed any open hostility between

Jeter and A-Rod, their mutual disdain was evident, especially in the years immediately following A-Rod's arrival in the Bronx.

I got the impression that the frosty relationship between A-Rod and Jeter thawed following A-Rod's admission of PED use early in 2009. Again, I'm no psychologist, but I always thought once A-Rod came (partially) clean about his cheating, he took a massive load off his chest and became more comfortable in his own skin. And that made him more at ease around Jeter and accepting of who and what Jeter was.

In addition to demanding loyalty from those around him, Jeter rarely let anyone into his private circle. While he was universally respected in the clubhouse by all factions, he held most of his teammates at arm's length with the exception of Jorge Posada, Tino Martinez, Andruw Jones, and one or two others. Jeter and I were together on the Yankees for 10 years, and toward the end of my stint in New York, he and I, being two of the elder statesmen on the club, formed a kinship. We spoke more frequently, hung out on the road more often, and would occasionally run in the same circles in New York, but I never felt like we were buddies. Still, I'll always consider it an honor to have played with the biggest winner in baseball over the last 30 years.

When the 2009 season started, I had a feeling it was going to be a watershed year for me. At 34, I realized I was on the back nine of my career and for the first time was starting to think about my legacy in the game. I already had nearly 350 homers, as well as an MVP and four second-place finishes. I realized that with a few more big seasons, I'd be within striking distance of the big 500 and a chance at baseball immortality. The only question was how much I had left. The 2008 season was the first time I felt human on a baseball field since I began taking PEDs, and I was curious to see if my downward trajectory would continue.

I felt that I came to a fork in the road with my PED usage prior to the '09 season. Between my salary and various endorsement deals that brought in several million dollars more a year, I had more money than I'd ever be able to spend. Plus, although I remained unscathed by the fallout from the Mitchell Report and A-Rod's saga, I knew the vise was tightening. At some point, I was bound to get busted, and fearful of wearing a scarlet letter for the rest of my life, I seriously considered giving up the juice. But the additions of Teixeira, Sabathia, and Burnett made the allure of a World Series as strong as ever and the mental image of my name on a plaque in Cooperstown was too much to resist. So, I decided to continue the charade Kenny and I had been running for nearly a decade. Though, by now, Kenny was on a $50,000 annual "retainer" and my regimen was composed exclusively of HGH, which was still undetectable through MLB's testing protocol.

The dimensions of the new Yankee Stadium were the exact same as its predecessor, including just 314 feet down the right-field line. However, the wind patterns in the recently completed ballpark were far different from what we had been used to, with a jet stream blowing out toward right field.

About half a dozen times in the season's first month I hit what I thought was just a loud out to right field but instead the ball kept carrying and ended up in the stands. Suddenly, I had 10 dingers and we were still in April. I kept thinking my home runs would taper off as the weather warmed up and the wind gusts died down, but that never happened. By Memorial Day, I had deposited 21 balls in the cheap seats, by July 4 that number had increased to 32, and on August 1 I was sitting on 40 bombs. Things climaxed with about a week to go in the regular season when I hit home run number 50 against Paul Byrd of all people in a 4-2 win against Boston. For good measure, I hit number 51 the next night against Luke Hochevar and the Royals as we clinched the A.L. East title.

As indicated by our 103-59 record, the 2009 Yankees were a well-oiled machine and the best team I ever played on. New arrivals Teixeira, Sabathia, and Burnett all made Brian Cashman look like a genius, especially Sabathia, whose 19 wins and 230 innings gave our rotation a much-needed ace. Nearly as vital as the two new horses in the rotation was the presence of young, hard-throwing relievers Phil Hughes and David Robertson for almost the entire season. With Mariano Rivera as effective as ever but already 39, Hughes and Robertson pitched a lot of high-leverage innings while providing an important bridge to our amazing closer.

Our starting pitching was dominant in the ALDS, with Sabathia, Burnett, and Pettitte allowing just one earned run in each of their starts as we swept the Twins in three games. In the ALCS, A-Rod finally proved his mettle in the postseason, hitting .429 with three home runs to propel us past the Angels in six games.

In the World Series, we came face-to-face against the Philadelphia Phillies. Led by the keystone combination of Chase Utley and Jimmy Rollins and southpaw Cole Hamels anchoring the rotation, the Phillies were in the middle of a five-year stretch in which they won consecutive N.L. East titles, including winning it all a year earlier. Utley was a boss in the series, hitting five bombs, including two apiece in Games 1 and 5, but we had all the mojo in the other four games. Jeter was Jeter with a .407 batting average, A-Rod continued his hot hitting by slugging four more extra-base hits, and I shook off a nightmarish 4-for-23 performance in the ALCS to hit .364 with three long balls. Finally, at 11:50 p.m. on November 4, 2009, Robby Cano fielded a ground ball off the bat of Shane Victorino, threw it to Teixeira at first, and the Yankees were world champions for the 27th time in history. I'd never been happier on a baseball field thinking that somewhere up there Michael Carter was looking down at me, smiling.

As if winning a World Series and all the trappings that go along with it, including a killer victory parade down Manhattan's Canyon of Heroes, weren't enough, I won my second MVP less than a month later. Fortunately, I was stateside this time when they made the announcement.

With 398 home runs, I made the conscious decision to go for 500. That meant continuing my HGH regimen even though it seemed guys were getting outed or busted left and right. I had my money and my World Series ring. Now I wanted to cement my legacy.

I started 2010 just as hot as I'd been in '09, with eight home runs in April, which enabled me to blow past the once-coveted 400 mark, and another 10 in May. Then, trouble struck. After an early June game against the Orioles, I was doing barbell shoulder presses when my right shoulder popped out of the socket. Although Nick Swisher was about five feet away and able to help me hoist the bar and weights back into place, the damage was done.

After I forced my shoulder back into place, I foolishly did another set. And another. Though not in excruciating pain, I felt this weird twinge deep in my shoulder. I decided to call it a day and see how I felt the next day.

The next day brought more bad news as my shoulder was throbbing from the moment I woke up. I tried over-the-counter anti-inflammatory pills to quell the pain, but they were worthless. Rather than tell the trainer and get the injury diagnosed and treated, I tried to muscle through.

That night, against Baltimore's Brad Bergesen and a trio of junkballing relievers, I went 0-for-4 with three strikeouts as my teammates pounded out 14 hits and scored nine runs. The next day was no better. Against Kevin Millwood, whose best days with Atlanta were a thing of the past, I took the collar again, striking out twice, while Teixeira and company belted 12 hits and plated six runs. After the game, Joe Girardi, who was one sharp cookie, accompanied by trainer Gene Monahan, came up to me with a concerned look on his face.

"You OK, Jack?" the skipper asked.

I hesitated just a second before responding, "Sure, Joe."

Girardi didn't miss a beat. "Don't BS me, Jack. You've looked like you've been swinging underwater these past two games. You're not yourself up there. What is it?"

"Ah, nothing. I just tweaked my shoulder."

That was all Girardi and Monahan needed to hear. Monahan whisked me immediately to his lair in the bowels of Yankee Stadium and immediately started to work on me. In no time, he assessed that I likely had a superior labrum from anterior to posterior (SLAP) tear, a diagnosis that was confirmed the following day when I underwent an MRI.

Because we were locked in a battle royale with the

pesky Tampa Bay Rays for first place in the A.L. East, the medical staff, baseball ops guys, and I agreed that after taking about a week off, I would get a cortisone shot and try to play through the injury until the end of the season. At that point, I would be reevaluated with surgery as a possibility.

Many people falsely believe that a cortisone injection is a panacea for a wide variety of sports injuries. While cortisone will help reduce inflammation and thus alleviate pain, it will not repair the underlying injury. In my case, although the pain from my labrum tear subsided within days after I received the cortisone treatment, much of the explosiveness from my swing diminished. The result was a severe drop in my power. In the 52 games before my injury, I had clubbed 19 home runs, but in the 99 games following my dislocated shoulder, I was able to hit just 11 balls out of the park.

The injury also adversely impacted my throwing, which forced me to DH regularly for the first time in my career. Yet, all was not for naught. I still hit 30 home runs and made the A.L. All-Star team for the 10th consecutive year, and my .294 average and .895 OPS were respectable. But most important, we made the playoffs yet again, sneaking in as the wild card with a 95-67 record.

We got medieval on the Twins in the ALDS, sweeping them in three games and outscoring them by a margin of 17-7. As a team, we hit .314 and slugged better than .500. Even with my bum shoulder, I was able to chip in by going 5-for-13 with a double, a home run, and four RBI.

After demolishing the Twins, we faced the Rangers in the ALCS, and the series quickly evolved into The Josh Hamilton Show. Hamilton was always a guy who fascinated me. The first overall pick in the 1999 draft by the then Devil Rays, Hamilton was a once-in-a-generation talent who could do it all, including hit the high 90s from the mound. He rose quickly through the Tampa Bay system until his career was derailed by drug addiction. After being out of baseball entirely for three seasons, Hamilton finally made his big-league debut with the Reds in 2007 and became an All-Star with the Rangers a year later. I used PEDs, worked out religiously, and as time went on monitored each morsel of food I ingested, but on my best day could never cross the 220-pound mark. Hamilton, despite taking enough drugs in his 20s to take out a small town, was built like an NFL tight end at six-four, 240 pounds.

I could never decide what was the most impressive thing about Hamilton—the fact that he could sit out three years only to become one of the most feared hitters in baseball or that he could ravage his body with all sorts of drugs and alcohol and still be built like Hercules.

Anyway, Hamilton beat us single-handedly in the ALCS. Even though we walked him eight times in the six-game series, he still found the time to hit .350 and smash four home runs and knock in seven runs. I guess I was too busy admiring Hamilton because I only collected three hits the entire series—all singles—and by Game 6 was taken out of the lineup because of my shoulder, which was starting to throb again.

The day after we were eliminated by the Rangers, I went to the hospital to get another MRI on my ailing shoulder, and the results came back exactly as I had expected. My playing for four months after I had hurt my shoulder had aggravated the injury, causing my labrum to be pulled from the rim. Although the joint could be repaired arthroscopically, it was an involved procedure, requiring a recovery period of up to six months.

I had the surgery a week after our season ended, wore a sling for three weeks, then underwent a six-week therapy program that focused just on flexibility to prevent stiffness to my shoulder. Around Christmas, strengthening exercises were gradually added to my program. When I reported to spring training in mid-February, I still wasn't cleared to resume baseball-related activities, meaning I would not be ready for Opening Day. I didn't begin hitting off a tee and light throwing until early March and finally saw game action a month later in extended spring training. After about a dozen games in extended, I began a rehab assignment with the Tampa Yankees in the FSL. Ironically, my first game for Tampa was in Lakeland, where I had played 15 years earlier. Man, I was getting old! After a week with Tampa followed by a week with Triple A Scranton/Wilkes-Barre, I was finally ready to rejoin the Yankees.

After coming back from my shoulder procedure, I had a newfound respect for pitchers who are Tommy John surgery survivors. I was going crazy after just several months of rehab; I couldn't imagine what it's like to be on the mend for upwards of a year.

There's nothing more monotonous than rehab. The same exercises day after day without a reprieve. Occasionally, a trainer will work with you or monitor your progress, but 90 percent of the time you're on your own. But as boring as rehab is, the worst aspect of it is being left at the spring training facility when the healthy big leaguers break camp and head north. It's just you, the other injured guys, a bunch of minor league guys not ready for full-season ball, and the trainers. Trust me, there's no better incentive to work your ass off than being left behind in camp.

When I did rejoin the Yankees, Girardi felt it would be best if he slowly eased me into game situations rather than start me every day right away. To be blunt, this was a dumb idea. I was a rhythm hitter who needed to be in there all the time to maintain my stroke, and by not playing me regularly, Girardi was prohibiting me from getting my timing down.

After about a month, Girardi started putting me in the lineup on a regular basis, and while I eventually started putting up decent numbers, it became obvious I was just a shell of the player I was two years earlier. I attributed my waning performance to the fact that because I had been preoccupied with rehabbing my shoulder the previous offseason, I couldn't dedicate much time to my traditional training regimen. It was no accident that 2011 was the weakest I had felt on a baseball field since 2000, and my diminished bat speed was the end result. Although my 22 home runs and .283/.385/.475 slash line in just 505 at bats (the least amount I'd had since 2000) were decent numbers, they were a far cry from what I had been used to and made me once again question how much time I had left in the game. I looked forward to 2012 and proving that I still had something left.

But before the calendar flipped to 2012, we still had the playoffs, which with the Yankees seemed like a birthright. In the ALDS, we faced the Tigers, who were buoyed by a fearsome rotation fronted by Justin Verlander, who would win both the MVP and Cy Young that year, and Max Scherzer. Despite Verlander's supersonic 100-mph fastball and tough-as-nails secondary offerings, I always considered Scherzer tougher to hit. That's because

Verlander's fastball was as straight as an arrow, while the lateral movement on Scherzer's fastball—usually in the mid to high 90s itself—made it impossible to barrel and his slider was just as devastating. Years later, Scherzer would add a curveball to his repertoire, making him just as tough on lefties as he was against right-handed hitters. After Pedro Martinez, Scherzer was the toughest righty starter I ever faced.

After we took Game 1 9-3, Scherzer and Verlander had our number in Games 2 and 3, respectively. Scherzer pitched six shutout innings in Game 2, while Verlander K'd 11 Yankees in Game 3. My four hits, including a three-run homer, and five RBI in Game 4 propelled us to a 10-1 victory in Game 4 that enabled us to force a deciding Game 5. But Doug Fister, another one of Detroit's stud hurlers, was money, and Scherzer made a cameo out of the Tigers' bullpen to seal our fate. Like all of our early playoff exits, the loss to the Tigers hurt, but my hot hitting (a team-best .381 with two dingers and eight RBI) was especially gratifying after my underwhelming regular season.

While apple picking on a beautiful Indian summer day in late October 2011 in upstate New York, I asked Kirsten to hand me a basket half-full of the Macouns we had just picked before moving on to try our luck with Braeburns. As Kirsten bent down to hoist the basket, she noticed a small black box wedged in between two apples. The instant Kirsten saw the box, she knew what was inside.

Though not an ice princess by any means, Kirsten was not the type to get all warm and gooey, even if some handsome, charming, witty, successful prince was asking for her hand in marriage. This probably explains Kirsten's

235

first reaction to the box, which was a quick sigh, followed by a "Jack, you didn't."

"Oh, Kirsten, yes I did."

"Well, this is definitely the most productive apple-picking trip I've ever been on."

"Me, too. Believe it or not, this is the only apple-picking trip I've ever been on."

"Such a romantic."

"It was either this or the batting cages. The amusement park's been closed for weeks."

With that, I grabbed the small box out of the apple basket then opened it, revealing a three-karat diamond ring. Obviously, nothing was too good for my baby. Then, as hundreds of millions of men before me had done, I got down on one knee and asked Kirsten if she'd be my eternal partner as I slipped the hardware onto her finger. With a glance at the ring and then a longer look into my eyes, Kirsten said yes.

It's weird. Maybe I was too high on myself, but I always had a certain vision of how the minutes immediately following my engagement would play out: My new fiancée, overcome with joy and emotion, can barely contain her excitement as she emits multiple primal shrieks and calls everyone she's known since middle school to tell them the amazing news. There are tears, laughter, hugs, and kisses, followed by more of the same. Amazingly, none of this happened with Kirsten. Instead, true to form, she merely looked at the ring once again and said, "You outdid yourself this time, Jack." Not until we got into the car for the drive back into the city did Kirsten start making calls. And when she told people, it was all very measured. No "Oh, my Gods!" or "You're not going to believe this!" or even "Guess what just happened!" but instead plenty of "So, I have news."

I suggested we take a few days and fly to the Bahamas to celebrate, but Kirsten was working on a big case and had to take a rain check. We couldn't even go out to dinner that night because she had a conference call with several partners to go over a big case they were preparing to litigate that week. So, on the night I got engaged, I hung out in bed alone as my new fiancée talked until past midnight with a bunch of other miserable lawyers.

I started to think how this was so different from what I'd always imagined and I wondered whether I'd made a huge mistake. But I then reminded myself how much of a catch Kirsten was and how many guys would have killed to have been in the same position as me.

Over the next several months, Kirsten, her mom, and the party planner the Hennesseys hired started planning the wedding. Because of the possibility that I'd be playing in the postseason, it was slated for the following November at Kirsten's parents' tony country club in Greenwich. The guest list was expected to rise well past 400, with many of the New York area's most gifted surgeons and well-heeled hedge fund managers expected to be in attendance.

In the run-up to this affair, Kirsten and I had to endure countless dinners with the Fairfield and Westchester jet set, and I quickly realized that I would be entering a brave, new world when I tied the knot with Libby and Albert's baby girl. It was obvious I was not their first choice. Nor their second, third, or fourth, as I'm sure they would have preferred someone with an Ivy League pedigree. Or someone who could at least hang a community college degree on his wall! But I had a feeling Mommy and Daddy Hennessey didn't want their only child to blame them years later for commandeering her ship so they kept quiet.

As the 2011–12 offseason came to a close, I could sense a palpable tension forming between us. I was a soon-to-be 37-year-old ballplayer winding down his career and she was a 28-year-old attorney trying to jump-start hers. Prior to heading to spring training, I had nearly unlimited free time, while her hectic schedule made going out to dinner or catching a movie an event. I was ready to have kids shortly after tying the knot, but she didn't want anything to do with the idea. And I thought "Kirsten Carter" had a great ring to it until my future bride informed me that she would be taking my name on the same day hell froze over.

The night before I left for spring training, I should have seen the writing on the wall. Kirsten and I had our biggest blow-up to date when I asked her when she'd be joining me in Tampa. Spring training is a pain in the ass with monotonous drills, long bus rides, and lots of down time, and it's even worse for the older guys who have families and significant others they may not see for up to six weeks. Anyway, Kirsten went completely turbo on me after I suggested she come down midway through camp.

"Why is this entire relationship about you, Jack? Like you're the only one with a career and things you want to accomplish? How about my career?"

"I'm not asking you to give anything up. I'm just asking that you come down so we can spend some time together. Just a week, heck, not even. How about just a long weekend?"

"Don't you ever listen? Do you have any idea how busy I am and how hard it is to make partner these days? Do you even care?"

"Of course, I do, Baby."

"Don't 'Baby' me, Jack. I'm not some groupie chick, and I am so sick of you treating me like one. I am just so fed up with so many things right now."

"Kirsten, what's the problem? Let's talk about this. I don't want to leave for Florida with you so upset. You want to be away from each other for six weeks after parting like this?"

"Jack, I don't know what I want at this point."

So, the next morning, I caught the first flight to Tampa without even kissing my fiancée good-bye. Then, I spent the next six weeks apart from her. Sure, we spoke on the phone, but the conversations were sporadic, brief, and forced. And there was never any mention of our wedding, which was just eight months away, or married life.

To make matters even worse, we opened the 2012 season on the road in Tampa Bay and then Baltimore, so I wouldn't get so see Kirsten for yet another week. On Wednesday, April 11, we had a night game against the Orioles, which we won 6-4. Usually, we would have flown home on Thursday, which was an off day for us, but because spring training had just ended and we hadn't been back to New York yet, our charter took off about an hour and a half after the game ended. We landed at Newark Airport around one in the morning, and when I opened the door of my apartment a half hour later, I had a wonderful surprise waiting for me.

I knew something was fishy when I first opened the door and saw a pair of men's Gucci loafers. Then I saw a pair of men's dress pants and a dress shirt and sport coat strewn across the floor as I made my way to the bedroom. The bedroom door was open, and though it was

239

the middle of the night, I could make out the silhouette of two bodies. I turned on the lights, waking them both up instantly. They had both been sleeping, stark naked, above the sheets. Kirsten, I must say, looked as amazing as ever, while he had to be in his late 40s with a hairy ass and king-sized love handles. Seriously?

"What the fuck, Jack?" Kirsten blurted out, as stunned as I was. "I thought you weren't coming home until tomorrow."

"Oh, I'm sorry. I hope I haven't inconvenienced you," I said sarcastically to my now ex-fiancée. Then turning to grandpa, I hissed, "And you, douche bag, get the fuck out of my bed and my apartment." As the loser pulled his pathetic body out of my bed, I saw he was wearing a wedding ring. Son of a bitch.

The adulterer was gone within milliseconds, well aware that if he took any longer I probably would have bashed his face in. That left Kirsten and me alone.

"You know what, Kirsten? If I hadn't seen that asshole's wedding band, I probably would have blamed myself for this. I would have told myself that maybe I was too self-absorbed or self-centered, maybe I didn't give you and your career enough attention. But now, all I see in front of me is a pathetic, lying, opportunistic bitch. Let me ask you something. That asshole—is he a partner at your firm?" No reply. Kirsten just sat up on the bed staring at a wall.

"That's what I thought," I said. "Get the fuck out. Get the fuck out now. I never want to see you again."

"Jack, it's the middle of the night. Where do you want me to go?"

"I don't care. Between your mommy and daddy and that fucking job of yours, I'm sure you've got enough money to find a hotel. Especially now that you're likely on the fast track to making partner. Come to think of it, I think you're better suited for a motel. You know, the ones the charge by the hour."

"Fuck you, Jack. I never loved you. It was fun in the beginning, dating a star baseball player, but it got old fast. And it's probably a good time to tell you this—I was never going to marry you. Not in a million years."

"That's great, Kirsten. Now get out."

In the following days and weeks, I did a postmortem of the relationship in my head and came to the conclusion that my relationship with Kirsten was doomed to fail from the start. But contrary to what you may think, it wasn't our nine-year age difference, Kirsten's stressful job, or our vastly different upbringings that were the culprit. Instead, it was far simpler than that. We were never in love. Kirsten clearly enunciated her side of things—I was nothing more than a fun diversion, while for me, Kirsten was the "anointed one." I was getting older and as my list of partners in crime dwindled, I thought it would be cool to have what my buddies had. Kirsten just happened to be in the right place at the right time.

I guess you could say that I got what I had coming. After years of playing chicks and using them merely for my own gain, I got played myself at a time when I genuinely wanted a legitimate relationship. While I wasn't heartbroken, I was saddened and my ego took a huge hit.

The 2012 season was the final year on my contract with the Yankees, and I knew it would be my last in New York. At 37, I was certain that Brian Cashman was going to go younger and would not offer me another multiyear deal. Although I had put up decent numbers in 2011, my worsening performance as the 2012 season wore on gave proof to the widely held belief that my best days were far behind me.

As a result, by midseason I had checked out of New York, both physically and mentally. Although I was still taking the HGH, I no longer worked out with the ferocity that I once had and also rarely took extra time in the cage. In earlier years, I would confront slumps head on, spending hours working with our batting coach on the tee and dissecting video to see what component of my swing needed repair. But now, I was content just to ride it out and let the baseball gods determine my fate.

My performance on the diamond wasn't the only part of my life that suffered after I caught Kirsten cheating. I packed it in socially as well. In the past, nary three days would go by in which I didn't go out, but during the 2012 season, weeks would go by without me hitting a bar, club, or restaurant. Whether home or on the road, I would just hang out in bed with my laptop catching up on *Mad Men*, *Sons of Anarchy*, or *Blue Bloods*. As much as I'd loved New York my first nine seasons with the Yankees, I couldn't wait for my time in pinstripes to end. With that in mind, you can imagine how pissed I was when we made the playoffs yet again after capturing the A.L. East title with a 95-67 record. Yep, you read that last sentence correctly—I wanted to get out of New York that badly.

We faced the Orioles in the ALDS and beat Buck Showalter's squad in five games as Derek Jeter once again proved to the world why he was the best money player in recent times by hitting .444. Raul Ibanez, a true pro and a guy I wished was my teammate for more than just one year, hit two key home runs to enable us to win the crucial Game 3 by 3-2. Ibanez hit the game-tying home run in the ninth inning against Baltimore closer Jim Johnson, then broke the Orioles when he sent one flying into the seats off tough lefty Brian Matusz. I had a decent series, hitting .300, though all six of my knocks were singles.

In the ALCS, we faced our new nemeses, the Tigers, and once again they prevailed. But this time they embarrassed us. It looked like Fister & Co. were going to blank us in the first game of the series, but down 4-0, we hit two home runs in the ninth inning, including a two-run shot by Ibanez off Tigers closer Jose Valverde to tie it. But in the top of the 12th, Detroit scratched two runs across to win 6-4. In Game 2, Anibal Sanchez, a righty who always gave me fits, blanked us, allowing just three hits in seven innings.

The series then moved to Detroit, where we didn't stand a chance against the dynamic duo of Verlander and Scherzer. We lost a 2-1 squeaker in Game 3 with Verlander throwing eight and one-third innings of three-hit ball, then got humiliated in the series-clinching Game 4 when the Tigers pounded out 16 hits en route to an 8-1 drubbing. Scherzer was at his best in that final game with his fastball crackling and slider dancing all over the place. In just five and two-thirds innings, he struck out 10, including me twice on just six pitches. And to add insult to injury, after fanning for the second time, I was booed by a bunch of Yankee fans sitting behind our dugout. This was not the end to my Yankee career that I'd imagined.

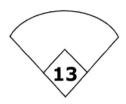

Kansas City or Bust

The 20 home runs I hit in 2012 gave me 470 for my career, just 30 shy of the big 500 that would pave the way to my immortality. I was sure I would need just two seasons to get those 30 measly homers, but Brian wasn't so certain. His rationale was that over the past five seasons, an increasing number of the analytically tilted front offices were placing more value on defensive metrics, a trend that did not look favorably on a guy in his late 30s who was never a defensive dynamo to begin with and whose offensive production was waning. Brian felt that whoever signed me wouldn't play me full time, leaving me with not enough at bats over the next two seasons to swat those 30 dingers. As a result, he advised me to seek a three-year contract.

Because I had recently relocated my winter hideaway from the hustle of South Beach to quiet Del Mar, right outside San Diego, the Padres were originally my first choice. But Brian again intervened. "Dude, between the stiff ocean breeze blowing in and those dimensions, it will take you until you're 50 to hit those 30 homers. Plus, you're gonna want to go to an A.L. club so you can get a bunch of at bats at DH." Case closed.

From the onset of the free agent signing period, the Royals showed the most interest. Their GM, Dayton Moore, was convinced that all the hard work he undertook during Kansas City's lengthy rebuilding process was about to bear fruit and a stable veteran presence and seasoned left-handed bat was all the club needed to contend. Moore demonstrated his interest by acceding to our wishes for a three-year deal by offering $7 million each year and promising me a starting job. However, after the Indians and White Sox entered the fray, Moore upped his offer to $8 million a year.

"You have to take this," Brian said.

Don't kid yourself; as intriguing as the opportunity to hit in a lineup full of up-and-coming young stars like Eric Hosmer, Lorenzo Cain, Salvador Perez, and Mike Moustakas might have been, I wasn't crazy about spending three years of my life in the heartland after spending the last 10 in the capital of the world. As miserable as I was that last season in New York, I didn't think I was ready to go from one extreme to another. But Brian and I agreed that Kansas City's deal, while being the most generous of the offers I'd received, offered me the best shot to win another World Series and get to 500 home runs.

There were so many new things to get used to after my move to the Royals. For starters, for the first time in my career, spring training would be in Arizona instead of Florida. This was a plus for several reasons. Not only was it just a short trip from California, but because all the teams that train in Arizona do so in the Phoenix area, bus

245

rides to exhibition games all last well under an hour as opposed to up to three hours in Florida.

As was the case in Detroit, the Royals were covered by a skeletal media staff. Kansas City was one of the smallest markets in MLB, and that was evident by the size of the media contingent covering the Royals. In addition to the beat writer from the *Kansas City Star*, KC's signature newspaper, you had the local TV and radio guys and occasionally a reporter from a smaller, suburban-based paper. That was it. Once the regular season started, it felt odd to come back to the clubhouse after the game to often find just one or two guys with a recorder or notebook walking around.

When I arrived in Kansas City, the Royals hadn't been to the postseason since their World Series victory in 1985. As a result, the culture was completely different from the vibe that emanated in the Yankee clubhouse. Despite Dayton Moore's best efforts to field a championship-caliber club, there weren't high expectations because the team hadn't won in generations. The youth of the club tied into this culture. Kids like Hosmer and Moustakas, as talented as they were, were just happy to be in the majors and focused most of their efforts on staying in the big leagues as opposed to injecting the clubhouse with a winning ethos.

The low expectations in the clubhouse carried over into the stands. After playing in front of 40,000 fans on a nightly basis in the electric atmosphere of Yankee Stadium, playing in front of 20,000 in Kansas City felt like I'd been demoted to the minors.

Getting acclimated to Kansas City itself presented me with the most daunting challenge. New York was the capital of the world, the city with unlimited potential, and in my 10 years there, I had squeezed every ounce of adventure out of it. Six months earlier, I couldn't wait to hightail out of there, but now I missed everything about the place. I longed for the fast pace of the city streets, the dry sarcasm of its inhabitants, and the ability to have anything from a steak to sushi delivered to my doorstep in the middle of the night. But now I was in Kansas City, a polite town in the Midwest, where the women wore sensible shoes, people drank pop, and all the stores and restaurants closed before 10. God help me.

In January 2013, the players' association and owners announced that they had agreed to HGH blood testing throughout the regular season. I interpreted this as a signal that my days of cheating had to come to an end. Immediately. The last thing I wanted was to end up like Rafael Palmeiro, who got busted in the twilight of his career, his Hall of Fame chances and his name forever soiled.

I may not have made it out of USC with a diploma, but I could do simple arithmetic. Entering the 2013 season, I was sitting at 470 home runs—all I needed was just 30 more bombs to become the newest member of the 500 Club. Even without the HGH, I was confident I could average 10 homers a year during the life of my contract with the Royals.

I considered myself both smart and lucky. I was smart because between paying Dr. Esfandiary for the PEDs and Kenny for the freight, I was down close to a million bucks. But I since I started using, I had earned over $185 million, not including tens of millions more in postseason bonuses and endorsements. Not a bad return, eh? And I was lucky because after 12 years of treatments, my organs still functioned as well as the day I took my first drug.

It turned out that the Royals weren't quite ready for prime time in 2013. Although the team enjoyed a 14-game improvement over 2012 and finished a respectable 86-76, the Tigers still owned the A.L. Central with a 93-69 record and the 92-win Indians came in second place. Still, with "Big Game" James Shields anchoring a much-improved starting rotation, a lights-out bullpen, and exciting core of young position players, it was obvious that Kansas City had all the pieces in place to make a deep run in 2014.

In my first year off the PEDs, I'd had a decent season and was still on pace to crack the 500-homer mark. Although my .267 average was the lowest since my days in Detroit, my .354 on-base percentage was good for second on the club and my .436 slugging percentage trailed only Hosmer's .448 mark. Most important, however, my 19 home runs meant I was only 11 away from a plaque in a certain museum in upstate New York.

Good news on the diamond aside, that first year in Kansas City was tough. Hosmer, Moustakas, left-hander Danny Duffy, and a bunch of the other young Royals were awesome dudes whose company I thoroughly enjoyed, but they were so young that it felt strange to hang out with them.

I remember hanging out in a bar in Southern California when I was in my mid-20s and noticing this one guy around 40 trying to party with all the other patrons who were so much younger than he was. This dude looked like such a tool that at that moment I promised myself that would

NEVER happen to me. So, nearly 15 years later, when I turned out to be "that old guy," putting them back with guys who were in grammar school when my big-league career was starting, I decided to call it a night and make a beeline for the exit.

With no contemporaries to hang out with, my first year in Kansas City ended up mirroring my last season in New York with a lot of Netflix and quiet nights in my apartment. At 38 and after a decade of partying in Manhattan, I was at peace with my new situation. The tranquility in Kansas City extended to the offseason in Del Mar. With all of my childhood buddies and many of my friends from within baseball married with children, I was content just to live the good life as a carefree bachelor and do the things that had always interested me. I took sailing lessons and ultimately bought a small boat, enrolled in a gourmet cooking class, hired a Spanish tutor, and even joined a book club. While I occasionally had to contend with bouts of loneliness, my life was richer and more gratifying than it had ever been. Nearing 40, I was proud of the man I had become.

It was clear from the moment I reported to spring training in Arizona that the 2014 Royals would be a special team. Many of the guys like Hosmer, Moustakas, Duffy, and Cain had come up through the minors together and won at every level but struggled when they got to the majors. However, after going 43-27 in our last 70 games of 2013, it was evident that the youngsters had turned a corner. You could sense a completely different vibe in camp with guys no longer content just to be in the big leagues. Now they wanted to win.

Curving Foul

The Royals were a different group from all those Yankee playoff teams I had been on. While power was the hallmark of all those great Yankee clubs, Dayton Moore clearly built the Royals with cavernous Kauffman Stadium in mind, emphasizing speed, defense, and a tremendous bullpen to pull out close games in the late innings. In Kelvin Herrera, Wade Davis, and Greg Holland, manager Ned Yost had a devastating trio of relievers able to blank opposing lineups in the seventh, eighth, and ninth innings. Each of these guys could scrape 100 mph, live on the black, and torment opposing hitters with their equally ferocious secondary offerings.

The most impressive thing about the 2014 Royals was our toughness. After the first 31 games, we were just 14-17, yet nobody panicked, which was unheard of for such a young team. After 100 games, we were only 50-50. Still, no one gave up. We caught fire in late July, going 19-4 in one 23-game stretch, and overtook the Tigers for first place. This was no small feat considering that Detroit's $164 million payroll was almost double ours. However, we petered out in September and had to "settle" for the wild card to secure Kansas City's first trip to the Octoberfest in 29 years.

Unfortunately, I didn't serve the role as "wise veteran leader whose steady voice in the clubhouse and potent bat in the middle of the order helped elevate the team to new heights." Instead, I was the schmuck who tore an ankle ligament while *jogging* around the bases after clubbing his 499th home run. What can I say?

On July 13, I had been 0 for my last 26 and stuck on 498 for the past two weeks when Justin Verlander, of all people, hung me a curveball—probably the first deuce he'd hung in five years—and I hit the snot out of it. The problem was that it had been drizzling all game and I was so amped up that I wasn't paying attention as I was rounding third base. Next thing I knew, I turned my ankle on the slick bag and suddenly felt this weird popping sensation. I was able to limp the last 90 feet to home plate but then collapsed and had to be carried into the clubhouse.

After an MRI was taken, the Royals' team doctor diagnosed the injury, gave me a set of crutches, and told me I'd miss the rest of the season. Go ahead, just say it. How can a guy who'd sent 100-mph fastballs into orbit, made leaping catches to rob opposing hitters of home runs, and done 30-30 tear up his ankle *while jogging around the bases after hitting a homer*? I'm still trying to figure that one out.

I will say this, though. The Royals played out of their minds in October while I was sitting in the dugout eating sunflower seeds. First, we overcame a 7-3 deficit in the eighth inning of the A.L. Wild Card game to beat the A's, then won seven straight games on the backs of our otherworldly bullpen to breeze through the ALDS and ALCS. Finally, in the World Series, we played the Giants to a standstill until Game 7.

The craziest thing for me about Game 7 was that San Francisco won by the modest score of 3-2, yet by the fourth inning, both starters—Tim Hudson for them and Jeremy Guthrie for us—had been knocked out of the game. At that point, I was positive we would win as our vaunted bullpen mix of Herrera, Davis, and Holland, which had been unhittable all year, would keep the Giants' hitters at bay while we somehow found a way to get two

251

runs across. However, what I didn't count on was the Herculean effort by Madison Bumgarner, who threw five shutout innings *just three days* after tossing a complete game shutout in Game 5.

As bitter a pill as *comingthisclose* to winning a World Series was, I didn't let it bother me that much. Maybe old age had mellowed me. Maybe I was more pissed off about having to wait another whole offseason to hit The Big One. Or maybe I recognized that we had a tremendous young team in Kansas City on the verge of even more greatness.

Regardless, I couldn't wait for 2015. Little did I know, however, that the book had not yet closed on 2014.

Chance Encounters

By early November, my ankle was fully healed and I was back to working out, running, and taking my mountain bike for long rides in the trails. One Saturday morning in mid-November, I woke up and decided to load my bike into my Jeep and head for the Del Mar Preserve, which was a collection of great trails about 15 minutes from my place. It was a gorgeous San Diego day, with temperatures hovering around 70 degrees, a light breeze, and not a cloud in the sky. I had bought the bike and started riding not long after moving back to California. Though not as cardio intensive as running, I found mountain biking a lot more enjoyable and a great way for me to clear my head while taking in some amazing views.

About 15 minutes into the ride, I started to descend downhill on a path I'd never taken before. This was the first time I'd been out with the bike since returning home from Kansas City, and I was probably going faster down the unfamiliar path than I should have been. Before I knew it, I saw a massive ditch about five feet in front of me. I tried to swerve around it, but because my bike was travelling so fast, I lost control and went flying, together with my bike, down an embankment at the side of the trail. My right arm was the first thing to hit the ground, followed by my head.

I lied there motionless on my stomach for what seemed like a long time until I heard a concerned female's voice resonate from somewhere behind me.

"Oh, my God, are you OK?"

I didn't move an inch. My right arm throbbed and I had a splitting headache. But all I could think of was Aaron Boone and his voided contract after I'd tripped him playing hoops. I was certain that mountain-bike riding wasn't permitted under my Royals contract, and since I was no longer the star I once was, there was no way the small-market Royals wouldn't void my deal. As I lay there in the dirt, I wondered if I'd ever get another crack at 500 home runs. Damn, first the torn ankle and now this!

"Hey, are you all right?" The chick was getting closer. "Please. Say something."

She was now right on top of me. Despite my wretched state and the fact that I hadn't yet laid eyes on her, I thought there was something eerily familiar about her. I could tell she was trying to use her cell but couldn't get a signal. Realizing I still had use of all my limbs, I decided finally to turn over and try to sit up. When I did, my rescuer and I were both in for the shock of our lives.

"Jack!"

"Jennifer?"

"Oh, my God. I can't believe this. Are you OK?"

Instantly, the pain in my arm and head went away and was replaced by a massive lump in my throat. Thirteen years later, she looked as amazing as ever. I wanted to say something, anything, that would reflect how I'd been feeling for years, but instead my mouth froze. I tried to get up but was wobbly. Suddenly, I felt lightheaded. I wondered if it was from the fall or from seeing Jennifer. A little of both, perhaps?

Jennifer, noticing that I didn't have all my wits about me, grabbed my arm, which I saw was bleeding heavily, as if to steady me. That induced a pit in my stomach about the size of a watermelon.

"Maybe that's not a good idea, Jack. You may have a concussion. Didn't you notice how fast you were going?"

I just looked at her and didn't say anything. Sure, I felt woozy, but there was so much more at play here. I decided to sit back down, cross-legged, and tried to regain my bearings. Genuinely concerned, Jennifer sat down as well, and we were both silent for what seemed like an excruciatingly long time.

Finally, I said, "I'm sorry, Jennifer."

"No sweat, Jack. I just think you better have someone look at you as soon as possible."

"No, Jennifer. You don't understand. I'm sorry. Sorry for everything." Quickly, without her noticing, my eyes shifted from that beautiful face to her left hand, where there was no ring, and back to her face.

She then looked into my eyes as she used to all those years ago and said almost with a laugh, "Jack, this probably isn't the right time or venue for this discussion. Anyway, you might have a concussion."

"No, Jennifer, I'm fine, and this is the right time. It's been the right time for a long time. I've made many mistakes in my life, but letting you go was by far the biggest."

Jennifer sighed, then said, "You *really* want to talk about this, Jack? Now? After all these years?"

"Yes."

Another sigh.

"Jack, what happened to you? One minute you were the world's greatest boyfriend, and the next you were acting like a cold, distant prick. Do you have any idea what I went through after we broke up? Do you know how much you hurt me? I cried myself to sleep every night for months."

Now it was my turn to sigh.

"Nothing *happened* to me," I started. "I was young, naïve, and had a lot thrown at me at once. The season we met, I was still a nobody, just happy to be playing in The Show. Then when I became a star, I began to need things I thought a plain-spoken, nice girl from Ohio couldn't give me. I began to emphasize things like glamour and flash over substance. And when the Yankees traded for me and I knew I was going to New York, forget it. Take what I just said and multiply it by 10."

"It's funny," Jennifer countered, her mouth breaking into a half smile as she spoke, "because my parents liked you, especially my mom. For a guy who grew up like you did, she was impressed with how polite you always were. But she also warned me about you.

When you first started flaking, she said, 'Jennifer, be careful with this guy. Here's someone who's come from nothing and for the first time in his life, he's getting all sorts of things thrown at him—money, fame, adulation—and at some point he may want to move on and test the waters.' I remember the phrase so vividly. 'Test the waters.' It made me so angry. Then, the night you were traded to the Yankees, she told me that you'd be flying the coup. Smart woman."

"Smart woman, indeed," I said. "How is your mom? And your dad?"

Jennifer's face saddened. "My mom died a couple of years after we broke up. Breast cancer. It was ugly. My father moved to the Gulf Coast of Florida not long after that. His golf game is better than it's ever been, but I can tell he's lonely. I go out to visit him a couple of times a year. I wished he'd move out here or at least to Arizona, but he's got his brother and a bunch of friends in his community and he's happy there."

"I'm sorry about your mom," I said.

"Thanks, Jack. So, was New York as amazing as you thought it would be?"

"It was, especially in the beginning. I fulfilled ev—"

"Don't be a dick, Jack," Jennifer interrupted, a hint of an edge to her voice. "That's not what I meant."

"No, it's important that you know this."

"Fine."

"In the beginning, I had the time of my life. The baseball was great, I made a cool bunch of friends, bought a beautiful place, and took full advantage of all that Manhattan had to offer. And, yes, I enjoyed the single life and had access to every type of girl imaginable. But then, as I got older, and the things that had excited me when I was younger didn't matter that much anymore. Instead of wanting a chick who was a regular on Page Six and preoccupied with going to all the 'in' restaurants and A-list parties, I just wanted a girl who asked me how my day was when I walked through the door and was cool eating pancakes in bed. And that's when I started to miss you. I never thought I could miss someone as much as I missed my dad, but I did. There were so many nights you were the last thing on my mind when I closed my eyes, and then in the morning you were the first person I thought of when I woke up."

Jennifer looked at me for a long second with those beautiful, big blue eyes and said, "There's something else my mom also told me. She said, 'At one point, many years from now, regardless of whether he's with someone, he will one day look back and think of you and your time together very fondly. So fondly, in fact, that he'll miss you.' It looks like Mother knew best, doesn't it?"

I could just nod my head.

"I know I hurt you, Jennifer, and whether you accept this apology or not, I'll always be sorry. Remember that you could always look in the mirror and know that you always gave our relationship 100 percent and there was nothing more you could have done. That became the toughest thing for me to deal with, knowing that I ran away from the only person who ever loved me as an adult. I loved you when things were amazing between us, I loved you the night I broke up with you, and I've loved you all the years since."

"I do accept your apology, Jack, because I never thought of you as a bad person. At times immature and perhaps misguided but certainly not a bad person. And I know that you loved me. Whatever happened between us, I don't feel any animosity toward you. I came to grips long ago that the timing simply wasn't right between us."

"I'm glad you said that," I said. "Selfishly speaking, it was always important to me to know that you didn't hate me. Though I never expected to have this conversation with you. What are you doing in San Diego anyway?"

"Several years after we broke up, I got back together with Kyle, my ex from high school. By then, he was a Navy SEAL stationed out here, so I moved to be closer to him. It's funny because had Kyle been stationed any closer to LA, I never would have moved out here—that should tell you something about the feelings I still had toward you. But I figured Coronado was far away enough from Newport Beach, and I was also ready for a change. It was rough because Kyle was called to serve a tour in Iraq just five months after I moved out here, but we made it work. We got engaged in 2007 and were supposed to get married a year later."

Knowing full well this story didn't have a happy ending, I just grabbed her hand and said, "I'm sorry."

Jennifer kept speaking, and as she did, her voice began to crack. I couldn't remember the last time I'd seen a woman this vulnerable. "I begged him not to go. It was his third tour and his first as squad leader. As well trained as he was, I always knew it was just a matter of time before the grim reaper came calling. About a month after he was in-country, his vehicle drove over an IED. He was killed instantly."

I held her hand tighter.

"It's weird, Jack," she said, with a solitary tear making its way down her left cheek. "I've loved two men in my life who couldn't have been more different, yet both ended up breaking my heart when they left me. You for all the glitz of New York and Kyle for some desert in the middle of nowhere."

Quick to change the subject, I offered, "I'm happy I saw you, even if it was under these conditions." I glanced at my arm, which now had caked blood all over it.

"Yeah, you better get that arm checked out. And that head of yours."

"Will do. Just one thing. If anyone asks, you never saw me here. I think my contract stipulates I'm not allowed to mountain-bike. The last thing I need is for them to void it."

"Yeah, I know. How would you hit your 500th home run then?" Jennifer shot back with a wink.

Even after all these years, she knew all the right buttons.

We slowly made our way back to her Jeep, and Jennifer graciously offered to drive me to mine. By the time we found it, the sun was going down.

"You realize," I said, "this was even longer than our first date."

"Why did I know you were going to say that?"

"Because even after all these years apart, you know me so well. How about we do this again sometime, but with tablecloths, some good wine, and a place with a catchy, French-sounding name?"

"How about not, Jack. Don't get me wrong because it was great to see you, but I don't think I want to go through that door again."

"Fair enough, Jennifer. I understand. Just one more thing."

"What?"

And with that, I leaned over to give her a quick kiss on the lips and said, "I love you."

Several weeks later, in the middle of a battle with a nagging head cold, as I was settling in for a night of Netflix and some homemade veal Milanese, my cell rang. Though the number was from a random area code, it seemed vaguely familiar, so I followed my gut and played a hunch as I answered it.

"Craving French food?" I inquired.

"*Oui*," came the response.

The veal Milanese could wait.

In the late-afternoon hours of Saturday, November 7, 2015, a crowd of about 170 gathered at Los Willows Estate outside San Diego to celebrate the wedding of the future Mr. and Mrs. Jack and Jennifer Carter. As I stood at the altar waiting for the arrival of my beautiful bride, I couldn't help but think about how amazing the last year had been. The unexpected rekindling of a romance with the love of my life followed by our engagement was only half of it. My 500th home run, which you read about in the intro, the Royals' victory in the 2015 World Series, and my subsequent retirement were the other half. As action packed as the last 12 months had been, I couldn't wait to ride off into the sunset with Jennifer.

Then I saw her, escorted by her father, as they made their way down the aisle. That hot chick I'd met all those years ago while waiting in line at Home Depot was now a stunning woman, and, more important, my wife-to-be. As proud as I was of everything I'd achieved during my career, those accomplishments paled in comparison to what went down on that beautiful November afternoon.

After the justice of the peace read us our vows and gave me permission to kiss the bride, I leaned toward Jennifer and whispered in her ear, "I'm sorry. This was about 12 years later than it should have been."

"Don't apologize, Baby," she whispered back. "Better late than never."

An hour later, with a ring on my finger and new wife at my side, I surveyed the scene at the cocktail hour and couldn't help but smile as I observed the many people who had played a major role in my life. At one bar table, Coach Orbison, still spry in his mid-70s, stood and held court as former players Bobby Rossi, Justin Finkelman, and Kenny Lapitka listened intently, hanging onto every word. Kenny, it should be noted, was holding two-year-old Lindsay, his fourth daughter from as many women. I am proud to say I was a main contributor to Lindsay's college fund.

At an adjacent bar table, *Detroit News* reporter Lynn Henning and Anne Honeycutt, my host mother from the Cape, were engaged in an animated political conversation, debating what would happen to Obamacare if the Republicans took the White House in 2016.

To the left of Lynn and Anne, C.J. Nitkowski was busy telling an amused Buddy Bell and Brad Ausmus and anyone else within earshot that his 0.00 ERA with the Mets gave him the franchise record. What he didn't tell them, of course, was that he only threw five innings for the club.

And behind them my agent Brian Goldstein and Jason Giambi were reminiscing about the '92 Olympic Team. No, not the Dream Team with Jordan, Magic, and Bird, but the '92 Olympic baseball team. Giambi, in only the way he can, was trying to convince Brian that it was the baseball team, with himself, Nomar Garciaparra, Jason Varitek, and Phil Nevin that was the *real* dream team.

I looked one more time at all my guests in the crowd and realized how wonderful my life had been. Sure, there had been struggles and a big mistake or three along the way, but I'd had the privilege of getting to know some amazing people and fulfilled all of my childhood dreams. And, now, with my career behind me, I was ready to embark on the second act with these same friends and one amazing woman. Children? A Hall of Fame induction speech? A new job? New hobbies? New friends? I was ready for whatever awaited me.

The Truth

It was a beautiful early April morning nearly two and a half years later and life was good. No, it was great. My son, Michael, all 18 months of him, had just gone to the bathroom and I had the honor of changing him. As I began tending to the molten goodness in his diaper, I thought I heard the doorbell ring over Michael's cooing but wasn't sure. Anyway, Jennifer would get it as I was busy dealing with bigger, though not necessarily better, things.

Five minutes later, as I was wrapping things up on my small son's changing table, Jennifer approached the doorway with a concerned look on her face.

"What is it, Baby?" I asked.

"Sweetie, there are two people here to see you," was all she said.

"Well, what do they want?"

"I think you should talk to them. I'll take the baby."

I handed Michael off to Jennifer, then made my way to the family room where I saw two women sitting on our couch. Jennifer, the perfect host, had already given them orange juice, which was in glasses that were resting on our coffee table.

As I got closer, I got a better look at our unannounced houseguests. The older one was skinny to the point of looking almost emaciated. She was well dressed and likely attractive in her day, but that day was a long time ago. I would put her age at about 70, but she was so sickly that I wasn't certain. I looked at her one more time and realized there was something vaguely familiar about her. I just couldn't put my finger on it. The lady next to her was tall with shoulder-length brown hair and had to be in her late 20s or early 30s. I suddenly tensed up. *I didn't knock this chick up in New York, did I?* I asked myself, but because there was no kid in tow, the fear quickly dissipated. What in the world could these two possibly want?

As I approached one of the chairs that was next to the couch, the older lady stood up and extended her bony hand.

"Jack Carter," she began, "you have a beautiful home and lovely wife."

"Thank you, ma'am. What can I do for you?" Something told me these two dames were not here at 10 a.m. on a Saturday for an autograph.

"Jack," the old lady continued, "you don't know me. I'm Helen Karalson and this is my daughter, Stacey. Please know how sorry we are to intrude like this."

"Not a problem at all," I lied with a pleasant smile on my face.

"Jack," the older one began again. "A minute ago, I said we had never met. That's only partially true and I'll explain in a minute. I don't know the best way to say this, so I'll just

Curving Foul

be up front. I've had an affair with your father."

That smile quickly evaporated from my face and was replaced by a half-quizzical, half-angry look. Just who was this old lady? Jennifer had put Michael in his playpen and had just sat down.

"Ms. Karalson, I'm sorry. You must be mistaken. My father's been dead a long time. A very long time, as a matter of fact."

"I know. Next week will be 33 years. I was with him right before he died in that car wreck."

Then it hit me like a ton of bricks. Stacey wasn't just Helen Karalson's daughter. She was also my half-sister. I looked at Stacey, and she must have been reading my mind because she quickly looked down at the floor, almost embarrassed. Jennifer put her hand to her mouth and said nothing. She was in as big a state of shock as I was.

"I-I d-don't understand," I stammered. "Why are you here now? Why are you doing this after all these years?"

"Because I'm dying," Helen said sadly. "I have lung cancer and the doctors have given me less than six months. You are the only family Stacey has and I wanted her to meet you before I'm gone."

More disbelief. What could I say?

Helen used this uncomfortable silence to continue telling her story. "I was a stewardess in the early and mid-1980s. I met your father on a flight to Portland, where he was attending a conference. I'm sure you won't want to hear the details, but we struck up a relationship and saw each other for over a year. The last time we saw each other—on the day he died—I told him I was pregnant and that I intended to keep—"

Helen's voice tailed off as she looked out into space.

Tears had begun to well in her eyes. I could tell how hard this was for her. Stacey grabbed her mother's hand and started to say something but stopped. Helen took a deep breath and continued.

"When your father left my house, he was in a bad place, more agitated than I had ever seen him, and I wondered whether I'd ever see him again."

Another deep breath. In addition to being distraught, Helen appeared to be in excruciating pain. But she pressed on.

"I knew your father had two small children at home. You and a younger sister, if I'm not mistaken. I felt horrible for such a long time and blamed myself for causing your father's accident. The guilt hurt so much that I decided to confess our affair to your mother. So, one day—it must have been a year after your father's death—I drove to your house. Your mother and the two of you were pulling out of the driveway. I followed you all to a clothing store. I was going to strike up a conversation with your mother, but instead I noticed that she didn't have enough—"

"Money to buy a pair of jeans, so you gave her $20," I completed Helen's sentence.

"You remember?" Helen asked, dumbfounded.

"Yes," I responded. "Like it was yesterday. And then you whispered something into my ear. Something to the effect of my father being a great guy and how I should be brave and take care of my mother." Helen nodded in agreement, visibly impressed that I was able to recall events from over 30 years ago.

"If you don't mind, Ms. Karalson, may I ask you something?"

"Of course."

"So, you and my father had an affair for over a year. Do you think he would have ever left my mom?"

Helen briefly closed her eyes as if she were deep in thought, then gave me her answer, meticulously choosing each word as if it would be her last.

"I don't know. Your father told me on multiple occasions how unfulfilled he was in his marriage. He and your mother had gotten married so young that by the time we met, he claimed all the passion had been drained from the marriage. But he loved you and your sister so much that it's hard for me envisioning him doing something that would have disrupted your childhoods.

"Looking back, I think your father would have preferred the status quo. Staying with his kids but seeing me whenever he needed some excitement. And me suddenly telling him that I was pregnant forced him to make a decision, one he didn't want to make. That's probably why he became so upset."

This seemed like the right juncture for this quasi-family reunion to end. Strangely, I wasn't at all mad at Helen. She was a dying old lady who wasn't out for money or any other type of material gain. She just wanted to introduce her daughter, who for all I knew might have been as lonely as I was at an earlier stage of my life, to the only family she had.

I helped Helen up from the couch and wished her the best. What do you tell someone with terminal lung cancer and just months to live? Stacey and I then hugged and exchanged numbers.

"As you can see," I started to say to Stacey with a facial motion toward Michael in his playpen, "I've got a lot going on. But it would be great if we could stay in touch.

My sister and I rarely talk, so Jennifer and I would love for Michael to have an aunt."

That brought a smile to both Helen and Stacey's faces. But I was already somewhere else.

Two hours later, Michael was taking a nap and I was sitting on that same couch in the family room deep in thought. Confused, angry, sad, my emotions were all over the spectrum. Jennifer, sensing I was in bad shape, sat down next to me and gave me a kiss.

"I can't imagine how tough hearing all this was for you," she said earnestly.

"Jennifer, I have something to tell you. Something that I've been meaning to tell you for over 15 years but never had the balls to say."

"What's that, Sweetie?"

"I cheated."

Suddenly, Jennifer went from sympathetic, caring wife to vicious predator at the mere thought of me straying. "Jack, are you kidding me?"

"I didn't cheat on *you*," I clarified.

"Then what are you talking about?"

"I cheated on the game. On baseball."

That drew a huge sigh of relief.

I then proceeded to tell Jennifer how all my accomplishments on a Major League field were a farce. I told her about the encounter with Griffin Dengler during batting practice in 2000, the trip to see Dr. Esfandiary at the Mexican clinic, Kenny Lapitka serving as my mule for over a decade, and all of my inflated numbers and accolades that were the by-product of my cheating.

I was unsure of how Jennifer would respond and was

therefore relieved when she hugged me when I was finished and simply said, "I don't care how much HGH or whatever else you took. I still love you and so does our son."

It was at that moment when I decided to write this book and come clean with what I had done. I had spent the last 30 years of my life idolizing a man who had lived a lie and did not want the same fate for my son. While my dad was a great father who loved me more than life itself, he was not without his flaws and it was important for me—even in my 40s—to understand this, just as it is important for my son to realize that I am not a superhero or a saint.

I realize I've risked my entire legacy by revealing the truth. The minute this baby hits the shelves, every single one of my 508 home runs, two MVPs, 10 All-Star Games, and two World Series rings will be lambasted, and my Hall of Fame candidacy, once considered a sure thing, will go up in flames. Not only will my entire big-league career be discredited, but also my name will be dragged through the mud and every guardian of America's pastime will do his or her best to eject me into instant obscurity.

But before anyone rushes to judgment, they should ask themselves what they would have done in my situation given all the facts presented on these pages. Am I the only person willing to take a chance by pushing the moral envelope to give myself a better opportunity at a lifetime full of happiness?

The day might come when the name "Jack Carter" will be synonymous with Shoeless Joe Jackson, Barry Bonds, and any other *villain du jour*, and someone will ask me whether I have any regrets about cheating. My answer then, as it is now, will be a resounding NO. I knew early on that a successful Major League baseball career would be the only way for me to escape the misery that had plagued me early in life, and sensing that opportunity was about to elude me, I did what I had to do. After all, I'm a survivor.

About the Author

Harris Frommer wrote MLBTalk.com's *Strategy Session* column and also covered baseball for *Bleacher Report*. He occasionally writes about all things baseball on his Infield Chatter blog. He is currently an economist in New York, where he lives with his wife Jessica and two children.

Made in the USA
Middletown, DE
04 June 2018